"My friends, our sweet Tibby is withering on the vine."

"But Winnie...Ralph Hopple's the only bachelor in Yaqui Springs," Henrietta Feeney ventured timidly. "He's sixty-five if he's a day. Besides, do you think Tibby wants us meddling in that part of her life?"

Winnie Toliver leaned closer and lowered her voice. "Tibby mustn't know. We have to find an acceptable single man between the ages of twenty-eight and thirty-five and somehow entice him to settle in Yaqui Springs."

"Who?" wailed Mabel. "And how?"

"Mabel, you sound like an owl," Winnie snapped. "I didn't say it would be easy. It will require a lot of thought and possibly some scouting. Let's meet again one week from today. I'll expect everyone to bring some workable suggestions."

Mabel jumped to her feet and clapped. "Winnie, you're right! I always said old age and treachery will win out over youth and skill any day!"

Dear Reader,

I was delighted to learn that *Sweet Tibby Mack* is the
launch book for Superromance's in-series promotion,
MATCHMAKER, MATCHMAKER. In some parts of the world, the
role of matchmaker is not taken lightly. Official matchmakers
present the prospective groom's offer to the bride's family and
negotiate the dowry. Here, it's an informal role—usually entered
into enthusiastically by well-meaning friends and family members.

Most women have experienced matchmaking, either aggressive
or low-key. To many it's a source of amusement, to others a
situation abhorred. But for some it works. My own marriage is
the result of my husband's sister bringing me in as a decoy to
break up a relationship he had with another woman. I'm not sure
the matchmaker expected her efforts to end in anything as
permanent as marriage, however.

But, alas, too often matchmaking doesn't go as fondly planned.
It's almost always fraught with problems—and frequently
backfires, as Tibby Mack's friends discover when they endeavor
to find her the perfect husband.

I hope you enjoy Tibby's experience—*and* her matchmakers!

Roz

P.S. I love to hear from readers. Write to me at:
P.O. Box 17480-101 Tucson, Arizona 85731

Books by Roz Denny Fox

HARLEQUIN SUPERROMANCE

649—MAJOR ATTRACTION
672—CHRISTMAS STAR
686—THE WATER BABY
716—TROUBLE AT LONE SPUR

SWEET TIBBY MACK
Roz Denny Fox

Harlequin Books

TORONTO • NEW YORK • LONDON
AMSTERDAM • PARIS • SYDNEY • HAMBURG
STOCKHOLM • ATHENS • TOKYO • MILAN
MADRID • WARSAW • BUDAPEST • AUCKLAND

ISBN 0-373-70746-0

SWEET TIBBY MACK

Copyright © 1997 by Rosaline Fox.

This edition published by arrangement with Harlequin Books S.A.

® and TM are trademarks of the publisher. Trademarks indicated with ® are registered in the United States Patent and Trademark Office, the Canadian Trade Marks Office and in other countries.

Printed in U.S.A.

My heartfelt thanks to Gloriajean and Jim Boone for recounting the joys—and less-than-joyous experiences—connected with building a public golf course on private land. May you have smoother sailing on the back nine.

For those readers not fluent in golf's bewildering language, I offer the information the Boones so kindly gave me: In golf, when it comes to score, less is best.

par: number of strokes set for a hole, depending on difficulty
birdie: one stroke under par
eagle: two strokes under par
bogey: one stroke over par
double bogey: two strokes over par
irons and woods: two types of golf clubs

PROLOGUE

"I SUPPOSE YOU LADIES are wondering why I called this emergency meeting of the Moped Mavericks." Winnie Toliver, the group's president, was a born leader. Energy all but crackled around her short gray curls as she paced the width of the Yaqui Springs recreation center.

The others immediately quieted.

"I'm concerned about our sweet Tibby," Winnie said, referring to the youngest resident living in their retirement community. Each woman present had had a hand in Tibby Mack's early upbringing. A few days ago she'd turned twenty-six.

"Gracious, Tibby isn't ill, is she?" asked Mabel Sparks, a retired teacher who had scheduled Tibby's home schooling from age ten through eighteen.

Yaqui Springs sat on the west bank of the Salton Sea in California's Imperial Valley. Since it comprised mainly retired citizens, the county saw no need to provide transportation to elementary or secondary schools. Outside of Tibby, the youngest person in the loosely formed community was fifty-six.

"Tibby's not sick," Winnie assured the others quickly, halting the murmurs of sympathy that threatened to disrupt the meeting. "Since her grandmother passed on, rest Lara's soul, Tibby's scarcely stopped running. Each week the child takes on more chores."

Ariel Pulaski patted her new perm. "You aren't suggesting she close the beauty shop, are you? It's so handy.''

"I know our men would hate to lose the coffee bar." Rosamond Gordon, a former concert pianist, frowned. "And we've come to depend on the post office. You aren't suggesting she give that up after Lara worked so hard to establish one for us?"

"Ladies, ladies, don't get me wrong. I love all the services Tibby provides. Mack's General Store has never been so well stocked. And who among us doesn't appreciate the organic fruits and veggies that sweet girl grows? With more people moving here each year, Tibby's newsletter is a blessing, too. But I ask you—what kind of social life does the poor girl have?"

"You're right, Winnie," chimed in Justine Banks. "Tibby hasn't attended one of my watercolor classes this year. Claims she's too busy."

"Justine, I'm talking social life as in dating. As in getting married and having babies for us to spoil. My friends, our sweet Tibby is withering on the vine."

"But Winnie...Ralph Hopple's the only bachelor in Yaqui Springs," Henrietta Feeny ventured timidly. "He's sixty-five if he's a day. Besides, do you think Tibby will want us meddling in that part of her life?"

Winnie leaned closer and lowered her voice. "Tibby mustn't know. We have to find an acceptable single man between the ages of twenty-eight and thirty-five and somehow entice him to settle in Yaqui Springs."

"Who?" wailed Mabel. "And how?"

"Mabel, you sound like an owl," Winnie snapped. "I didn't say it would be easy. It will require a lot of thought and possibly some scouting. Let's meet again one week from today. I'll expect everyone to bring workable suggestions."

Rosamond waved her hand. "Couldn't Joe and the others take her golfing more often over to Bogey Wells? I hear the resort hired a new golf pro."

"Yes!" Winnie clapped her hands to cut through the excitement that had erupted. "Joe plays there daily, as do Pete, George and Fred," she said, speaking of their mates. "We'll check out the new pro. Although he's forty-something, I think."

"My dentist is younger," piped up Henrietta. "Thirty-eight. Maybe he'd like to move his practice out here from Indio. He's talked about slowing down."

"See." Winnie beamed. "Already we have prospects. One week from today we'll meet here and study our options."

"LADIES, COULD WE HAVE quiet, please? We've got a lot to discuss. I realize our one week ran into three, what with Yale O'Donnell's funeral and all. If we hadn't stepped in, the poor man wouldn't have had a decent burial. His daughter-in-law only showed up to try and get her mitts on his fortune. I'm glad he just left her a token amount."

Ariel snorted. "He left the bulk to his grandson. If you ask me, Cole's no better than his mama. She, at least, attended the funeral."

Winnie shushed the women, who'd begun to chatter among themselves. "Cole is out of the country. You know he designs resort golf courses. After Henrietta and Justine give us their reports, I'll tell you what else I dug up on Cole O'Donnell."

Teased by the promise of juicy gossip, Henrietta stood. "I made a special trip to my dentist. Tibby drove me. Scratch him from our list. On the way home I pumped her to see what she thought of him. You know how Tibby never says anything bad about a person?'' Henrietta paused. "She said he was stodgy."

"She's Lara's granddaughter all right." Mabel smiled. "Tibby was twelve when she asked me what stodgy meant. It's how Lara described Ralph Hopple."

Justine exchanged places with Henrietta. "We're in trouble, ladies. There's only one bachelor registered at the resort in Bogey Wells. A forty-year-old bird-watcher from Connecticut. If there's a term meaning beyond stodgy, he's it. And forget their golf pro. Winnie and I agree he's nothing but a Don Juan."

"Oh, no." Rosamond wrung her hands. "I have worse news. I saw Tibby poring over brochures for a nutritionist's program they offer at San Diego State. You don't suppose she's thinking of leaving Yaqui Springs?"

"Wait." Winnie silenced the twitters. "Don't you want to hear the rest of my news?" Her blue eyes sparkled as she produced a creased golf magazine from her back pocket. Quickly she thumbed it open to a dog-eared page and made a circuit of the group so all could see.

"He's a dish," someone murmured.

"A dreamboat. Who is he?" demanded another.

Winnie fairly smirked. "Don't you recognize him? This, ladies, is a grown-up Cole O'Donnell." Once all the whistles and you're kidding's tapered off, Winnie let the silence drag out until she had everyone's attention. "According to the article he's still single. If I remember correctly, he must be just over thirty."

"I see it says he lives in Hollywood," interjected Justine, who'd grabbed the magazine. "He's not...funny, is he—well, you know what I mean?"

A ring of anxious faces turned to Winnie. "No. In the fine print it alludes to one of his aims being to start a family someday. Now, hush and let me get to the good part. You know how Joe and the others fuss, having to drive to Bogey Wells every day to play golf?'' Seeing all the nods, she continued, ''Last night at dinner, out of the blue Joe says, 'It's too bad young Cole O'Donnell doesn't come to Yaqui Springs and build a golf course on all that land Yale left him.''' Winnie paused to let that sink in. ''Well, I said, calm as you please, 'You're head of our recreational-development committee, Joseph. Get up a petition on behalf of the residents' association and send it to Cole.'''

Mabel jumped to her feet and clapped. ''Winnie, you're a genius! I always said old age and treachery will win over youth and skill any day. As I recall, our Tibby used to be quite smitten with that boy. Let's all go sign Joe's petition.''

''Tibby may have been enamored of Cole once, but ten years is a long time. Until we see how they get along, mum's the word,'' Winnie cautioned as the Moped matchmakers left the rec center.

CHAPTER ONE

TIBBY MACK smiled to herself as she loaded the last of the homemade baskets, each of them filled with bright spring blooms, into the back of her aged station wagon. She could almost feel her grandmother's presence. Hanging May baskets on the front doorknobs of all the Yaqui Springs residents was a yearly event Lara Mack had lovingly observed. Though Gram had been gone nearly a year, Tibby knew that if the kindly old lady were ever to smile down from heaven, it would be on May Day.

Running late as usual, Tibby slammed the tailgate and hurried into the store to shed her gardening gloves. If no one caught her distributing baskets and stopped to chat, she might get back to open the store and coffee bar on time. Although she'd promised to feed Ariel Pulaski's Afghan hounds for a few days, and they had to be worked in before she drove Mabel Sparks to the airport...

"Uh-oh. Looks like I didn't move fast enough." Clutching the Closed sign, Tibby tossed her thick braid over one shoulder as she watched a car leave the main highway and speed toward the general store. A racy sports car. She frowned. No one she knew drove anything remotely that upscale. Had it been a local, she would've given him a key, and trusted him to leave a list of what he took. As it was a stranger, she had no choice but to leave fast or chance letting the fragile blossoms wilt.

Flipping the sign to read Closed, she sprinted toward her vehicle.

The approaching stranger squealed his midnight blue Jaguar to a halt in front of Tibby and hopped out almost before the full-throated growl of the engine quit.

She froze, her breath trapped in her throat. The world tilted crazily. Not a stranger. Cole O'Donnell. Someone she'd steeled herself to see at Yale's funeral—and then he hadn't shown up. After she'd spent days foolishly worrying that she wouldn't recognize him. Tibby would have known his thick acorn brown hair and beachboy tan at ten times the distance. But why was he here now? She automatically smoothed her wrinkled skirt and grappled for composure.

"Well, hel-lo," he drawled, flashing a smile that warmed his gray eyes. "It's a thirsty drive from the coast. I'm dying for a cup of coffee." He glanced expectantly from the still-swinging Closed sign to the woman's lush goldenrod hair. "Things *have* changed in Yaqui Springs. I'd heard Mrs. Mack passed away. She ran the store as far back as I can remember. Are you the new owner?" Cole didn't think the attractive blonde was the new owner's wife. He noticed that her left hand was bare of rings.

Hurt that he didn't recognize her, Tibby slipped on a pair of sunglasses. Yet it shouldn't surprise her that he didn't. Their last meeting—the spring she'd finally found the courage to invite him to the Date Festival in Indio— he'd been an older man of almost twenty to her sixteen. Oh, he'd looked at her, but he hadn't really *seen* her when he carelessly turned her down. It embarrassed her now to think how often she'd haunted his grandfather's place, waiting for snippets of news about Cole. If Yale ever guessed what prompted her many visits, he'd never let on.

That grand old gentleman had taught her bookkeeping skills, which allowed her to run the store during her grandmother's long illness and after. He'd also taken her golfing to keep her spirits up.

Now Yale, too, was gone. A fact that didn't seem to bother the man standing before her, flaunting his sexy, easy smile.

"You're a little late for your grandfather's funeral," Tibby said coolly. "We buried him six weeks ago."

The accusation cut through Cole like a hot knife. Anna, bless his mother's callous soul, hadn't seen fit to let him know. Until he'd returned from Italy to a backlog of mail, he'd remained unaware he'd lost the person he loved most in the world. At first he'd been too shaken to even deal with the inheritance. Then one day about a month ago he'd received a note from the Yaqui Springs recreational committee, along with a petition asking that he build a golf course on his grandfather's land. *His* land now.

Owning his own golf course was Cole's "someday" dream. Gramps had taught him to play the game and love it. What better tribute to the old man's memory?

Who was this woman? Cole shaded his eyes against the sun. And if the set of her shoulders and the twist of her lips were any indication, she didn't like him.

"Hey, wait," he called as she climbed into a wood-sided station wagon and prepared to leave. "Have we met?"

"Blue moons ago, whiz kid. I'm Tibby Mack." Slamming her door, she pushed the key into the ignition and gave it a twist. Tibby thanked her lucky stars that for once the wagon started without a sputter. "I hate to run, but I'm delivering May baskets to the residents. Then I have Pulaski's dogs to feed and Mabel Sparks to take to the airport. Afraid you'll have to get your caffeine fix elsewhere.''

Tibby Mack. Lara Mack's granddaughter? Cole's jaw nearly hit the asphalt. That skinny kid who wore pigtails and had braces on her teeth? Maybe the moss green eyes were familiar, but now they appeared in a whole different package. He hadn't seen her for—what?—at least ten years. The summer he'd been a college sophomore. Hot stuff. Nineteen going on thirty. His friends had spent their spring break in Palm Springs. Gramps had wanted him to come to Yaqui Springs—and after all, Yale had paid for his education. If memory served Cole, his vacation hadn't turned out half-bad. He'd met an ''older woman'' of twenty-five. A tennis instructor working the resort at Bogey Wells. She'd greatly enhanced his education—and not just in tennis.

Cole stared after the disappearing car. ''Well, whaddaya know.'' Though he hadn't been back since, he'd spent most previous summers in Yaqui Springs. He remembered the year Tibby Mack had come to live with her grandmother. The kid had looked so lost and forlorn. Because Cole understood loneliness, he'd taken her fishing and given her rides on his moped—until she'd gotten one of her own.

Cole checked his watch. The store sign said she opened at eight. Was business so good she could take off on a whim? Not by the look of the big empty parking lot. It was all pretty much as Cole remembered, except for a new building Gramps must've put up. Even that needed a coat of paint. If Tibby's eye was on progress, it didn't show. Maybe she'd become the type to flit around living off inherited money because it was her due—like his mother, he thought bitterly. Old news, Cole reminded himself. No longer affecting him. Nor did anything about *Tibby* affect him.

Cole jerked his thoughts back to the mission that had brought him here—Joe Toliver's letter. It'd come at the right time. Tired of traveling, he'd been giving serious thought to settling down and starting a family of his own. He even had a lady in mind. Cicely Brock, an actress. They got along well. Plus, when the two of them walked into a room, men stepped all over their tongues. A guy could do a lot worse.

Cole wasn't going to let one rude woman deter his plans. He'd survey his grandfather's property, then visit the committee who'd asked him here. Those old boys just might have themselves a first-class golf course.

BY THE TIME Tibby had finished delivering her fiftieth May basket, she'd nearly ground the enamel off her molars. If one more person brought up Cole O'Donnell's name, she thought she'd scream. First of all, she didn't see how anyone could forgive him for skipping his grandfather's funeral, let alone roll out a red carpet for the man.

"Yoo-hoo, Tibby!" Henrietta Feeny came out onto her porch to collect the May basket hanging from her doorknob. "Tibby dear, have you heard the news?"

"What news, Henrietta?" Tibby fidgeted on the bottom step. She was afraid she knew exactly what Henrietta would say.

"Yale's grandson is back in town."

"Do tell. Amazing how fast bad news travels," Tibby muttered.

"Bad? But he's so handsome, dear." The plump woman preened a bit. "Why, if I were thirty years younger..."

"Yes? And what about Fred?" Tibby knew that Henrietta and Fred had been married forty years. They still walked hand in hand when they came into the store.

"Oh, you know what I mean."

"No, Henrietta, I don't. Am I the only one who cares that Cole didn't show up to pay his respects to his grandfather?"

"He couldn't help it. The dear boy's been working out of the country. Tibby, you have dirt on your dress. Will you have time to change before you open the store?"

"Change?" Tibby blinked. Her mind stalled on the information about Cole. How on earth did Henrietta know where he'd been? Was there a full moon or something? Her friends were acting very strange. Absently Tibby scrubbed at the spots on her skirt. "It's honest dirt, as Gram used to say. I'll put on a smock at the store. No one'll notice."

"Tibby, about those smocks. They were all right for Lara. But they make you look…frumpy."

"Frumpy? Thanks a lot, and happy May Day, Henrietta. I wish I could stay for more hot fashion tips, but I've got a very full schedule today."

"You shouldn't do so much, Tibby. I'll take Mabel into Palm Springs and get her to the airport."

Tibby had almost reached the street, but the remark gave her pause. Henrietta's eyes were so bad she had trouble telling red peppers from green; she certainly couldn't identify traffic lights. And she probably hadn't driven in five years. Far-fetched though it sounded, Cole O'Donnell had apparently cast a spell on the women of Yaqui Springs. *Some* of the women, Tibby corrected. *She* saw through him.

"I'm not doing too much, Henrietta," Tibby said more gently, worried that the woman might truly take it upon herself to drive Mabel to the airport. "Maybe you should

go in out of the sun. Drink a cup of chamomile tea.''
Tibby checked over her shoulder after starting her car.
Was Henrietta exhibiting some form of mild dementia?
Ginkgo encouraged blood circulation to the brain. She
made a mental note to bring her friend a supply at the
earliest opportunity.

Before Tibby finished delivering the remaining baskets,
she decided half the town needed ginkgo. Either that, or
she needed the spring tonic. Men and women alike bub-
bled excitedly over Cole's sudden appearance.

Tibby drove past the O'Donnell house on her way back
to the store. She craned her neck and saw Cole surveying
the property. At the funeral, she recalled, his mother had
mentioned that he'd inherited virtually everything. Tibby's stomach tumbled. Was he planning to sell Yale's
place?

To whom? she wondered. Since his land bordered hers,
any sale concerned Tibby. If only she could swing buying
twenty or so acres. Yaqui Springs expanded every year—
it'd be nice to have space between the store and any new
dwellings. Except for the nearby bird sanctuary and the
state park, the smattering of retirement communities dotting the shores of the Salton Sea were loosely zoned. A
few oldtimers like her grandmother and Yale had built
permanent homes; most others lived in mobiles or prefab
homes that had sprung up willy-nilly.

Tibby parked and got out. She didn't understand how
Cole could sell and never lay eyes on Yaqui Springs again.
Everything that mattered to her was right here. Un-
locking the door, she flipped the Closed sign around to
read Open.

She stood there for a minute and drew in a deep breath.
Thyme, rosemary and ripe oranges blended with the
lemon oil Grandmother Mack had taught her to use lov-

ingly on the old wood counters. To some the store with its many additions might look like a hodgepodge. To Tibby it was home—and had been since shortly after her tenth birthday, the spring her missionary parents died in a Brazilian mud slide. She loved every nook and cranny of the rambling house and the store. Both were solid structures. Safe.

Happy as she'd once been in Brazil, fond memories were overshadowed by the frightening pain of loss. People lived to a ripe old age in Yaqui Springs. As Tibby ran water for the coffee, she took comfort in that thought.

A group of coffee-bar regulars, townsmen who stopped to sample her special blend and her cardamon or poppy-seed rolls before they went to play golf at Bogey Wells, arrived before the coffee finished perking. They seemed unusually ebullient—Cole O'Donnell again?—but Tibby was too busy catching up on her work to eavesdrop. Besides, the point of her newly installed tea-and-coffee bar was to run itself. Ideally people filled their own cups and bussed the tables afterward. She made fresh rolls and sandwiches daily, placing them in a refrigerated case for easy access. She'd installed a small microwave in the alcove for her patrons' convenience. If she was busy in the office, pharmacy or beauty shop, folks were more or less left on the honor system. Lara Mack had operated on trust, and Tibby saw no reason to change.

Midway through the morning, after the men had gone, she busily wrapped tomato-and-sprout sandwiches for the lunch bunch. Justine Banks, Yaqui Springs's resident artist, strolled in, passing through to what was once the store's sunporch. Last year Tibby had made it a pharmacy of sorts. She carried Band-Aids, ointments and a number of simple holistic remedies.

"My hay fever's acting up," Justine called. "That elder-flower tea worked wonders. And Pete asked me to pick up another bottle of purple-sage mouthwash.''

''Really?'' Tibby poked her head around the corner. ''I thought you said he wouldn't give up his commercial brand.''

Justine winked. ''I said he didn't *want* to give it up. There's a difference. To convince a man, you have to work things around to where it appears to be *his* idea. Remember that advice, Tibby. Someday when you get married, you'll find it useful.''

''Married?'' Tibby wrinkled her nose. ''Me? When would I find time for a husband? That's supposing a candidate just dropped out of the sky.'' Tibby stilled, recalling a time she'd dreamed of marrying Cole O'Donnell.

Justine plucked a few more items off the shelves and carried them to the counter. ''Did you know the O'Donnell boy is back in town?'' she asked casually.

Tibby rang up the purchases without comment. ''Your total is eight dollars and forty-nine cents, Justine.''

The older woman handed her a ten. ''Yale's house has been closed up for weeks. Did you leave a May basket there? Lilacs mixed with lemon balm would freshen musty rooms, say, if someone planned to stay at the house awhile.''

Crossing her arms, Tibby sent Justine a withering look. ''Somehow I don't picture Cole O'Donnell as the lilac sort. Lavender, to remind him of a French boudoir, maybe.''

''What's gotten into you, Tibby? It's unlike you not to be neighborly.''

''Yale was my neighbor. If you want to take Cole a bouquet, here're the shears.''

Justine pouted. ''I'm offering to watch the store while

you take something over. It'll do you good to get out more."

Tibby stripped off her worn serviceable apron. "Thanks for the offer, Justine. Otherwise I'd have to close the store while I run Mabel to the airport. This way, I'll have plenty of time to stop and feed Ariel's hounds. I'll be back to relieve you by three."

"But, Tibby. That's not what I—" Tibby moved very fast, and Justine was left looking bewildered.

All the way to the Pulaski house, Tibby fumed. A testament to how upset she was, she fed the hounds canned food, instead of the kibble Ariel had requested. *Darn.* Too late now. Genghis Khan and Alexander the Great licked their dishes clean and looked as if they'd start on her toes next. They wouldn't, though; Tibby knew the dogs were lovable. "Good boys. Tonight we'll run," she promised, refilling both water bowls.

Every time she fed and exercised the hounds, Tibby thought about getting a pet for herself. Evenings, especially this past year, seemed unbearably lonely.

Escaping two large dogs who hadn't laid eyes on a human all day wasn't easy. Tibby tossed tennis balls across the yard and quickly ran out through the gate. Still panting, she started her car and drove the four blocks to Mabel's neat double-wide mobile home. So help her, if Mabel mentioned Cole even once on this trip, no matter how innocently, she could darn well walk to the airport.

"Sorry I'm late." Tibby hopped out and opened the back of the station wagon. She brushed aside flower petals before stowing Mabel's suitcase.

"You're not late, child. It's sweet of you to do this. I don't know what any of us would do without your selfless generosity."

They buckled up and Tibby drove off. "Are you kidding? You set up my school curriculum and taught me how to read. Everyone in Yaqui Springs contributed to my education. If I gave back twenty-four hours a day, I could never repay half of what I owe.''

Mabel gazed at her with kind eyes. ''It's not a debt, Tibby. Don't you know? You gave us purpose again. You needed skills we had that we thought no one would want again. Retirement isn't all it's cracked up to be. Joe Toliver didn't ask to quit the chemical-engineering firm he worked for. He was forced out. Teaching you math and chemistry was a boost his ego needed. Just ask Winnie. And Rosamond's arthritis kept her from playing concert piano. Giving you music lessons made her feel worthwhile. The same with Justine. In teaching you art, she realized she still had enough talent to begin selling her work again.''

''I guess I always thought you did those things as a favor to my grandmother.''

''Lara did us a favor by sharing you, sweet Tibby.''

''I don't know about that.'' Embarrassed, Tibby stammered. ''I...I was homely as a mud turtle and twice as awkward.'' Quite suddenly she saw herself as Cole O'Donnell must have seen her.

''You were a duckling, all arms, legs and eyes.'' Mabel smiled. ''We knew some day you'd be a beautiful swan.''

''Pul-leez!'' Never one to field compliments well, Tibby drove in silence for the remaining miles. While searching for a parking place, she brought up Mabel's return trip. ''If you stay past Sunday, call me. Otherwise I'll be here at nine.''

''Then you aren't planning a move to San Diego while I'm gone?''

Tibby gasped. ''Whatever gave you that idea?''

''Someone saw you poring over college brochures.''

"I'm looking at correspondence courses in nutrition." Tibby set Mabel's case on the scale at the check-in counter. Idle chatter fell off as the reservations agent stamped Mabel's ticket and gave her a boarding pass. During the short walk to the concourse, Tibby picked up where they'd left off. "Organic foods and fresh herbs are a start toward good health, Mabel, but I'd like to provide the residents with more. I want all of you to live to be a hundred."

"You already take good care of us, Tibby. It's time you gave some thought to taking care of yourself."

Tibby blinked. "I do exercise and try to eat right."

"Oh, dear, they're calling my flight." Mabel patted Tibby's smooth hand with her wrinkled one. "Longevity stems from more than a healthy body, dear. How long has it been since you've enjoyed the company of anyone your own age? Someone like that nice-looking Cole O'Donnell, for instance." She winked. "Goodness, last call already? Look after yourself, Tibby. I'll see you Sunday. And Tibby? Don't forget the two essentials of happiness—something to do and someone to love."

Mabel's words nagged at Tibby on the drive home. It seemed a curious statement for anyone who knew her to make. When had she ever had companions her own age? Occasionally, during the summers, if any of the residents' grandchildren visited. Mostly the girls had been silly and giggly, the boys cocksure and pushy. All except Cole, who at four years her senior, had let her tag along sometimes. Him she'd worshipped. Then came the year she'd desperately wanted him to notice she'd grown up.

Which, of course, he never did.

Speaking of the boy wonder—as she passed Yale's cedar ranch-style house, she saw him amid a cluster of colorful mopeds. The women of Yaqui Springs seemed entranced, watching Cole's teeth flash white in the afternoon sun.

Tibby snorted in disgust. No wonder Henrietta, Mabel and Justine were smitten, watching him ooze charm. He seemed to be going out of his way to enchant them.

Why, Tibby wondered? It wasn't as if he intended to join the community.

Her whole body was tense by the time she reached the store. Fortunately Justine was too busy to ask questions, and Tibby was soon able to forget Cole O'Donnell *and* Mabel's provocative exit line. In between waiting on customers, the mail came. Tibby hefted the bags, dashed to the post office, sorted and tucked mail into the residents' boxes. Justine had taken off shortly after Tibby returned.

Around four—still two hours to closing—she found a minute to sit down with a cup of blackberry tea. The aroma soothed her and the sweet flavor took the edge off her hunger. Normally she ate a piece of fruit for lunch. Today there simply hadn't been time. Now it was too close to dinner.

She'd just taken a sip when the bell over the front door jingled. Tibby glanced up, then all but choked on the hot tea. Cole stood in the entryway shrugging into a T-shirt. Her lungs threatening to collapse, Tibby caught a glimpse of bronzed corded muscles and a line of dark silky hair that disappeared under low-riding jeans.

Before he finished tucking the shirt into his jeans, Cole spoke. "I've just surveyed my grandfather's land. Are you aware that your outbuilding—the post office I understand Lara had built—sits squarely on his property? Er…my property."

Tibby saw him carelessly muss his sweat-damp hair. Heat pooled in her stomach. Obviously her tea needed more time to cool.

He stalked toward her. "Well, don't you have anything to say?"

"Would you like a cup of blackberry tea?" she offered breathlessly.

Cole scowled. "I'd like to discuss this problem."

"There isn't any problem. Coffee's around the corner if you'd rather have that. Soft drinks and water in the front case. Consider it my treat."

Leaning both arms on the coffee bar, Cole forced her to look up. "When you have a structure a good twenty feet onto land belonging to me, I call it a problem."

"Your grandfather donated the property to us—to my grandmother for the post office. I guess you don't remember when residents had to drive all the way to Brawley to pick up mail. This is much nicer."

He drummed his fingers on the wood. "Donated? Do you have that in writing?"

"Probably. Someplace. Yale was meticulous when it came to business." There *had* been a letter. Tibby didn't think it mentioned that she'd won the parcel in a golf wager. Yale loved to play. He'd taken over Tibby's training after Joe Toliver taught her the rudiments. He bet outlandishly and rarely lost—except to her. The other golfers in town referred to her win as a fluke for Yale's sake, but everyone knew the truth.

Cole waited, but she didn't elaborate or offer him her copy. "Um…Gramps filed every receipt and every scrap of paper that ever crossed his desk," he muttered. "There's an entire room full of five-drawer file cabinets. I wouldn't have the foggiest idea where to begin looking. It might take me weeks to find the documentation."

"More like months," Tibby said, averting her gaze. "I know. I frequently helped file his backlog."

"Look, the burden of proof lies with you. His lawyer

sent me copies of deeds, land grants and a plot plan. There was no reference to any donation. I need that section. You'll have to tear the building down and relocate it on your own land."

Tibby's temper flared. "I don't know who you're selling to, but surely they won't miss one worthless hill." She folded her arms. "Besides, isn't possession nine-tenths of the law?" she added flippantly.

"Says you. And for your information, I'm not selling. I'm planning to build an eighteen-hole golf course. That worthless hill is a prime location for my clubhouse."

"A golf course?" Tibby blanched. "Why? Everyone plays at Bogey Wells."

"Are you saying you aren't aware that the people of Yaqui Springs want their own course? I find that hard to believe when your store seems to be the headquarters for gossip."

So that's why everyone was ecstatic when Cole showed up. Tibby couldn't imagine why she'd been left out of the loop. That knowledge hurt. As possible reasons whirled through her head, she rose and watched Cole wander around the store, picking up a few food items. Bread, cheese, coffee, a selection of fruits and vegetables. Finally he threw in a six-pack of light beer.

"Anna must have cleaned out Gramps's cupboards when she was here," he said stiffly. "They're bare as old Mother Hubbard's."

"Anna? Oh, your mother." Tibby rang up items automatically. Her brain retraced what Cole had said about building a golf course. Even if he designed one, who would run it? Did that mean he intended to sell to a resort developer? Yaqui Springs would never be the same if he did.

"Regarding that so-called letter..." Cole said as Tibby

bagged his groceries. "I'm staying at the house. If you turn up something, you can drop it off there."

Tibby ignored that. "Talk to the people who invited you here. They know Yale contributed the land. In Brawley the post office never let any one person from here collect everyone's mail. It placed a hardship on residents who didn't drive. Having our own postal service was Gram's dream. But unless she tore out the gardens or the orchard, her property wasn't suitable. Yale's land was the perfect solution. Why don't you put your clubhouse someplace else?"

"I don't expect you to understand the layout of a golf course. I'm afraid you'll have to take my word for it. And time is money. I'd like to start excavation. If you need help tearing that shack down, I'll be happy to assist."

"Shack?" Tibby leaped out of her chair. "Take *my* word for this, O'Donnell—touch one stick of wood in that *federal* building, and I'll contact the authorities." Tibby lowered her voice as Winnie Toliver strolled through the front door. The pert woman eyed the two who stood rigidly, glaring at one another.

"Afternoon, Cole...Tibby," she said, inclining her neatly cropped hair. "The Moped Mavericks rode past the cemetery today. The fresh flowers look beautiful, Tibby."

Tibby relaxed. "Thanks. It didn't seem right to decorate just my grandmother's plot. Not when she gave May baskets to everyone."

Cole, who'd reached the door, stopped. "I meant to ask who decorated the graves. This morning I paid my respects to Gramps. Your flowers brightened the place and made my visit easier," he said, his voice rough with feeling.

Tibby hitched up a shoulder. "You're welcome," she mumbled, avoiding his eyes. "He needs a headstone,

O'Donnell. The kind with a built-in vase. Your mother only authorized one of those cheapie markers.''

"Tibby.'' There was a note of shock in Winnie's tone.

Tibby frowned at Cole. "I can't help it. The marker is tacky. It's not like Yale was a pauper. He deserves better.''

Cole wrenched the door open. "Anna didn't mention needing a stone. Actually she didn't mention Gramps had died, either. Consider it done, Ms. Mack. The kind with the vase. Two damned vases if you'd like.''

Winnie jumped as the door banged sharply on his dramatic exit.

Tibby didn't bat an eye. "Of all the arrogant, insufferable, overbearing—''

"Why, Tibby!'' Winnie's eyes widened. "This is so unlike you.''

Ashamed of letting her feelings show, Tibby closed her eyes and massaged her temples. "Sorry, Winnie. I don't know what's come over me.''

"I do. You've been working too hard. You were by our house at six this morning, and I'm sure you rose earlier to cut all those flowers. You probably stayed up half the night making baskets, too.'' Her face softened. "They are pretty, though. Made out of wallpaper, aren't they?''

Tibby nodded. "Last time I went to buy stakes for my tomatoes, one of the paint stores in Indio was selling sample books,'' she said. "Wallpaper holds up better than construction paper for heavier flowers like lilac and jasmine. This year the trees are overloaded.''

"I noticed that the desert verbena's beginning to bloom, too. And the smoke trees are starting to leaf. The Mavericks rode south toward El Centro today. I wish you'd been with us, Tibby. I remember how you used to love finding the first burroweed blossoms.''

"That was before Gram got so sick. I honestly don't know how she managed the gardens, the orchard, the store, plus the housework. Especially at her age."

"She devoted her whole life to this community after she lost Leo. It became her obsession after your parents were killed. But, Tibby, you're too young to bury yourself in work. You haven't lived yet."

"This is certainly the day for everyone to lecture me. First Henrietta, then Mabel and now you. Have I turned into such a terrible grouch?"

"No, sweet Tibby. But all work and no play makes for a dull life." Winnie left, giving Tibby no chance to respond.

Tibby wondered if Winnie had dropped by just to scold her. *Was* she working too hard? No. And right now she had better things to do than speculate. This week she was scheduled to print the newsletter. In addition to that, she had to find where Grandmother Mack had put Yale's letter. Frankly, Tibby would've liked nothing better than to shove that document in Cole O'Donnell's face, along with a copy of the scathing article she planned to write in the newsletter denouncing his golf course. Couldn't the residents see that this was exactly the kind of development that'd make Cole a millionaire—and Yaqui Springs just another toilet bowl for the rich?

CHAPTER TWO

THE NEXT EVENING Cole took his sandwich and cup of coffee to the screened porch. The setting sun gave off just enough light to see. He and his grandfather used to have some great talks out here. The old man had been able to debate both sides of any issue and do a convincing job of it. Cole wished he'd known about his grandfather's heart condition; he'd have turned down that last job. All the hours they'd spent together, and Gramps never once mentioned being on high-blood-pressure medicine or having to use nitroglycerin tablets. Joe Toliver had supplied that information yesterday.

The people of Yaqui Springs had really loved Gramps. They made Cole see the value of belonging to a close-knit community. They looked after their own; they really *were* a community. At his condo complex on the coast the residents had iron grates on their doors and windows, and he knew barely any of his neighbors. Yes, sinking roots in Yaqui Springs appealed to him.

For no reason at all Cole recalled the baskets of flowers Tibby had placed on everyone's door yesterday. Every door except his. After visiting the Tolivers, Fred Feeny and Ralph Hopple, Cole had to admit he'd more or less expected to find one at his place. Winnie had expected so, too. She'd lent him a vase. Apparently she didn't know *sweet* Tibby as well as she'd led him to believe.

Weird how everyone called her *sweet Tibby Mack* as if it was her name. She hadn't shown *him* any sweetness.

Swallowing the last bite of sandwich, Cole leaned back to enjoy his coffee. Boy, Tibby Mack was a classic case of a caterpillar turning into a butterfly. She used to be skinny as a post, and so bashful she'd made Cole nervous. Even then, her eyes had resembled huge moss agates, always watching him from the shadows.

Yet...if he hadn't met Cicely, he might be tempted to ferret out that sweet personality everyone raved about. But he *had* met Cicely. Which reminded Cole of how lonely he'd been this past year. When they'd begun dating two years ago, a loose relationship suited them both. Cicely wanted freedom to pursue her acting career, and he flew off on short notice to design golf courses for conglomerates. The last time they'd spoken, Cole suspected Cicely's career had stalled. Now here he was with the chance of a lifetime dumped in his lap. And with him staring thirty-one eyeball to eyeball, and Cicely a couple of years older... By the time his course opened, they should both be more than ready to settle down and start a family.

Assuming he could begin excavation soon.

Cole slammed his mug down on the glass-topped table. There was still the little matter of that prime land his neighbor had usurped. He checked his watch. Eight o'clock. Was it too late to have another go at talking her around? Rising, he carried his plate and cup into the kitchen. From there he had a fair view of the Mack house, where lights still blazed. Maybe he hadn't approached Tibby the right way yesterday. What if he offered to compensate her for the cost of rebuilding elsewhere? Not that he owed her. But if it'd facilitate things, Cole guessed he could bend a little.

TIBBY WAS ELBOW-DEEP in printer's ink when someone knocked at her back door. "Come in!" she yelled, hoping it'd be Pete Banks. He was Yaqui Springs' all-purpose mechanic. Someday she hoped to be able to afford a computer and laser printer. Then, putting out the newsletter would be a snap. For now, she had to nurse this ancient printing press along.

She glanced up as Cole O'Donnell poked his head hesitantly around the door. What was *he* doing here? Tibby suffered a moment's panic. Black ink covered both her hands and no doubt smudged her face. She knew her reaction was pure vanity, yet she'd rather *anyone* but this man caught her looking like a chimney sweep.

"Why would you shout 'come in' when you had no idea who was at your door?" Cole stepped inside. "An unlocked door is asking to end up a murder victim."

"Do murderers generally knock?"

"Some might. That isn't the point."

"Come on. This is Yaqui Springs, not Hollywood."

He gazed critically around the room. Quilting frames stood in one corner, ablaze with color. Dusty golf clubs in another. On the far wall a dry sink overflowed with sweetpeas. Surprisingly the effect was warm and inviting. Cole's stomach tightened. A crazed stranger could destroy this trusting woman.

"Crime is no longer exclusive to big cities," he said.

"You're right, of course. It's a habit I picked up from Grandmother Mack that I should try to break. But I'm sure you didn't drop by to discuss my bad habits. What brings you here, O'Donnell? Forget something at the store? Or dare I hope you've come to tell me you've decided against raping our land?"

"Raping? Now see here. Golf courses are considered

greenbelts. And greenbelts are pleasing to the eye. They enhance a residential community.''

"Tell that to the birds, the snakes, the ground squirrels, coyotes and other desert animals your pleasing-to-the-eye greenbelt will deprive of homes. To say nothing of destroying plant life and marsh grasses so vital to the lake. I assume you plan to use a section of the lake?'' Tibby's nose itched. She rubbed it and knew at once she'd left a black mark.

"Eventually. But I'll have to comply with the state's environmental policies. As a matter of fact, I faxed them my proposal this afternoon. I should hear something soon.''

"Busy boy. You drove to Brawley and back just to send a fax?''

"No. I have a fax machine in my car.''

Tibby arched a brow. "I should have known. The ultimate yuppie. Look, I'm busy. Why don't you speak your piece, then leave?'' She didn't want him accidentally picking up one of the papers she'd already run off, as she'd written a pretty inflammatory article accusing him of wrecking the ecological and social balance of Yaqui Springs. Tibby would rather he received the news in the morning, along with everyone else.

He spread his feet and crossed his arms. "All right. I'll get to the point. There are always normal delays in construction projects of this size. The people who petitioned to get this golf course off the ground are anxious. I'm willing to offer some monetary support in relocating the post office you've erroneously built on my land.''

"No part of that building is erroneous. Gram had a permit, and the plans passed all inspections. Do you mind showing me this almighty petition?''

"Gladly." Cole dug a folded piece of ruled notebook paper from his wallet.

Tibby accepted it without a word. Signatures covered both sides of the paper. Good heavens, every resident in Yaqui Springs—except her—had signed the thing. They'd skipped her on purpose. Her friends? Surrogate parents, practically. Wounded, Tibby refolded the damning evidence and thrust it back at him.

"Well?" He stuffed the smudged paper in his pocket and waited.

"It changes nothing. You probably dangled the idea before them like a carrot in front of a horse. We'll see how they feel tomorrow after they read my article. Here." Perversely Tibby pressed a drying newsletter into Cole's hands and urged him toward the door. "It'll make good bedtime reading. I hope it keeps you awake."

Cole found himself standing on her porch almost before he realized what had happened. At least she'd locked the door, he thought as he heard the dead bolt slide home. Holding the paper up to the porch light, he skimmed the front page. The smile that had formed when he heard the lock engage died the moment he read headlines accusing him of hoodwinking the town. "She wants war." He crushed the page. "Well, then, that's what she'll get," he muttered to himself. "If Gramps gave land away—and that's a damned big if—there's got to be a record. I'll check every scrap of paper in the house even if I have to stay up all night."

Why was he hanging around out there? Tibby peered between the sunny yellow café curtains she'd stitched up last week. A sigh slipped out as Cole finally stomped down her back steps. With the moonlight dancing off his broad shoulders, he threw a long shadow across her herb garden and onto a big old apple tree. The tree where she'd spent many a summer spying on him—where she'd once foolishly carved their twined initials in a heart.

Tibby dropped the curtain after Cole had disappeared from sight. Lord, but his muscular legs and narrow hips still had the power to stir her blood. Stir her blood, and make her yearn for...for nonsensical things she didn't have time to dream about. Impossible things...

Brushing at a tear, Tibby went back to working on her press. She wanted to run all the copies tonight and deliver them before daylight. The residents ought to have time to digest her article before they invested in Cole's folly. They must have known she'd object to their forking over their savings to the whiz kid's venture. Why else would they have gone behind her back? Cole must have persuaded them by playing on their esteem for Yale. The injustice had her inking rollers with a vengeance.

COLE STOOD in his grandfather's study and popped the top on a can of beer. Where to begin? There must be thirty file cabinets. The first drawer he slid open seemed well organized, but it started the year Gramps had moved to Yaqui Springs. "Mm." He tried to gauge the age of the post office. Definitely newer than the store. Roughly five years, he guessed. Otherwise he'd have to start with the most recent date and work backward—which really could take all night.

It was slow work, but interesting. In a way, the receipts gave a history of his grandfather's life. The old man had bought stock low and sold high. He'd dabbled profitably in bonds and money markets. He'd bought, sold and traded a lot of land in the Imperial Valley, underscoring Cole's belief that his grandfather wouldn't *give* property away.

Cole tensed and downed a slug of beer. Gramps had

spoken highly of Lara Mack—but come to think of it, he'd mentioned Tibby more often in their later correspondence.

Hadn't Tibby admitted spending time here doing his filing? Cole fought a queasy feeling in his stomach. Was bilking people Tibby's game? A lonely old man was a prime target.

Cole laced his fingers behind his head and tried to imagine Tibby Mack in action. That thick braid of sun-streaked hair swishing across her hips as she talked animatedly. Green eyes filling a heart-shaped face. There wasn't a damn thing wrong with Gramps's eyesight. Tibby possessed a willowy frame and small firm breasts that moved seductively when she walked. A swift surge to his loins jackknifed Cole into a sitting position. Now why would he have *those* kinds of thoughts about a woman who accused him of fraud?

Hurrying to the oak rolltop desk, he yanked up the telephone. Eleven o'clock. It wasn't too late to call Cicely. Thrusting aside thoughts of Tibby, he went through his billfold until he found Cicely's number. Then it struck him. This was a woman he thought he was serious about, and he didn't have her phone number committed to memory. He knew the numbers of ten places that would ship sod anywhere in the world, and the numbers of twenty or so subcontractors. What did that say for his love life?

That he spent too damned much time involved in business, Cole decided as he punched in the sequence of numbers.

The phone rang repeatedly. He was ready to hang up when a sleepy voice answered. "Cicely?" he said. "Sorry, did I wake you? Who? Cole. Come on, it hasn't been *that* long since we talked. No, I'm not calling from Italy. I'm in the States. Right here in California, to be exact. At my grandfather's place out near the Salton Sea. He passed away." Swallowing hard, Cole listened to her conventional murmurs of sympathy.

Between yawns she asked when he'd be back in Hollywood.

"I'm building a golf course in Yaqui Springs. I called to see if you'll drive out for the weekend.... Oh, you have plans for Saturday? An audition? Well, come afterward," he said. "We have blue sky and clean air. I'll cook all the meals," he promised. Cicely hated to cook. Cole sensed the moment she began to weaken. "Good. Good. Try to get here before dark, or you may miss the road." He gave directions, then listened to her grumble. "It's not the back of beyond, Cicely. But it *is* secluded," he added, his voice husky with longing. "You'll love Yaqui Springs."

After hanging up, Cole leisurely finished his beer. Then he strolled into the kitchen to take stock of his cupboards. Tomorrow, first thing, he'd hire someone to come in and clean. He wanted everything perfect. Dinner on the screened porch. Candlelight, wine—the whole shebang. Cicely counted calories and fat grams, but he made a pretty fair Mediterranean pasta, which he figured she'd find acceptable. He reached for another beer. Did Mack's General Store carry things like feta cheese and angel-hair pasta?

Wondering that brought Cole full circle to the one person he'd been trying to forget. Tibby Mack. Striding to the window, he peered out. The fool woman's house was still lit up like Christmas. How many of those damned tabloids did she print?

Mood greatly deteriorated, Cole dumped the rest of his beer down the drain. Snapping off the lights, he made his way to bed. The avid golfers of Yaqui Springs wouldn't make any of their decisions about the course based on one small article, he reasoned. All she was doing was spinning her wheels. He almost felt sorry for her.

TIBBY HAD FOLDED the last newsletter and was carting the final batch out to her car when Cole O'Donnell's house went black. My, look how quickly she'd begun to think of it as Cole's house, considering that it'd belonged to Yale for as long as she remembered.

Had Cole found a copy of the note his grandfather had signed giving her that wedge of land? Tibby frowned. What if neither of them turned up a copy? Then Cole could stir up a lot of trouble. She was afraid he'd like nothing better.

Tired though she was, Tibby decided to search her grandmother's papers. An hour later she closed her eyes and rubbed at the insistent ache attacking her shoulders.

Lara Mack kept records. She kept everything. It was just that nothing was in any kind of logical order. Important papers were thrown in drawers. Some were boxed but not labeled. Others had been tossed haphazardly into expanding folders. Tibby uncovered what amounted to a couple of years' worth of correspondence between her grandmother and the office of the postmaster general. Mostly letters concerning the feasibility of establishing a postal center in Yaqui Springs. Lara's theme—Tibby laughed over the unintended pun—was that driving approximately forty miles into Brawley every day to pick up mail constituted a hardship for senior citizens.

There were applications and receipted filing fees that Grandmother Mack had paid out of her own pocket. From all indications, she had worked harder than anyone to bring postal service to Yaqui Springs. And Tibby intended to do her level best to keep it there. Maybe she should suggest dedicating the building to her grandmother. Yes, that would rally the residents. Why hadn't she thought of it sooner?

She carefully gathered all the papers she'd found. Before the week ended she'd carve out time to drive to the courthouse and check on deeds. She'd call on her grandmother's lawyer, too; it couldn't hurt to pose a few questions regarding where she stood legally. His office was in Brawley. Yaqui Springs had no lawyers—or any other kind of professionals, either.

Slogging through her normal nightly routine, which consisted of little more than brushing her teeth and washing her face, Tibby crawled into bed and lay for a long time listening to the creaks and groans of the old house settling. She felt a wave of loneliness and stared into the darkness, weighing again the pros and cons of getting a dog for company. Not that she was afraid to stay alone. In spite of Cole's lecture, she'd never felt nervous in this house. But every time she cared for Ariel's hounds, she enjoyed talking to them. They'd cock their heads to one side and woof a time or two as if responding. Her next trip into Brawley, she'd go by the animal shelter and just look at dogs.

The alarm shattered the stillness, rousing Tibby from a pleasant dream—an unreal dream in which she and Cole O'Donnell were drifting around the Salton Sea in, of all things, her ancient canoe. Lord, it was pitch-black out. She reached over and shook the small alarm clock. Then she remembered. The newsletter. She wanted to deliver it early. She yawned. It seemed as if she'd just gotten to sleep.

Tibby dragged herself into the shower. The water, a bit on the chilly side like Grandmother Mack had always advocated, perked her right up.

Once she went outside and saw that a faint moon and a few stars still shone in the sky, she decided her moped might make less noise. It took only moments to transfer the stacks of folded papers to her saddlebags.

When she returned from making a circuit of the sleeping town, golden fingers of sun had begun to brighten the eastern sky. Her sixth sense told her that everything was going to work out to her advantage.

By seven o'clock it was abundantly clear that her sixth sense needed a complete overhaul. The early-morning golfers, who took coffee in her alcove before they headed to Bogey Wells to tee off, were embroiled in arguments with Winnie's band of moped travelers. Ladies who rarely if ever saw the sun rise—except for today.

"Winnie, dear," Joe Toliver said, sounding terribly condescending, "surely you didn't think Cole would just sink cups out among the sage and call it a golf course. Naturally he has to *clear* the land."

His wife stood her ground. "Frankly, when we signed the petition, I had other things on my mind—if you recall," she snapped. "Tibby brings up a good point in her article. What provisions have you men made for preserving our wildlife?"

"What wildlife?" broke in Fred Feeny. "Snakes and field mice?"

Winnie pursed her lips. "You know very well that on our nature hikes we've seen coyotes, rabbits and ground squirrels. Even gray fox and bobcats."

"Big deal." Pete Banks snorted. "Anza-Borrego Desert State Park is only minutes away. Those animals will find homes quick enough."

His wife, Justine, normally a pacifist, elbowed her way into the fore. "Clients ask for paintings of our desert chaparral. Who'd buy a painting of a golf course? Why does Cole need so much land?''

Pete gave her a cup of coffee and pointed her toward the door. "For God's sake, Justine, a top-notch eighteen-hole golf course takes two hundred acres. Would you rather he sold out to one of the truck farmers in the Imperial Valley? Then we'd stare at miles of tomatoes or dates or whatever.''

"I assumed the golf course would be for those of us who already live here. In her editorial Tibby says if Cole advertises, we might have to contend with an influx of snowbirds. What if they decide to stay?''

"Snowbirds don't like the heat, dear heart,'' Ralph Hopple interjected. "Neither do they like snow. Hence their name. When the snow flies in their home state, like migrating birds they travel in droves to the sun. But when the desert hits ninety and the snow melts at home, they leave us again.''

Rosamond Gordon sniffed. "We're not dumb, Ralph. We know what snowbirds are. Some of us *were* snowbirds once. *We* settled here permanently, didn't we?''

Tibby listened to the quarrel heating up around her, growing more distressed by the minute. Her article had created all this discord. Never had she heard her friends disagree so violently. While considering whether to intervene—wondering if she could even make them listen—she saw Winnie Toliver beckon her group to the door.

"Come ladies, it's time to rethink strategy. Let's buy a loaf of Tibby's zucchini bread and we'll make a pot of decaf at my house.''

Tibby quickly bagged a loaf and followed them out. "Would anyone be free to watch the store later in the week? I have business in town. I'd like a full afternoon.''

"I'll be glad to,'' Justine offered. "Especially if your

business concerns the wildlife issue. I'm so mad at Pete. He can't see beyond the end of his golf club.''

Tibby worried her lip. ''Don't blame the men. They must get tired of making the drive to Bogey Wells. I'm sure it's Cole's fault—for dangling this opportunity under their noses. He should be ashamed. Yale isn't even cold in his grave.''

The women gazed at one another guiltily. The look went by Tibby. She continued to firm up plans with Justine. Then, as she turned to go inside, Tibby saw Joe Toliver and Fred Feeny measuring the post office. Pete, who obviously didn't realize Tibby was watching, said in a voice that carried, ''What if we jacked her up, put her on skids and sort of scooted her this way? She's only resting on pier blocks.''

Joe shook his head. ''The post office would still be too close to Cole's property line for the county to issue him a building permit. We'll have to brainstorm. Come on or we'll be late. Let's discuss it in the car.''

Tibby shrank into the shadow of the doorway. How dared they assume they had the right to move the post office her grandmother had built! ''No more *sweet* Tibby Mack,'' she vowed, watching them leave. ''I'll find a dog, all right. A guard dog.''

She was still in a foul mood when the man she blamed for the unrest in Yaqui Springs sauntered through her door a few moments later. Tibby finished cleaning up a mess of spilled sugar and crumbs at the coffee bar. Ignoring Cole, she ground beans for a fresh pot of coffee.

''Mm, that smells good.'' He came up behind her and sniffed over her shoulder. ''Is it for your use only or do you sell that by the pound, as well?''

Tibby turned and found herself at eye level with his chin and gently curved lips. Luckily for her he had his eyes closed and missed the start she gave when her knees caved. "I, uh, sell a variety of specialty coffees. They're on the far side of aisle four. This is vanilla bean. I stock almond and raspberry. Great after-dinner coffees. All decaffeinated. Most of the residents have high blood pressure, so they need to avoid things like caffeine. *And situations that cause stress,*" she emphasized.

His eyebrows shot up. "Are you saying I'm causing them stress? Golf is one of the least stressful activities. It gets people outside in the fresh air. Cardiologists everywhere recommend golf as a method of reducing blood pressure, in case you haven't heard."

"You're a regular medical encyclopedia, O'Donnell."

He shrugged expansively. "I'm here to buy groceries, not engage in debate. I have a guest coming for the weekend who's a fussy eater. Do you carry things like feta cheese, fresh basil and bulgur for making tabbouleh?"

"Yes." Tibby rolled her eyes. "A chef now. It must be nice to be a jack-of-all-trades."

He leaned a hip against the coffee bar and studied her through half-closed eyes. "Are you aware that the residents refer to you as *sweet* Tibby Mack?"

Tibby released her breath and spun away. She'd been anything but sweet to Cole since he'd arrived. But when he stood as close to her as he was now... "You said you came here to shop, O'Donnell. Why don't you hop to it and quit harassing the management?"

Cole tugged on one ear. Lowering his gaze, he racked his brain, trying to think of something he might have said or done to make her so prickly. In the end he decided the problem, whatever it was, lay with her. Since it was out of his control, he grabbed a cart and started down the aisle.

Glad to be free of the tension stretching between them,

Tibby puttered while Cole made his selections. She watered the hanging baskets of fuchsia and geraniums that brightened the dark wood walls. She snapped dry leaves off the pothos and trailing ivy that lent a homey feel to the coffee bar and small beauty shop. Yet she knew at all times exactly where Cole was.

A few minutes later Tibby rang up Cole's purchases and sent him on his way with one of her most professional smiles. Thankfully it was the last she saw of him all day.

When the golfers popped in that afternoon, they weren't as talkative as usual. Pete and Fred muttered that as far as the wildlife went, she was making mountains out of molehills. They reminded her there were rabbits on the greens at Bogey Wells.

That night Tibby went to bed with a splitting headache.

It hung on for the rest of the week. A steady stream of travelers kept her unusually busy. So busy, she barely spoke to any of the men who came for coffee every morning.

During a lull that occurred on Saturday—the day Tibby finally decided business had slacked off enough for her to go to town—Cole dashed in. "I forgot to buy candles," he said. "Do you carry the short fat kind? And I'll need a bottle of good white wine."

Tibby directed him to the proper aisles. She didn't want to serve him today and checked her watch for at least the twentieth time, waiting for Justine. She was eager to get on with her mission.

Time dragged. No other customer came in to offer distraction. Cole walked up to the counter in that easy way of his that sent a whistle of awareness through Tibby's midsection. Her best defense was to get mad at him and stay mad.

Fortunately he provided the opportunity as he took the

first item from his basket and placed it on the counter. "I asked around like you suggested. No one remembers my grandfather donating land for the post office."

"What?" Tibby stopped feeding prices into the cash register. She gripped a bottle of expensive coastal wine by the neck. "Who'd you ask, for pity's sake?"

Cole rubbed his jaw. "The group that headed out to play golf this morning. I met them on the road and we stopped to talk."

"You mean Joe Toliver, Pete Banks and Fred Feeny didn't set you straight?"

"They were among the people I spoke with, yes."

Tibby felt a stab of anger. Those men knew the truth. Why on earth wouldn't they stand behind her? Had they forgotten what it was like driving forty miles to pick up mail? "I know the land was donated," she said angrily. "So do they."

Cole tugged a folded paper from his back pocket and dropped it on the counter. "This is a rough layout of the golf course, clubhouse and pro shop. If the interest is what I predict, later I'll add a restaurant. So you see, I need that property desperately."

"Need all you want. I wouldn't start breaking ground if I were you unless you put the clubhouse somewhere else. You aren't touching that post office, O'Donnell."

"Look, I pawed through most of Gramps's files over the week. He has receipts of transactions dating back twenty years and not one shred of evidence that he gave you the land. Unless you show me proof, I plan to start clearing."

They were nose to nose, shouting, when Justine Banks scurried in. "Sorry I'm late, Tibby. We met at Winnie's for coffee this morning. You know how she is when she climbs on her soapbox. Is something wrong? You two having a quarrel?''

Tibby stuffed Cole's groceries in a sack. "That's putting it mildly. Instead of entertaining out-of-town visitors he should close up Yale's house and return to Hollywood, where sneaky double-dealing is a way of life."

"Resorting to slander now, I see. I do have a witness." Cole turned to Justine, and the older woman sort of puddled at his feet.

Tibby shoved the sack into his arms. "I believe you were leaving?" she said with sarcastic sweetness.

"Gladly. And don't hold your breath waiting for me to darken your door again. I'd sooner drive the extra miles to shop in Brawley."

Justine's head whipped from one to the other like a baby bird seeking a worm. "My," she said as the door slammed on Cole's heels, "it's like Winnie said not five minutes ago. Our community cohesiveness is going to heck in a handbasket."

"It goes to show that the person who said one bad apple spoils the barrel knew what he was talking about." Tibby glared at the door through which Cole had departed. "But don't worry, Justine." She patted the older woman's arm. "Maybe later today I'll have news to mend this rift once and for all."

Justine blinked owlishly behind her round glasses. "Yes, Winnie made that same comment. What time will you be back, dear?"

"I hope by four. Help yourself to lunch and try some of that new raspberry-and-rosemary tea I bagged today. I think you'll find it calming. You'll need to make sandwiches for the lunch crowd. There are still two loaves of seven-grain bread and one of sourdough. Tomorrow I'll bake again."

"You go run your errands. I'll do fine, Tibby. Take some time and pamper yourself. You're always doing for us, child. Do something for yourself for a change."

"Like what?" Tibby balanced on the balls of her feet near the door.

"Oh, a manicure or a new hairdo. You've worn a braid since you were fifteen."

"It's easy-care and keeps the hair out of my face when I work in the gardens or stocking shelves. What's wrong with my braid?"

"Nothing, child. But if you gussied yourself up a little, maybe the O'Donnell boy would be more amenable to putting his clubhouse somewhere else. According to Emily Post, a man can't refuse a well-turned-out woman *anything*."

"First, I'm not a child and Cole O'Donnell isn't a boy. And nobody goes by that old bunk today. There's equality between the sexes now. And I, for one, don't want Cole to put his clubhouse anywhere in Yaqui Springs. I'd rather he did sell to truck farmers. End of discussion, Justine. If I don't hurry, I won't be back in time for you to start Pete's dinner. I know you like to have it ready when he comes home."

"Not tonight. I'm mad at him, too." She flushed. "My waiting on him is part of that old bunk you mentioned. I think I'll give him a taste of this equality thing."

Frowning, Tibby marched back to the counter and collected her sunglasses and the drawing Cole had given her of his proposed golf course. "Isn't that pretty rash, Justine? Pete isn't exactly a nineties man."

The woman smiled and patted her gray chignon. "Don't fret, dear. After nearly forty years of marriage, I know exactly how to enlighten him."

CHAPTER THREE

TIBBY COULDN'T BELIEVE she'd forgotten it was Saturday, and the land office was closed. Fortunately Gram's attorney was in, but that visit proved nearly as fruitless; Lara had never mentioned the land transaction to him. However, the elderly Mr. Harcourt did provide Tibby with one ray of hope.

"I imagine there are strict rules and regulations concerning the relocation of a U.S. post office, Tibby. I'd be happy to file an injunction against O'Donnell to tie his hands until you get a ruling from the postmaster general's office next week. However, it takes at least two working days to process an injunction. If I file Monday, it'd be Wednesday or so before the county served him."

"Even that would help, Mr. Harcourt. He's not at the digging stage, and I didn't get the impression he'd rip out the building. He's pressuring me to move it. But there's no room on my property unless I stick it in the middle of my parking lot."

"I'll start the ball rolling, then. First thing Monday you get on the horn to Washington and see what they suggest. Meanwhile I'll draft a letter telling O'Donnell of our intent to file the injunction. Sometimes that alone makes a person back off. If you're going to be in town awhile, drop by later and pick it up."

"I do have other things to take care of. I've decided to adopt a dog. The house is so quiet without Gram. I thought maybe a pet... Please point me in the direction of the shelter.''

"A pretty woman like you shouldn't have to resort to canine companions. What's wrong with the young men out there in Yaqui Springs?''

Tibby's heart took a sinking dive as she thought of the only *young* man in Yaqui Springs. "It's largely a retirement community, Mr. Harcourt. Not too many men my age retire.''

"Humph. Then if I were you, I'd sell Lara's store and move. I recall her saying she wanted you to go away to college. Unfortunately, as we discussed after she passed away, she was badly advised financially and lost the bulk of her nest egg.''

"I love living in Yaqui Springs and I love running the store. I'd never sell it. I hope eventually to take some college correspondence courses. I've been checking into San Diego State. Now, about the animal shelter, Mr. Harcourt...''

"Yes...yes. But a dog hardly seems a fitting alternative to dating. Tell you what, my wife's in charge of our church socials, and she teaches the young-adult Sunday-school class. I'll have her send you an invitation to the next event. No matchmaking, understand. Just come and enjoy the company of men and women your own age.''

"That'd be nice. Thank you.'' Tibby doubted she'd accept the offer. Unless the social was during the day. It was a dark lonely road to travel at night.

Harcourt drew her a map to the shelter. She thanked him again. "I'll run by for the letter, say, at three?'' He nodded and escorted her to the reception area.

Walking along the street to her car, Tibby caught her reflection in the window of a shoe store. Her steps slowed. Was her braid outdated? Or was it her loose-fitting cotton

dresses? She'd noticed that both the secretary and receptionist in the attorney's office wore suits with shorter
skirts. No, by darn. Tibby gripped the shoulder strap of
her purse. She liked her hair long, and she'd grown up
wearing dresses. They were cool and comfortable, good
for bending and stocking shelves.

Tibby stopped at a café for lunch. The place was
crowded. The harried hostess acted as if it was a crime to
eat alone when Tibby asked for single seating. Once they
managed to squeeze her in, Tibby felt as if she *had* come
with a crowd, since the tables were pushed so close together. Two couples on her left knew the people on her
right, and talk more or less flowed over her.

As she dug into her salad, she realized that a majority
of the men and women in the restaurant were paired up.
Contemplating that, Tibby pretended interest in her fork-
ful of greens. Before Justine and Mr. Harcourt had pointed
out her social impairment, she'd never given it much
thought. Was that how Cole saw her? Naive and inexpe-
rienced? A country mouse? He must know a bevy of so-
phisticated women.

Embarrassed at the thought, Tibby requested her check
and left the majority of her lunch untouched. Awareness
of her own inadequacies always made her heart trip over
itself.

Only after she was safe in her station wagon did her
heart settle and the trembling stop. Flirting wasted time.
She had no need for such skills. A dog was what she
needed to keep her company, and a dog she would have.

Less than half an hour later, she pulled into the shelter
parking lot. Sharp barks and mournful baying pulsed from
the building. Goodness, she thought as she entered the
reception room, this might be a bad idea. So many dogs
needing homes—how would she ever choose?

"May I help you?" A pretty girl with soft brown eyes greeted her over the din.

"I want to adopt a pet," Tibby explained. "A dog."

"A puppy, you mean?"

Tibby gave the question some thought. "Do you have any that are young but already trained?"

"We have a beautiful Pekingese. Very well mannered. Her owner died, and the woman's daughter lives in an apartment where they don't allow pets."

"Oh, how sad." Tibby's heart turned over. "I had in mind something bigger, though. Like a guard dog."

"That's too bad. Peek-a-boo only has another twenty-four hours." The girl's brown eyes misted. "I've tried so hard to find her a home, but everyone I know is full up. I'll even throw in food and a doggie dish."

Tibby's forehead puckered. "I know an elderly lady whose Yorkshire terrier died. She'd had her sixteen years. I wonder... She was brokenhearted. Still is."

"Oh, do you think?" The girl sounded hopeful. "Could you call her?"

Tibby smiled. "I believe I'll surprise her. It's too easy to say no over the phone. It's much harder to refuse a gift."

"You're a woman after my own heart. But I've given so many dogs as gifts, I'm almost out of friends." The two shared a conspiratorial grin. "Now that Peek-a-boo has a home," the receptionist said briskly, "let's go choose you a pet."

Tibby shook her head. "Do you mind picking one and bringing it out here? If I go in, I'll want them all."

"We have a young Great Dane. The man who brought him in claimed that when they got him they didn't realize he'd grow so fast. It was a family of four, and all of a sudden they had twins. Between two babies and a growing pup needing attention, I guess it was too much." She shook her head. "There are laws against giving away your kids, but people don't think twice about dumping their pets."

Tibby couldn't bear to imagine what happened to throwaway pets. "The Dane sounds fine. May I see him, please?"

The girl disappeared through a set of double doors almost before Tibby finished speaking. The din rose unbearably. Tibby wondered how many dogs they had. A short time later the attendant returned. She cuddled a pug-faced champagne-gold dog. At her side trotted a sleek but massive tan dog with dark velvet eyes. He got down on his belly and wriggled toward Tibby. Then he raised a paw and rolled over. Tibby's heart was lost. She knelt and scratched his chest, then his ears. "He's perfect. What do I have to do to adopt him?"

The young woman explained the shelter's policy, and Tibby paid the nominal fees. "I almost forgot," she said, stowing her receipt. "Does my dog have a name?"

"Ah, uh, you might want to change it. The boys in the family named him Exterminator." The girl made a face.

"Exterminator." Tibby tried it out. A smile twitched. Perhaps Cole O'Donnell wouldn't be so cavalier about bulldozing his way over her property faced off against a dog called Exterminator. "But it's just a name, right? I mean, he wouldn't, you know, really go for the jugular or anything." Tibby's smile faltered.

The attendant laughed. "Just don't hold red licorice close to a main artery. According to his former owner, the Dane has a sweet tooth. I guess that was the last straw. He ruined one of the kid's birthday cakes. He can smell chocolate a mile away, and it's hazardous to a dog. Our vet had a box of M&Ms in her purse. Exterminator nosed open the zipper and had the pack out by the time she caught him. Darn—they told me not to mention that. Now you'll want to give him back, I expect.'' She sighed.

Tibby considered for a moment. She stocked very little candy. Some of the residents were diabetics. She baked using raisins and blueberries. On rare occasions, carob chips. "Not a problem," she said at last. "He can't eat what isn't there. As of now, he's a health-food dog."

Pulling away from the shelter, she wondered if it was safe to leave the dogs in her car while she ran in to Mr. Harcourt's office to collect the letter. A needless concern, as it turned out. Both were apparently seasoned travelers. Exterminator claimed the rear of the station wagon and Peek-a-boo the front. The small dog made three revolutions then settled close to Tibby's hip as they headed home. If Millie didn't want her, Tibby decided, she'd take them both. She had a big house and no one with whom to share it.

The sad fact brought a catch to her breathing—heightened by a fleeting vision of Cole O'Donnell as he looked today. But he'd always been ruggedly handsome. She was the one who'd changed. Matured. Still, she was nowhere near as comfortable in her skin as he was in his.

Cole hadn't said who he was entertaining this weekend. But he planned to serve angel-hair pasta and fine wine. Tibby would bet the store it wasn't a male associate. She exhaled harshly as her spirits plummeted.

Exterminator reached over the back of her seat, whined and licked her ear. "Ooh." She hunched a shoulder, then stroked his cold nose. "If you're saying I should forget that charming rat, you're absolutely right. But it's easier said than done."

The dog whiffled in response and placed a paw on her braid. Their two heads bobbed together in the rearview mirror. "Why do I need a man when I've got you?" she murmured. Apparently reassured, he bounded off to stare out the rear window again.

Once Tibby reached Yaqui Springs, her first stop was at Mildred Hopkins's small mobile. As usual Millie sat rocking on her tiny porch. There was a time when her vegetable gardens had flourished. She'd let them go to seed after her husband died and stopped working in them altogether after losing her pet—as if she'd given up on life.

Braking outside the peeling picket fence, Tibby instructed the Dane to stay. The older woman ceased her listless rocking as Tibby climbed from her car.

"What's that you're bringing me, Tibby Mack? If it's another casserole, you may as well take it home. The last two are still in my freezer."

"No food today, Mildred." Although it was on her list. After Henrietta mentioned that Millie had stopped cooking for herself, Tibby made it a point to drop by with nutritious offerings.

Peek-a-boo yawned sleepily and squirmed in her arms. Tibby strove to juggle dog, food and dish in order to close the gate. She knelt and slipped everything except the dog behind a wilting bush. "I went into town today, Millie, and I stopped by the animal shelter to get a dog. You know how I rattle around in Gram's big old house by myself."

Mildred's eyes focused inward, as if she'd drifted away a moment. "Don't pay to get attached to man nor beast, girl. Comes a time when they all leave you."

"Not by choice, Mildred. The world is full of people and animals who could use a friend. Take Peek-a-boo, for instance. If I hadn't gone to the shelter today, she would've been destroyed." Tibby set the little dog down. The dog leaped right into Millie's lap and snuggled in.

"Git. What are you doing? I'm not your mama. Tibby is."

Tibby noticed the weathered fingers tugging gently at the dog's silky ears. And she also noticed the doggie smile on Peek-a-boo's face. "I wanted a bigger dog, Millie. I chose a Great Dane. But I couldn't bear to walk away and leave this one to her fate." Tibby sighed. "I'm afraid I promised to find her a home."

"Oh, well…maybe Winnie and Joe."

"No. They're always flitting hither and yon. Peek-a-boo lived with a retired lady. She's content to sit and rock."

"Mabel, then." The woman scratched the dog under the chin.

"She's off baby-sitting her grandchildren too often to take really good care of a dog, don't you think?"

"Yes. Yes, I suppose she is. I'd take her myself, but—"

"Would you? Mildred, you're a lifesaver. Or I should say, a dog-saver." Tibby suppressed a grin. "She comes with food and a dish. She's been spayed and has all her shots." Tibby grabbed the things from where she'd stashed them and piled them on the porch. "Well, I'd better run. Justine's watching the store, and I've been gone longer than I'd planned. The dog's name is Peek-a-boo, remember."

Tibby all but ran from the yard. She didn't want to give Mildred time to reconsider. As it turned out, she probably needn't have rushed. Looking back as she pulled away from the curb, she saw Millie talking nonstop and the Pekingese's tail waving like a flag in a stiff breeze.

"Yes!" Tibby punched the air with a fist. "It's a match

made in heaven, Exterminator,'' she murmured smugly, rubbing her pet's huge square nose.

Her good humor evaporated a bit as she passed the O'Donnell place. Cole stood with two men—strangers— on a hill of blooming sage. All three checked clipboards they held, then gestured wildly. Tibby wondered what the trio was up to. If she wasn't so late, she'd stop and deliver Harcourt's letter. It was well after four; surely he couldn't start tearing up the landscape tonight.

Parking in her normal spot, Tibby hopped out and hurried into the store. Exterminator padded at her heels.

Justine's eyes nearly popped out of her head. ''Tibby, don't look now, but there's a small horse following you.''

Tibby laughed. ''Meet Exterminator. He's one reason I went to town.'' She spread a car robe behind the counter, then filled a bowl with water for the thirsty dog.

''Exterminator?'' Grabbing her purse, Justine ducked out the other side. But the dog was too busy lapping up water to pay her any heed. When he lifted his head, water dribbling from his muzzle, he did look ferocious.

Tibby started to explain that he was really a pussycat. Suddenly she changed her mind. After all, what good was a guard dog if everyone knew he was a phony?

''Thanks, Justine. Drop by tomorrow. I'll cut and color your hair for free. I know your time is worth more, but it's something I can do in exchange for your watching the store, since you won't let me pay you.''

''I like doing it. This gives me a break from painting and lets my creative juices flow again. 'Sides, I'll never turn down a free haircut.'' They both laughed as the door opened.

Through it burst a man carrying a huge bouquet of roses. ''Tibby Mack?'' he inquired, helpless to see around the greenery.

Tibby cast a stunned glance at Justine, who avoided her eyes.

"Don't look at me," Justine mumbled. "Check to see who sent them."

Tibby continued to stare at the flowers. "There must be some mistake," she said weakly.

"No mistake." The man plunked the vase on the counter. "Sign here, please. It's a long drive out from Brawley."

Hands shaking, Tibby scribbled her name on the line he'd indicated. "But I don't know anyone anywhere who'd send me flowers," she insisted.

"Whoever sent 'em paid a mint for delivery," said the driver as he tucked the pencil behind his ear and headed for the door. "We soak 'em for mileage."

"Well, don't just stand there," Justine admonished when he'd gone. "Honestly, Tibby, I'd have that envelope shredded by now."

Tibby touched one of the dark red buds. Then she leaned over and sniffed. "They're gorgeous. No one's ever sent me flowers, Justine. I can't believe they're for me. Let me appreciate them a minute, in case it's all a horrible mistake."

"Tibby, you're too much. Florists aren't in the business of making mistakes."

"I suppose." Almost reluctantly Tibby plucked the white envelope from its forked stake. Even then, she turned it over several times and patted her dog's head before she finally slipped a fingernail under the flap and pried it open, never noticing that Justine had apparently lost interest.

Tibby frowned after reading the message. "They're from Cole." She tossed the card on the counter. "He says, 'Sorry for everything. Forgive me, Cole.' Ha! More than likely he had to run into Brawley for some piddling spice he forgot and realized how inconvenient it is.''

"Now, dear, he probably feels guilty about shouting at you earlier. Men have a tendency to speak first and think later. Why not enjoy the roses and let bygones be?''

"They are lovely, aren't they?'' Tibby's features softened.

Smiling, Justine angled toward the door. Before she reached it, the bell over the top tinkled again. A pretty woman, pale-skinned with shoulder-length blond hair, poked her head tentatively into the store. "Excuse me,'' she murmured in a smoky voice, "I'm hunting for Cole O'Donnell's country home. I must have taken a wrong turn. Could someone direct me?''

Tibby and Justine exchanged glances, Justine's one of surprise, Tibby merely rolling her eyes as if to say, *Country home, oh, brother!*

"You can see his house through that window.'' Tibby pointed. She shushed Exterminator when he loped to the end of the counter and barked. "Driving there is trickier. If you'd like, I'll show you on an area map.''

"Would you? And do you have any cold mineral water? It's so hot out.''

"Hot? It's barely eighty-seven. But yes, I have mineral water, juice and iced herb tea.'' Tibby directed the newcomer toward the cooler.

The woman pushed her sunglasses up into her hair and stepped fully into view. "Thank goodness you seem civilized. I was afraid to stop in any of the dingy little towns I passed through.'' She shrugged a delicate shoulder while inspecting the case.

Tibby took the opportunity to study the woman. She had wide violet eyes enhanced by liner and mauve eye shadow, and she wore a filmy little purple top and a fluttery short skirt that would have stopped a train on a dime. Good thing she'd driven straight through. Those poor farmworkers would've died of shock.

Silver hoop earrings and matching bracelets jingled when she reached into the case. If it'd been a man checking out those long bare legs, Tibby thought peevishly, he'd probably have swallowed his teeth.

"You known Cole long?" Tibby asked as she dug through a cluttered drawer in search of the map. She hated the hint of jealousy in her tone.

"A couple of years. I'm Cicely Brock, by the way. If you get an L.A. paper and read the entertainment section, you may have seen me. I'm in a new TV series."

"Winnie gets the *L.A. Times*," Justine said. "I'll mention it to her on my way home. How long will you be in Yaqui Springs, Ms., uh, Brock? In case Winnie would like your autograph."

Cicely broke into a smile. "I'm only going to be at Cole's till tomorrow afternoon. But I'd be happy to sign something. I don't expect to be back. He's usually on the continent working for classy resorts. I can't imagine why he's designing something out here in the boonies." The woman took a dainty sip of her mineral water, then fanned herself, which set her bracelets dancing. "Are you *sure* it's not closer to a hundred degrees? I can't afford to get sunburned. My agent would have fits." She gazed at Tibby as if seeing her sun-streaked hair and evenly tanned skin for the first time. "My goodness, don't you worry you'll wrinkle?"

Justine made a strangled noise in her throat, which she quickly turned into a goodbye thrown at Tibby.

Saying nothing, Tibby bent to find the elusive map. Triumphant at last, she turned with it clutched in her hand, only to find Cicely eyeing the card that had come with the roses. Tossing two dollars atop the card, Cole's visitor stormed out of the store, not waiting either for change or for directions to his lane.

Tibby felt her stomach lurch. Until that very moment, she'd been unwilling to admit that, in spite of their latest battle, she longed for more than an adversarial relationship with Cole O'Donnell. Even when he'd gone away to college, she'd known there'd be women. But they'd remained nameless faceless women. Easy to dismiss. It was pretty hard to disregard Ms. May Centerfold.

Tibby knew it wasn't very nice, but she hoped Cole burned the pasta or that the wine he'd selected had been on the shelf long enough to turn to vinegar.

She sneaked a peek out the window to see if Cicely had reached Cole's house yet. If she stood on tiptoe she could tell. "Uh-oh." Justine still stood in the parking lot, in a cluster of Moped Mavericks. The way Justine waved her arms, Tibby knew the ladies were getting a blow-by-blow account—of everything from the roses to Cole's girlfriend. It certainly wouldn't do to let that bunch see her spying. Jerking back, Tibby fussed with the shelves. Darn, she *was* tempted to take Exterminator out to explore. Stoically she resisted. Besides, her friends would see right through the flimsy ploy.

COLE RACED HOME after leaving the heavy-equipment contractor and the county inspector in charge of issuing permits. Since he owned the land, the inspector saw no problem with starting to clear it. The permits themselves would take a few weeks. Technically, county planners had to approve the drawings. Cole was confident his would pass muster; after all, it was how he made his living.

But he'd been a lot later winding things down than he'd planned. He hadn't showered, let alone started the pasta sauce. By his calculations Cicely should be rolling in soon. Cole's intent had been to have everything done except tossing the salad, so they could sit out on the patio and share a relaxing glass of wine without intrusion.

Stripping, he stepped into a cool shower. There was still one potential oil slick to mar his smooth sailing. Tibby Mack's blasted post office. He hadn't mentioned that little snafu to the inspector. Jockeying the location of his clubhouse entailed redrawing the entire plan and resubmitting it. Plus, he'd planned on using her traffic light. It was the only one in Yaqui Springs. As this wasn't technically a town, he didn't relish the thought of talking the county into installing another. He could just imagine it—weeks of costly traffic studies that would end with him paying some outrageous price for putting in a light. If the powers-that-be deemed a light was necessary.

Cole washed his hair, rinsed off, then blindly grabbed for a towel. He regretted having lost his temper with Tibby earlier. Unfortunately Tibby Mack had a way of setting him off like no other woman he'd ever met. He owed her an apology for this morning. And he'd have delivered it, except she'd been gone all afternoon. Where to? he wondered. Not that what she did was any of his business.

Irritated by his turn of thought, Cole took care laying out his clothes. Cicely liked a man's slacks pressed and his shoes shined. She was big on people wearing the right weight for the right season, too, he recalled as he quickly discarded one shirt and selected another.

Heading for the kitchen, he strapped on his watch. Once there, he uncorked the wine to let it breathe, then decided to set the table on the patio while it was still light. He'd bought a candle in a shallow dish for a centerpiece. Nothing he hated more than breaking his neck trying to see the person seated across from him.

Was he nervous? Probably. It'd been nearly five months since he'd seen her. Cole didn't kid himself that Cicely had sworn off dating while he was in Europe. They'd had no real commitment then. If things were to change, it was imperative that Cicely like Yaqui Springs, dinky or not.

Straightening, Cole gazed out through a ruff of pine trees toward the Mack place. Tibby seemed acclimated to the slower pace. Even when she was busy, she didn't give the appearance of rushing. Her braid sort of floated lazily out behind her when she walked, the honey gold strands catching fire in the sun.

But why was he dreaming about Tibby's hair when Cicely was due any moment? In fact—he cocked his head—was that someone at his front door? It sure sounded like it. Damn, now he'd be cooking, instead of relaxing. But maybe she'd like to shower and rest after the drive. Cicely had a tendency to be high-strung.

Cole skirted the couch on his way through the living room. When he reached the entry, he flung open the door, prepared to greet and be greeted with a lingering kiss.

Instead, Cicely exploded through the door, tromping on his new Italian loafers. Her spine carefully rigid, she paced the room in circles.

"Wake me at midnight, beg me to come for a romantic interlude—or at least that's what I *thought* your call implied, Cole. Did you think I wouldn't find out you've got another woman stashed in the wings? I guess you did, since it was quite by accident I found out." She flung a hand dramatically toward the south wall. Silver bracelets skittered up and down her slender arm.

"Cicely, hold it right there. I have no idea what you're raving about."

"Ha! I'm *raving* about the dozen roses you sent that…that…funky…person, when you've never sent *me* so much as a carnation."

Cole stared at her. "You told me flowers make you sneeze. That's why I haven't sent you any. But I haven't sent them to anyone else, either."

"Ha!"

"Will you quit saying that?"

"Don't lie to me, Cole. I read the card. Some drivel about how you're sorry and would she please forgive you. I could hardly miss it. She left it on the counter for the whole world to see. What are you sorry for, I'd like to know?"

"She who?" Cole reached for Cicely, but she pushed him away.

"That woman at the country store. The one wearing the kiddy braid and sweet-as-apple-pie smile. That *she who.*"

"Tibby?"

"If that's her name, yes." Cicely sniffed and inspected her nails.

"Listen, I don't know what you think you saw. I swear I did not send her flowers. We'll go over there right now and get to the bottom of this."

"You go. Get the card. I'd like to hear you explain how your name got on it."

"All right, I will. I've opened a bottle of wine. Help yourself. Relax. I'm sure there's a simple explanation." Cole steered her to the kitchen, where he pointed out the wine.

"Ha!"

Since she insisted on sounding like a broken record, he stalked out the back door, past the table he'd so carefully set and down the back steps. At the trailhead, he met Winnie Toliver. She clutched a crystal bowl full of green salad. Probably on her way to a potluck. Joe had mentioned that the residents held quite a few. Cole would have passed her with a brief greeting, except that Winnie grabbed his shirtsleeve.

"I hear you have a dinner guest, Cole. Shame on you for not telling us sooner. A man entertaining a lady shouldn't have to cook. I'll just leave this salad on your counter, shall I? Henrietta's making you manicotti. Rosamond promised a dessert to die for. If you're on your way to the store, pick up a nice bottle of red wine. A full-bodied red goes best with pasta."

Cole started to object. Then he held his tongue. He didn't know how long this mission would take. It'd be nice not to have to cook dinner and spend the time pacifying Cicely, instead. Smiling, he capitulated. "Thanks. Her name's Cicely. I'd appreciate it if you made her feel welcome. I want her to like it here, if you get my drift."

Winnie squeezed his arm. "You can count on me and the girls to explain the ins and outs of Yaqui Springs. Oh, and Cole—take your time. It's better not to rush girl talk, if you get *my* drift."

Feeling better, Cole watched her disappear down the path. He thrust his hands in his pockets and whistled softly as he sauntered toward Tibby's store.

CHAPTER FOUR

WINNIE RAPPED SMARTLY on Cole's back door before breezing into his kitchen. "Hi," she said, setting her dish on the counter next to a surprised Cicely. "I'm Winnie Toliver, one of Cole's neighbors. He's such a dear. Everyone here thinks so. We're delighted that he's decided to come live in his grandfather's house."

"Live here? Cole?" Cicely plunked her wineglass down next to the bottle. "Oh, no. It's far too remote. He has a nice condo just blocks from Wilshire."

Winnie looked properly sympathetic. "It's not so bad once you learn how to cope with the heat, mosquitoes and such. I see Cole set a romantic table for two out on his screened porch. I hope he remembered to spray for scorpions. The house has been closed up since his grandfather died. Where *is* the dear boy?"

Cicely's mouth opened and closed like a fish taking bait. "Out," she managed before another loud knock precluded anything else she might have said.

Henrietta Feeny bustled though the door and set a steaming pasta casserole and a foil-wrapped package of bread on the stove. "So you're Cicely," she gushed. "Welcome to Yaqui Springs. Any friend of Cole's is automatically a friend of ours." She nudged Winnie. "I see we have our work cut out to fatten this young lady up. Ah, here's the very person to add those calories. Our Rosamond." Henrietta beamed at Cicely. "I don't know what decadent delight she's brought, but knowing Rosie there'll be at least a thousand calories per bite. Would you believe? All of us were once as skinny as you." She patted her ample girth.

Winnie opened the screen. "Four-layer raspberry torte. Rosie, you outdid yourself. Here, let me put it in the fridge. I'll pop the salad in to cool, too."

Rosamond waved the rich confection under Cicely's nose as Winnie made room on the top shelf. Closing the refrigerator gently, Rosamond introduced herself, then said she had to run. "If you don't mind, I'll leave by the front door. I remember Yale—that's Cole's granddaddy," she clarified for Cicely. "Yale had problems with rattlers nesting under his rear steps. Some say it's too early in the season, but I'm a total basket case when it comes to snakes. Have a good visit, Cicely. We'll see more of you, I'm sure."

"Hi, everyone." Justine Banks barged in without knocking. "Sorry to be so late. Rosie, don't rush off. We can all walk out together." Justine let the screen slam behind her as she thrust a tray of hors d'oeuvres into Cicely's bejeweled hands. "Oh," she said, catching hold of the younger woman's fingers. "Those rings are pretty. And matching earrings." She touched the hoops. "Dear me, Winnie, I hope someone warned her to put her jewelry in a safe place tonight."

Cicely snatched her fingers back so fast she almost dropped the tray. "Safe? Safe from what?" Her eyes glazed a little.

Justine pursed her lips as she rescued the tray and made room for her quiche puffs on the shelf below Winnie's salad. "Pack rats, lovey." She closed the fridge door decisively. "Yale had quite a time—the little thieves. Clever they are. Carted away an expensive watch, a ring and one money clip that I know of. But Yale was so forgetful. You'll be fine as long as you remember to keep everything shiny put away.''

The women pressed close to Cicely, all nodding and smiling.

Winnie snapped her fingers. ''I believe this welcoming mission has served its purpose. Come, ladies, we don't want to intrude. Cole will show up soon.''

''I'm sure he will,'' said Justine. ''I passed him going into the store. In addition to the chives I needed, I found the item you requested, Winnie.'' Justine discreetly tucked a small white card into Winnie's pocket. Two pair of twinkling eyes met.

Cicely teetered beneath the arch as the women started for the front door. She twisted her bracelets nervously, peering into shadowy corners. ''Please, will you wait a minute? I just remembered a prior engagement at home. Let me leave Cole a note. Then I'll walk with you to my car.''

''You're not staying?'' Winnie pretended shock. The others *tsked* softly until their leader spoke again. ''Well, if you must go, you must. Poor Cole will be so disappointed. I vote we leave him the food to compensate.''

Everyone agreed it was only fair.

THE MINUTE COLE STEPPED into Tibby's store, he saw the roses he'd supposedly sent. The bouquet was gaudy in his estimation. Not at all like what he'd choose. Small buds in soft pink would be his preference.

Bending to inspect the flowers more closely, Cole jumped back when a menacing growl raised the hair on the back of his neck. A dog—a humungous beast—trotted around the corner of the counter, teeth bared.

''Good boy. Where'd you come from?'' Cole knelt

down slowly and stretched out a hand. He liked animals, although he'd never been in a position to own one. Another thing he'd do if he sank roots in Yaqui Springs— get an Irish setter.

The dog edged closer and sniffed. Cole scratched him between the sleek pointed ears. A pink tongue lapped at his wrist, and the long curved tail wagged.

Tibby backed out of her storeroom, arms laden with jars of honey. Seeing Cole making overtures to her dog sent a stab of hunger to her heart and a blast of fire to her cheeks. "Exterminator," she hissed, "fine guard dog you are. Bring a burglar in and show him the silver."

"This bruiser is yours?" Cole failed to conceal his surprise.

"Yes. I plan to teach him to attack on command. Come here," she ordered, and was greatly relieved when the dog left Cole's side to flop at her feet, his nose tucked between his paws.

"The store is closed. I assumed Justine would lock up on her way out. But maybe she saw you heading this way. I usually try to accommodate residents. If you don't mind, I'll shelve these jars while you find what you need."

"I came about the roses."

Tibby stammered slightly. "Oh. A-and I didn't even thank you. Um, I guess we both flew off the handle this morning. The bouquet is gorgeous, Cole. Really, though, I never meant for you to drive all the way to Brawley for your groceries."

Every line and feature of her expressive face softened when she gazed at those damned flowers. Cole wished he *had* ordered them, the change in her was so radical. And…she wasn't going to like what he had to say. "I, ah, didn't send the roses."

He glanced away from the embarrassment that quickly

replaced the pleasure in her eyes. "The first I heard of them was from Cicely. She's upset. Do you mind if I take a look at the card?"

"Help yourself. But…I don't understand. If you didn't send them, who did? And why would anyone use your name?"

"I don't know. But the florist does."

"They came from Brawley." Visibly shaken, Tibby thumped the jars of honey down on the counter.

Cole fingered the empty pick centered in the bouquet. "Where's the card?"

"There, beside the vase."

He lifted the vase and peered underneath. "It doesn't seem to be here. Did you put it in your pocket?"

"Why would I, for goodness' sake? It's not as if I had romantic illusions or anything. Look on the floor. Maybe it blew off when your girlfriend flounced out. What have you done with her? I thought you said you were cooking dinner."

Cole felt his ears grow warm. "Eating takes second place to clearing up this mess. Cicely's sort of…well, she's, ah, jealous." The last he muttered as he dropped to his knees to search the floor.

Tibby smothered a grin. "I'm sure that feeds your ego."

"Are you laughing?" Cole glanced up from his undignified position.

Tibby couldn't hold the laughter in. "No…oo…ooo."

"Dammit, if this is your idea of a joke, it's not funny." He scrambled up. "A lady I'm trying to impress thinks I sent you roses."

Tibby curbed her mirth. "You *can't* believe I'd send flowers to myself. Oh, and I suppose I have a crystal ball to tell me precisely when your movie queen would waltz in here this afternoon. Don't flatter yourself, O'Donnell.''

"Then help me find that card so I can call the florist and clear this up once and for all.''

"Oh, sure. I'll turn out my pockets while you search through the trash. I use that five-gallon ice-cream bucket behind the counter.''

"Is this the only rubbish you have?'' Cole asked a few minutes later, after he'd checked every envelope and torn receipt in the round cardboard barrel.

Tibby swept one hand toward the coffee bar and another toward the back room. "Two more trash cans, plus the dumpster at the end of the parking lot. I'd help, but I wouldn't want you saying I found it and kept it from you. I'm taking my dog home to feed while you dig around. Have at it!''

She showed up again just as Cole emerged, looking slightly unkempt. "No luck?'' she asked, truly surprised to see he was empty-handed. "Well, I wonder what happened to the dumb thing. I swear it was right beside the vase. I figured it'd caught on something and made its way into the trash.''

Stepping around him, she yanked open one of the drawers behind the counter. There lay the map she'd held when his girlfriend took off like a shot. Tibby shook it, but nothing fell out. Perplexed, she said, "Why would anyone spend that kind of money playing a practical joke? And who, for goodness' sake?''

"Beats me.'' Cole cast a darkly troubled glance out the window. "I guess I'd better get on home. Maybe I'll buy a second bottle of wine. Red, if you have it.''

"Sure. Top shelf, last row.'' Tibby watched him choose one. "If the card appears, I'll tuck it in your front screen. Otherwise I'll go through the Brawley phone book I have at home and find the number.'' She gave him change and bagged his purchase. ''I do feel bad, Cole.''

''Thanks. It's a puzzle, and I'm stumped. I'm a fan of mysteries and usually figure out whodunnit way before the end.''

''Really? I read them, too,'' Tibby said. ''In fiction the next step after something like this is to find a dead body.''

''I'll just have to hope Cicely's not so steamed that it turns out to be my dead body.'' Smiling crookedly, Cole left. Almost at once he stuck his head back inside. ''Don't forget to lock the door.'' Then he was gone again.

She not only locked up but snapped off the front lights. Even in twilight the roses were pretty. Although a dull ache crowded out the joy she'd experienced when she'd thought Cole had sent them.

Closing her eyes, Tibby rubbed at a niggling headache. Obviously it didn't take much to turn her head where Cole was concerned. Well, if she needed a dose of reality, she could visualize him and Cicely Sleepover. That'd do it.

Steps slower, Tibby snapped off the remaining lights. She welcomed the night as she made her way next door to a solitary dinner with her dog. At the door she realized she'd passed up another opportunity to give Cole the letter from Mr. Harcourt. But what did it matter? His mind wasn't on clearing his land this weekend.

THE MINUTE TIBBY DOUSED the store's lights, Cole was swallowed by darkness. He skidded to a stop where their properties joined to let his eyes adjust. His weekend certainly wasn't going the way he'd planned. Instead of a nice romantic dinner, he had one woman ticked off at him and he'd inadvertently hurt another. The look on Tibby's face when he told her he hadn't sent the roses bothered him. It dredged a memory from the past. Her birthday.

Her fifteenth. No, sixteenth. She'd invited him to a play at the Date Festival—*Midsummer Night's Dream.*

He resumed walking as memories surged in. If he hadn't been so hot for that tennis instructor, he probably wouldn't have been so abrupt with Tibby. Recalling the pain in her eyes, he felt guilty.

Why? That was ancient history. She probably didn't even remember. And Cicely was the one he should be worried about. Come to think of it, why *hadn't* she believed him when he said he hadn't sent those roses? A lack of trust ruined relationships. Cole had seen it erode more than one friend's seemingly solid marriage.

He and Cicely had a few things to discuss.

Now. Tonight. Over dinner. His mind made up, Cole jogged along the path and up the steps. Judging by the mouth-watering aromas drifting from his kitchen, it was evident that Winnie's pals had been there. He stopped to light the candles on the porch. Making up promised to be fun. Who could stay mad amid candlelight and moon glow?

Not him.

Cole gave a start as he snuffed out the match. Those were green eyes he envisioned in the candlelight. Cicely's eyes were violet. Frowning, he snatched up the sack with the red wine and strode across the porch and into the kitchen.

"Cicely, I'm home." Odd—the house seemed awfully quiet. Yet her nearly full glass sat beside the open wine bottle. Ah, a note. Obviously she'd come to the same conclusion as he—that jealousy was immature—and she'd gone to unpack.

Confident that time would iron things out, Cole snatched up the note as he set the bottle on the counter. "Cole." His name on the front was dressed in feminine curlicues. Inside she'd written: "I remembered an appointment back home. If you get tired of playing Davy Crockett and return to civilization, look me up. We'll have a drink for old times' sake. Cicely."

She left? Just like that? Cole sank into a chair. Before long his temper simmered on the edge of anger. Just as suddenly loneliness slipped over him like a coastal fog. But scarcely a minute had ticked by before he felt a vague sense of relief. And on its heels, a harsh stab of guilt. Talking about honesty—hadn't *he* been slightly deceptive? The reason for his urgency in coaxing Cicely to visit was that he'd found himself thinking far too often of Tibby Mack. Yaqui Springs's one-woman-salvation show. The very last woman he should let bewitch him.

Regretting the way he'd used Cicely, Cole smacked the counter with his fist. He would never forgive himself if anything happened to her. In a couple of hours he'd phone and apologize. Whether or not she forgave him, at least he'd know that she arrived home in one piece.

Why was hindsight always clearer? Cole saw now that he'd blown their feelings for each other seriously out of proportion. And from her not-so-subtle comment in the note, it was apparent she'd never be happy here.

While Cole plowed through some hard truths, his stomach let out a mournful growl. The smell of pasta and garlic bread reminded him that he'd skipped breakfast and lunch. He poured Cicely's wine down the sink. Not in the mood to drink alone, he placed her glass in the dishwasher, corked the bottle and opened the fridge to set it inside. Holy Toledo, every shelf overflowed. Food enough for a small army.

A damn shame to let it go to waste. To say nothing of his candles and the moonlight, he thought ruefully.

Brushing a thumb thoughtfully over his chin, Cole

gazed out the kitchen window. Through no fault of her own, Tibby's feelings had been hurt. And here he was…

The worst she could say was no.

When he located the phone book, he found her still listed under L. Mack. The Yaqui Springs section of this scrawny phone book barely covered two pages. The listing of restaurants in Hollywood's directory was ten times that. For several quickened heartbeats he stared at the *A* to *M* page. Afraid of losing his nerve, he punched in her number.

"Hello." She sounded somewhat out of breath.

"Tibby, uh, Cole here. Look, I know this is sudden, but Cicely had to, uh, leave unexpectedly. I have tons of food. I…well, if you haven't already eaten, you could help me out." The silence stretched so long Cole thought she'd hung up. "Tibby?"

"Is this your idea of payback? I told you I had nothing to do with those roses."

"No. Believe me, I feel as bad as you do. Really, I have all this food and only me. Please…come as you are." He didn't want to sound desperate, but was awfully afraid he had.

A delicious shiver wound up Tibby's backbone. She gazed helplessly at the baggy sweats she'd donned after work to do her yoga exercises—which had been interrupted by Ariel stopping by to say she was home and thank Tibby for feeding the hounds. Now this. Covering the mouthpiece, Tibby whispered, "Don't leave, Ariel. Cole O'Donnell invited me to dinner. But I can't go. I need you to give me some pointers on training my dog—now.

"What? I didn't hear what you said. No, not you, Cole. I have company. Hold on a sec."

Tibby put down the phone. "Ariel," she said firmly,

"if I went over there, I certainly would not put on makeup and a nice dress." Tibby didn't tell Ariel, but *she* knew she was Cole's second choice. "Please stay," she begged. "Yes, I know you all think I don't socialize enough. But eating next door hardly classifies as a huge social outing. OK," she grumbled, "it probably *is* the neighborly thing to do. Even so, I'll take him at his word and go dressed as I am."

Ariel waved and left, saying she'd drop off some videos and obedience-training manuals. Only then did Tibby clear her throat and turn back to the telephone. "Cole. Are you still there...? Oh. I thought maybe you'd given up. Of all the people you might have asked, why invite me?"

"Because..."

When he didn't finish the sentence, Tibby tightened her grip on the receiver and shrugged. "I haven't eaten. If...if this is a genuine offer, I'll come. What can I bring?"

Cole hadn't realized his stomach was knotted until it uncoiled. "Nothing. I told you, I have everything. I know dinner won't make up for— What I mean is, I'd welcome the company. We'll avoid the subjects of golf courses and roses. OK?"

Tibby twisted the phone cord around and around her index finger. There went her chance to give him Harcourt's letter. "All right," she said, fighting a thickness in her voice. "Just give me some time to run my dog."

"Run him on over here. I promise not to feed him under the table."

She laughed. "He's too big to fit under the table. Are you sure you want me to bring him? I can't vouch for his manners. I just got him today."

"Tibby, bring the damned dog."

"OK. Bye." Releasing her breath, Tibby plunked down

the receiver, leashed the dog and dashed outside before she could change her mind.

All along the inky path, her thundering heart drowned out normal night sounds. Just yesterday she'd imagined facing Cole O'Donnell across a candlelit table. But that was silliness. He might light candles for Cicely, but not for her.

The minute Tibby cleared the first step, she saw through the screen that he'd done exactly that. A candle glowed warmly on a table set for two. Others flickered in glass holders scattered about the patio. Definitely a romantic setting. Tibby panicked. Shifting from foot to foot, she scraped futilely at loose strands of hair that had fallen from her braid during her exercises. A little late now to be worrying about how she looked. Darn, why hadn't she listened to Ariel?

Without warning, Cole appeared in the doorway leading to the kitchen. "Hi. I thought I heard a noise." He waved a spatula, motioning her in.

Telling the dog to behave, Tibby herded him in first. As soon as she noticed Cole's silk shirt and crisp slacks, she felt even more self-conscious and kept to the shadows.

"Come have a glass of wine. The casserole and garlic bread needed reheating. It'll only take a minute. We can start with salad if you're starved."

"Uh, no. Whatever you want is fine." Tibby swung her arms to and fro. Aware the gesture showed her nervousness, she told Exterminator to stay while she stepped determinedly out for Cole's inspection.

He gave her worn jogging suit the once-over. "You weren't kidding about going out for a run. I used to jog for exercise, but when you live in hotels like I've done, it's easier to use the fitness room."

"I don't run regularly. Only when I tend Ariel Pulaski's

dogs. I'm sorry I look so grungy. You *did* say come as you are.'' Her tone was defensive.

His eyes made a slow feast of her. "That I did. And you look fine. Better than fine. Now, what would you like—red wine or white?"

Her heart sped erratically under his slow perusal. "I don't know. I rarely drink anything but fruit juice. Whichever. Don't pour me very much. When you aren't used to liquor, a little goes a long way."

"In that case, I recommend the white. It's already chilled.'' Shrugging, he bent quickly to remove the casserole from the oven. "I got back from the store to find Cicely had vanished," he said in a burst of honesty.

"Oh." Tibby moved fully into the kitchen then stopped dead. She'd been to enough potlucks in Yaqui Springs to recognize the array of cookware spread across Cole's counter. Winnie's signature salad, Justine's hors d'oeuvres, and if her eyes didn't deceive her, that was Henrietta's pasta Cole had just pulled from his oven.

"I thought *you'd* cooked dinner," Tibby exclaimed.

"I intended to. I bought all the stuff. Well, you know that. Apparently Joe told Winnie I was expecting a guest. She and her friends fixed all this to welcome Cicely. Since they were so thoughtful, how would it look if I took everything back? That's when I decided to call you. It's OK, isn't it? I mean, they aren't horrible cooks or anything?"

"No," Tibby murmured, struggling with jealousy. "They're excellent cooks. Outside of Winnie and Joe, most of them have high blood pressure because of it. I try to encourage them to eat more fruits and veggies. Less meat, eggs and cheese. Rich food was your grandfather's problem, too. He had heart disease for years and wouldn't alter his eating habits."

"I didn't know. About the heart disease, I mean. I knew

he loved to eat, and he did enjoy an after-dinner cigar.''
Cole handed Tibby her small glass of wine, his fingers a
bit unsteady. ''It's hard being here without him. Crusty
as he was, he always had time for me. He listened.'' Cole
lost himself in memories. ''I never knew my dad. He died
of a rare blood disorder when I was two. His long illness
left us broke. Gramps could have walked away—but he
didn't.'' His voice changed and bitterness crept in.
''Anna—my mother—felt he owed her a living for bearing the only O'Donnell grandson.''

Cole's stormy eyes widened as if he'd only just become
aware of Tibby's presence. ''Hey, I don't want to bore
you. I'm sure we can find better dinner conversation. If
you'd take the salad to the table, I'll bring the pasta.''

Tibby nodded, her mind jumbled. Yale had rarely mentioned his son or his daughter-in-law, but he'd constantly
bragged about Cole. Lovingly called him the whiz kid.
Oh, he'd been proud of his only grandson, all right.

After they were seated, Tibby took only a small helping
of salad and a little manicotti. She chose the thinnest slice
of bread.

''Don't overeat,'' Cole teased.

''I generally eat my biggest meal at lunch.''

''Ah. That's the way they do it in Italy. But they nap
all afternoon. I happen to know you're on the go all day.''

''I'm rarely sick, though. So, tell me about Italy and
Spain. Your grandfather loved getting your postcards. He
read them so often he knew their messages by heart.''

''You obviously spent a lot of time with him.''

Tibby toyed with her food. ''You're right—he did listen. Gram was pretty sick, and I was scared. Yale understood. And didn't he have a great sense of humor?''

Cole noticed how her face softened as she spoke of his
grandfather. His stomach tightened in resentment of their

easy relationship. Or was it guilt that she'd been here at the end and he hadn't? That prompted a nasty thought. "I imagine a lonely old man would be easy prey for a sweet smile."

Tibby straightened. "What do you mean?"

"Nothing." He let their gazes clash. "Then again, maybe I do. So far, I have only your word that Gramps *gave* you that land."

Exterminator opened a sleepy eye and growled as Tibby half rose from her chair. "I don't think I like what you're implying. Besides, you promised we weren't going to discuss the golf course. So much for your word."

Cole dropped his gaze first. "Sit," he muttered. "I did promise. Erase everything." He picked up his glass of wine. "What would you like to know about Italy and Spain?"

Tibby eased down on the edge of the chair again, grabbed her glass and took a bracing sip. Their eyes locked, and she stared into his until she judged him to be sincere. "I want to know everything you saw in Rome, Venice, Barcelona and Madrid."

"Tall order." He hooked an arm over the back of his chair. "Each is so different. Rome is warm reds. Old architecture mixed with new. Venice is layers of gray. A city struggling against ruin. Attempts at restoration may be too little, too late. Madrid pulses with people. Loud, friendly, colorful. Barcelona...let's see." He rolled the wine around his glass and took another sip. "Mostly I remember the government red tape. I'd never needed so many permits to build a golf course. The finished product was fantastic, though. Marble floors in a clubhouse with twenty-five-foot ceilings and ten chandeliers." His enthusiasm seemed to wane. "The club was so exclusive they wouldn't even let me play the course before I left."

Tibby glanced up sharply. "You're good at golf, I suppose."

"Fair," he said, not being one to brag. "I don't get to play nearly enough."

"Somehow I thought tennis was your game."

Cole choked on the pasta noodle he'd just swallowed. Was that some kind of double entendre? Well, if she *wasn't* aware of the accommodating tennis coach, he sure wasn't going to clue her in.

"Are you all right?" she asked. "Henrietta uses a lot of stringy mozzarella."

"She does. But it's good. Have a second helping, or I'll be eating it warmed up for a month." Deftly Cole steered the conversation off the subject of tennis.

"I couldn't. But maybe I'll take more salad."

As Cole passed her Winnie's crystal dish, his eyes ran appreciatively over her slender pale-gold neck and the flyaway curls nestled there.

She glanced up and caught him staring. "Do I have salad dressing from ear to ear?" She set down the bowl and raised her napkin to her face.

"Do you ever wear your hair down?" he asked without warning.

Tibby shook her head. "Only at night when I'm sleeping."

Cole experienced a jolt as he imagined how her hair would look spread over a pillow. His pillow. A man who appreciated textures, he reached across the small table and picked up the tail of her thick braid. Thumb and forefinger separated the strands. In the flicker of the low-burning candles, he watched the variegated shades sparkle.

Slowly his eyes lifted to hers.

Tibby shrank from the tingle in her breast as his fingers inadvertently grazed her fleece-covered nipple. Her heart went into overdrive. "What are you do...ing?" Her voice crumbled. She was mesmerized by the darkening in his gray eyes.

Cole's long tanned fingers continued to play with the braid. His thumb rhythmically stroked the tip. "Mm... nice," he murmured. "Feels like silk," he said huskily. "But then I suppose all men tell you that."

"I, uh, no, they don't." Tibby wasn't inclined to let him know she'd only ever had one date in her life, and it had been disaster. A woman her age should be more adept at fielding compliments. She knew from reading women's magazines that she should be reserved but clever. Unfortunately she found herself ill prepared for the trembling that seized her body. And Cole's crooked smile—Lordy, it made her light-headed.

Feeling every bone in her body turn to grease, she yanked her braid away. "It's...getting late," she stammered. "I have to pick Mabel up from the airport at nine tomorrow morning." As she climbed awkwardly to her feet, her knees threatened to give out. Magazines made all this dating stuff sound so easy. They should give detailed instructions.

Cole rose, too, thrown off-kilter by her swift retreat. "Wait! You can't leave before dessert. The coffee's already perked. It's decaf," he added, anticipating a claim that coffee would keep her awake.

He seemed so anxious she had no choice but to sink back onto her seat. Besides, with the uncomfortable moment past, would it hurt to share a few more minutes with him? Added memories for when she was alone again.

Cole brought the coffee first. "I'll serve dessert if you pour," he said, clearing a place on the table for the carafe. Not waiting for her response, he removed their dinner plates and hurried away.

Tibby had just replaced the carafe when a chill walked up her spine. She sensed Cole behind her, his lips all too close to her ear.

His breath fanned her cheek. "Something tells me you'd taste sweeter than this raspberry thingamajig," he murmured, his fingers brushing her neck as he placed a small plate in front of her. Smiling benignly, he brandished his plate aloft.

Next thing Tibby knew, some ninety pounds of Great Dane skyrocketed across the room, hit Cole broadside and knocked him flat at her feet. Deep growls filled the room as the dog slurped at the raspberry-topped torte that had landed on Cole's chest.

Leaping up, Tibby tried to pull her pet away. "Don't let him eat that whole thing," she panted. "It'll make him sick."

Don't let him? Cole's only aim was to avoid large snapping teeth. It felt like an hour, but really only seconds passed before he regained his feet. His silk shirt was ripped and stained. His hair, he knew, had raspberry goo in it. Cole glared at Tibby. "You said you were going to teach him to attack—not that you already had."

"It was the torte. The girl at the animal shelter said Exterminator loves sweets. Oh, my poor baby." Tibby wiped the dog's sticky nose and dabbed a napkin at his red paws. "If he throws up, it'll be your fault."

"*My* fault? Who's the injured party here?" Cole's gestures drew Tibby's frantic gaze to his ruined shirt.

"You said to bring him. I'm sorry, Cole, he—"

Cole stalked to the screen door and yanked it open. Outside, the crickets stopped chirping. The silence served to remind him of Cicely's precipitous departure. "It's been...an evening to remember. But I just remembered something else—it's time I phoned to see that Cicely got home safe and sound.''

''I never pegged you for a spoilsport,'' Tibby huffed to cover feelings of green-eyed envy. ''Come on, Exterminator, we've overstayed our welcome.'' She shoved the big dog through the door before he could get a hankering to devour the second slice of torte.

Twice Tibby paused on the dark trail to look back. Obviously Cole intended to wait on the porch until she made it home safely, too. Hastening her steps, she tried not to dwell on Cole's warm breath on her neck or how much she would've liked him to kiss her. *Had* he been planning to kiss her? Maybe. There was no telling what would have happened if Exterminator hadn't intervened.

No telling at all.

Have you forgotten, warned her good sense, *that you were Cole O'Donnell's second choice?*

Yes, she had. And it would pay her to remember.

CHAPTER FIVE

TIBBY AWAKENED to a terrible racket. A vibrating roar. At first she thought Yaqui Springs was in the throes of an earthquake. One arm of the San Andreas fault did run close by. Winnie had shown her evidence of the historic shift that separated the Salton Sea from the Pacific Ocean—petrified saltwater fish embedded on a ridge high above the current level of the water. A few years ago the basin had been badly shaken by a quake centered in the Yucca Valley. Stock had fallen off Tibby's store shelves, and two favorite pieces of glassware belonging to Great-grandmother Mack had shot out of the breakfront and shattered.

Burrowing under the pillows, Tibby waited for the rocking to begin. The latest safety information said to lie quietly in the middle of the bed. More fully awake now, she yawned and willed her panic to evaporate. She hadn't slept well because she'd spent the night obsessively raking over her evening with Cole O'Donnell.

Exterminator. Tibby scrambled to the edge of the mattress and peered over. The dog lay on the floor, nose flat to the rug, paws covering his ears. Odd. He wasn't whining. Pete Banks said that dogs, sensing the shift of a fault long before the shaking started, barked a warning. Come to think of it, although the bedroom hummed, she didn't feel any sway. Nor was her stomach giddy from the kinetic energy like last time.

Minutes passed. When nothing happened, Tibby ventured out of her bed. Shrugging into her robe, she ran to the window. It was light. Barely. Five-thirty, according to the clock.

"Oh, my stars!" Two giant bulldozers and a grader threw dirt and rock and desert scrub brush to the four winds. Clouds of dust billowed toward her house, burying her gardens under a fine silt. Tibby quickly slammed her window shut before the grit and grime filtered inside.

She leaned her head against the cool glass, forcing her brain to function. This was Sunday, wasn't it? Yes, she was sure of it. *Cole!* How had he managed to bribe a construction crew into working on a weekend?

Darn it all, she'd assumed she had until Monday to deliver the letter. Mr. Harcourt said it might be three days after that before the courts actually processed an injunction. At the rate they were moving earth and clearing land, all could be lost by then.

Her head reeled. Had Cole decided to change the location of his clubhouse? Given his expertise, he could sketch it in anywhere. If he *had* moved it, her injunction served no purpose. Tibby's stomach clenched. Something like that, you'd think he'd have told her last night, even if they had agreed not to discuss the golf course.

Turning away from the window, she hurriedly fed the dog. Then she took a quick shower and threw on a denim jumper. As she brushed and braided her hair, she decided she owed it to herself to deliver the letter and find out what was going on.

She collected the envelope and went out by the back door. A sick feeling engulfed her. Her herbs and vegetables were unrecognizable under the layer of dust. The fruit trees wept dusty blossoms. Red tomatoes, ready for pick-

ing, were streaked a dirty brown. And her strawberries—
Tibby didn't even want to look at them.

Angry, she summoned the dog and charged forward.
Darn, she'd left in such a hurry, she'd forgotten to leash
him. The two of them plowed through dusty ruts to reach
the path that led to Cole's house. Tibby saw him before
he noticed her.

He stood on his porch clad only in a pair of gray chinos.
Barefoot and tousled, he clutched a steaming cup of coffee
in both hands. It took her a moment to stabilize her stomach and forge ahead.

Noticing her at last, Cole turned and cracked the screen
door ajar.

Tibby shied away from so much tanned flesh. She
stayed where she was on the second step, shouting to
make herself heard above the ruckus of his dozers. "I trust
you have a permit to desecrate the desert, O'Donnell."

"Of course. And it'll be an oasis when I finish. Try to
picture grassy slopes and waving palms."

She flung out an arm. "Right now, sand and dirt are
blowing everywhere!"

"Sorry. Because it's so dry here, I have to contour the
course for water retention. As soon as the men finish today, they'll wet the ground good."

Tibby's hands settled on her hips. "That's too late.
They're ruining my gardens."

"Construction is messy," he said, shifting his cup to
more easily take a drink. "Especially this first phase.
Next, I'll tap into Gramps's wells and lay the irrigation
pipes. Once that's done, I can begin to sod."

"Wells? California environmental regulations are strict.
You're competing with farmers who need water for irrigation. Battles over water here are legendary." She
brightened at the prospect.

"Gramps owned the mineral and water rights on all his land. His wells are deep and clear. I plan on pumping into a holding tank."

Exterminator darted off through the trees. Tibby called him back to no avail. Giving up, she said to Cole, "Even if water's no problem, I can't believe you relocated your clubhouse, redrew the plans, submitted them and had them approved this fast."

Cole's expression gave him away.

Tibby saw the shadow of guilt pass over his face. "You didn't change anything!" she accused. "You're still planning to build on the site of our post office. A facility my grandmother worked until her death to establish." She exaggerated somewhat, but hey—it was in a good cause.

Cole's jaw jutted. "Is that a deed you're clutching? Clear title is the only thing that'll make me back off."

"Is that so?" Tibby closed the distance between them and slapped the letter from her grandmother's attorney into his outstretched palm. "Try an injunction, bud. Move one blade of that dozer near the post office, and you'll be sorry."

Cole set his cup down and tore open the letter. Reading it, he swore soundly. "So you found their agreement?"

"The attorney said I didn't need it. Once Gram cut through all the bureaucracy to have Yaqui Springs declared a bona fide postal-service center, the site and the building automatically came under the protection of federal law."

"The building, I can see. But not the land. You can't build a post office on someone's private land just because it suits you and the community."

"I'm not going to argue, Cole. I'm going to the airport to pick up Mabel Sparks. Tomorrow, talk to Mr. Harcourt. If your golf course depends on that piece of property, you

might want to call off your crew and go back to the drawing board.''

"Delay tactics," he said, folding the letter and returning it. "Even if your grandmother and my grandfather had
some sort of gentlemen's agreement, it won't hold up in
court. Why don't you admit that's all it was? You may
be eligible for some federal aid to move the building, you
know."

"Why can't you get it through your thick head that it
was more than a gentlemen's agreement?" Tibby tapped
a thumb to her chest. "I'll have you know I won—"

Cole had opened his mouth to cut her off when Tibby's
dog came yipping into the yard, claiming their full attention.

"He sounds hurt," Tibby said. She rushed down the
steps. The dog danced in circles, his cry sounding human.

"What is it?" Cole descended, coming as close as he
dared in his bare feet.

"His muzzle is full of barbs. Oh, my poor baby," she
crooned.

"Hold him still," Cole said. "Did he meet a porcu-
pine?" Serious gray eyes probed Tibby's watery green
ones.

"More like a cactus. Prickly pear? There's too many
spikes for me to try and pull them out. I'll have to take
him to a vet." She tried to pick up the dog to carry him
home, but he was squirming too much, and far too heavy.

"Let me grab a shirt and shoes and I'll help," Cole
offered.

"OK, but hurry, please."

Cole wasn't gone sixty seconds. He clattered down the
stairs, sneakers untied and shirt unbuttoned. Murmuring
soothing words, he scooped up the frightened animal. The

dog's head hung over one arm, rump and tail the other, but Cole seemed oblivious to the weight.

Tibby led the way down the path, her concern over the dozers forgotten for the moment. Her hands shook as she opened the back passenger door of her station wagon. "You'll have more room here than in front with me."

"How far to the vet?" he asked once he had Exterminator settled across his lap. The Dane's sides heaved and he continued to whimper.

She started the car before answering. "The one Ariel uses is a few miles the other side of Mecca. But it's Sunday, and I don't have an account there or anything. Oh, my stars! Money. I have to go find my purse. Heavens, I'm in such a state I'd have driven off without a driver's license." She dashed off, leaving the vehicle running.

Cole shook his head. Not only didn't she lock her house, but she left her keys in the car for someone to come along and steal.

"Cole, I've got another problem," she announced on her return. "I'm supposed to get Mabel at the airport in a little over an hour."

"Maybe Joe and Winnie—"

"Sunday is their couples' golf game. They tee off at seven."

"Surely in all of Yaqui Springs there's someone who owes you a favor," Cole snapped.

"We don't keep score. That isn't the point."

"What *is* the point? It seems to me you run yourself ragged for them. Isn't turnabout fair play?"

She ignored his sarcasm. "The few who still drive have standing commitments on Sundays. Oh, poor thing," she said, trying to comfort the dog, unable to stand hearing his pathetic cries. Then she put the car in gear and drove off in a cloud of dust. "I'll call the airport and page Mabel. She'll understand. I just hate to make her wait. Visits to her daughter are stressful enough.''

"Then why does she go?"

"Duty. Love. A constant hope that this time will be different.'' Tibby glanced at him in the rearview mirror. ''Her daughter's married to a big-shot lawyer. They're too cheap to hire a sitter when they go away on business. Yet they stuck Mabel out here because it was inexpensive compared to retirement places closer to them in Carmel. And they expect her to come at the snap of a finger. What burns me is that they even make her pay her own airfare.''

Cole grimaced. "Nice folks."

"Yeah. Take her story and multiply it by forty or so. Other than the couples who moved here because they used to vacation by the Salton Sea, their stories are remarkably similar.''

Cole met her sad gaze in the mirror. Something stirred in his chest. Tibby Mack truly cared about these people. Cole's fingers tightened in the dog's soft ruff. "Look." He cleared his throat. "There's no reason we can't take care of the pooch *and* Mrs. Sparks. If you trust me with your car, I'll leave you at the vet's, then go on to the airport.''

"Would you? That'd be great." Tibby's fingers relaxed on the steering wheel. "Why wouldn't I trust you with this old heap? You, the owner of a Jag?''

"You're kidding. Don't tell me you have no idea how much this old woody's worth?''

She laughed. "This junker? Sure, and I've got a bridge to sell you.''

"You don't know," he scoffed. "There's quite a group around the country who restore them. Every year they meet in Santa Monica to swap stories and car parts. It's a big convention. The interior of your wagon's in top shape. If you washed it and gave it a coat of wax, you might get, say, thirty to thirty-five thousand for it.''

"Dollars?'' Shocked, Tibby took her eyes from the road a moment.

"No, pesos. Of course, dollars.''

"Wow.'' She patted the dash. "My grandfather bought this car new. Grandmother didn't drive, and Winnie taught me when I was fifteen. The wagon had years of crud built up on her by then. Her tires were mush. But Gram could never bring herself to part with it, even though Grandpa died the year before I came here to live.''

"So you begged her to let you fix it up, huh?''

"No. She gave it to me for my sixteenth birthday. The residents secretly spiffed it up and bought new tires. The odometer only had eight thousand miles on it.'' It came back to her in a flash. If Cole had accepted her invitation to the Date Festival, he would have been her first passenger—and the ultimate birthday present. "Enough about me,'' she said briskly. "How's Exterminator doing?''

"He's a trooper. There must be twenty-five of those burrs stuck in his snout. Those things hurt like the very devil. I remember getting three in my leg once. Gramps told me not to go exploring unless I put on jeans. I wore shorts deliberately. Somehow I bumped into a cholla. Boy, did I hate to ask for his help,'' Cole admitted wryly. "He never said I told you so, though he must've wanted to.''

"I doubt that,'' Tibby said softly. "Yale told me once how much he wished you lived with him, like I did with Gram. But I guess I don't have to tell you that your mom insisted you stay in Hollywood where you'd have the best schools and a classy place to live.''

"Anna insisted? She didn't give a damn about me, just

Gramps's money," Cole said. "He had the power to tell her no."

Tibby let her gaze rest briefly on him in the mirror. "He didn't, Cole. Your mom threatened to marry some guy from Vermont and take you away for good."

"You mean Wendell Severson, the syrup king? She wouldn't have married him. He was too crude. Anyway, Gramps must have known I'd never have gone."

"How could he be sure?"

"I never made any secret of how I felt. I wanted to stay here."

"Really? A few years ago when Yale thought you were coming for Christmas, he got so excited. I spruced the place up because he was sick. I even decorated a tree. You phoned at the last minute and canceled. Didn't sound to me like you cared."

Cole appeared bewildered. "I'd received a great offer to design a course abroad. I was torn trying to decide what to do. The job meant a lot to my career, but I didn't want to hurt Gramps. He insisted I go. I had no idea I'd be building three courses back to back—or that I'd never see him again." Cole's chest shuddered.

"We're here," Tibby announced unnecessarily. What in heaven's name had made her say those spiteful things to Cole? Until now she hadn't realized that a part of her blamed him for the decline she'd observed in Yale from that day on. Still, she had no right to hurt Cole. It wasn't like her. And Yale would never have approved.

Stopping the car, she reached back and stroked the dog. "You sent postcards, which most families of our seniors don't even bother doing. I probably condemned you more than Yale did when you didn't come for that visit. I thought you were ungrateful, after all he'd done for you. I just assumed you knew he wasn't well."

She flew from the car. It felt good to get that off her chest, and better to have learned the truth. Perhaps Cole would see why her feelings for him were ambivalent. Knocking on his window, she pointed. "The sign on the vet's door says to pick up the phone and dial twelve for an after-hours emergency. He must live on the premises."

Cole nodded, still struggling with what she'd said. He opened the door and slid out, doing his best to minimize the dog's pain. No wonder Tibby had shied away from his touch last night. From the sounds of it, she thought he was a real jerk.

Not that he claimed to be perfect. Far from it. But Cole wasn't used to such honesty from a woman. He climbed slowly from the car, gazing at her through new eyes as he carried the dog to her side.

Tibby hung up the phone and glanced around expectantly. The veterinarian—Dr. Carlyle, presumably, as that was the name emblazoned on the building—trotted across the lot from a house nestled in the trees. He was tall. Leaner than Cole. Much younger than Ariel had led her to believe.

"Ow, that looks nasty," he said, running a practiced eye over Exterminator's thorny nose. "Thank goodness you found him right away. Some animals try to rub the spikes out on grass or a bush. They only succeed in jamming them in deeper." Taking a key from his pocket, he opened the door and led them into a noisy office. "Use examining room one," he instructed, shouting over the cacophony of barks and meows that greeted them.

"It sounds as bad in here as it did at the animal shelter. How do you stand it?" Tibby asked, hovering in the doorway.

The young vet shrugged. "These animals are going

home soon. Those at the shelter sometimes aren't so fortunate.''

''I know.'' Tibby sounded stricken. ''Yesterday I wanted to take them all with me. As it was, I adopted an extra. A Pekingese I forced on Millie Hopkins.''

''Really?'' The doctor pushed a tanned hand through unruly black curls. ''Good for you.'' He gave Tibby an admiring glance as he retrieved his lab coat and shrugged it over his broad shoulders. ''Mildred needed a new pet. I was on duty when she lost her old dog. You must be a miracle worker. She wouldn't listen when I suggested a new one. Well, well, maybe I'll take a run out there some evening to see how she's doing. Do you live in Yaqui Springs? I've never met anyone from there who's a day under sixty.''

''Not true.'' Tibby laughed. ''Several are in their late fifties.'' She cocked her head. ''Are you new to this clinic? No offense, but from the way Ariel Pulaski talks, I expected you to be much older.''

Cole had never heard Tibby's laugh sound quite so carefree. He glanced from one speaker to the other. Oddly enough he wanted to hustle Tibby out of there. Immediately.

''That'd be my father,'' the doctor said, disregarding Cole. ''I have a practice in Palm Springs. In November a horse kicked Dad. He's had complications, so I left my office in my ex-wife's care and came to help out. It wouldn't take much to convince me to stay.'' He smiled at Tibby.

Cole elbowed his way between them to lay the Great Dane on the examining table. Tibby seemed to have forgotten her friend at the airport. Cole wasn't anxious to leave her alone with this smooth talker, either. Maybe he wouldn't. ''Tibby, you know the Palm Springs airport much better than I do. Why don't I stay with Exterminator while you collect Mabel? The doc may need a strong arm to help hold this rascal's head.'' Cole cradled the dog's square jaw.

Tibby stepped closer to the table. "Appealing offer, since I can't stand the thought of him being hurt worse. But that wouldn't be very fair of me. Exterminator is my responsibility.''

Cole drummed up a smile. "Yes, but so is Mabel. If I try and pick her up, she may crack me over the head with her umbrella.''

"No way. First, it isn't raining. Second, she'll be thrilled. A little bird told me Mabel thinks you're *nice-looking*," Tibby said dryly.

Dr. Carlyle spread out an array of instruments, using the time to size Cole up.

Embarrassed, Cole wanted to bolt. "I have it on good authority that some people in Yaqui Springs hold less flattering opinions of me.'' He yanked the keys from Tibby's fingers and gave her a hard smile. "I'll hurry back. Anything special I should know about your car?''

Tibby dropped her purse on a chair and took his place beside the whimpering dog. "One thing. Any speeding tickets you get, you pay, O'Donnell.''

That was as good an exit line as he was likely to hear, Cole decided. He flashed her a cocky grin and jogged toward the door.

"Cole...'' Rushing around the table, she caught his arm.

The tremor in her voice, more than the zap he experienced from her touch, slowed his steps.

"Thanks for putting aside our differences long enough to help. I couldn't have managed this alone.'' Giving his arm a last squeeze, she went back to her pet.

Heat seemed to bubble along Cole's skin. He felt the imprint of her fingers all the way to the car. It took him three tries to get the key into the ignition. "You fool," he muttered to himself. "Didn't you hear what she said? I think you'd better concentrate on those differences, pal." After all, they weren't easily set aside. That building she was so protective of sat on the ideal spot for his clubhouse. Until they got the little matter of who owned that land squared away, it'd be crazy to pursue anything personal.

Try to forget her as he might, Tibby's wide eyes and sweet smile lingered in his thoughts until he merged with the traffic headed into the airport's short-term parking. Once he'd parked and locked the vehicle, his attention shifted to the problems at hand. Man, this place had grown. Joe Toliver said the Palm Springs golf courses had long waiting lists. Cole had dismissed it as exaggeration when in fact it must be true.

When he'd offered to come to the airport, Cole hadn't figured it'd be a problem finding Mrs. Sparks. He ended up waylaid by a host of travelers rushing in all directions; that cost him ten or so minutes. He only hoped he remembered what the woman looked like. He was glad Tibby had mentioned that Mabel'd been visiting in Carmel. According to the directory, her plane had just touched down.

Cole dumped his keys and loose change in a tray near the security checkpoint. Luckily his belt buckle didn't set off buzzers as it often did. Last time it'd been something to do with his shoes. He hated half undressing in the midst of a group of strangers who all shied away as if he was carrying a hidden weapon. Today, nothing. Hallelujah! Smiling at the attendant, he refilled his pockets and jogged up to the gate in time to see the last of the passengers leave the plane. One woman he vaguely recognized.

"Mrs. Sparks." Cole walked over and introduced himself.

"Why, as I live and breathe—Cole O'Donnell." Mabel smoothed a hand over a neat coil of white hair. "How nice to see you again. Are you taking this flight out?"

"No. I've come for you. Do you have bags checked?"

"One. I expected Tibby. She's not sick, is she?" Pale eyes searched his face.

Cole explained the situation as they fell into step and followed the crowd.

"A dog. Humph. That girl needs a Great Dane to care for like she needs a cross-eyed bear. Instead of tying herself down with more responsibilities, Tibby ought to let down her hair and swing a little."

Cole made a noise he hoped passed for agreement. He disliked gossip with a passion. Yet he had a hard time shaking the image of Tibby letting down her hair.

"Tell me what your bag looks like," he said politely. "You wait here, away from the crowd. I'll retrieve it."

"How thoughtful, Cole. I am exhausted. Hard to believe I used to keep a classroom of thirty in line. These days, two preteen grandchildren wear me out."

"Kids are different today."

"Kids are the same. It's the adults who are different. As I see it, the problem started with parents wanting to be buddies to their kids, instead of parents. They don't demand respect, so they don't get it."

"Ah. I'll have to remember that if and when I have children." With this idle comment, Cole left her and made his way to the baggage carousel.

His watch had ticked off nearly fifteen minutes by the time he returned. "Phew! That took longer than I imag-

ined.'' He plunked a flowered bag down at her feet.
''They must've unloaded a million cartons of golf clubs
off that plane. I wonder if there's a tournament in town,''
he said offhandedly, steering her toward the exit closest
to Tibby's station wagon.

Mabel didn't respond. Instead, she bounced back to his
earlier remark. ''You said *if* you have children, Cole.
Don't you like children?''

''What?'' He'd all but forgotten the brief exchange.
''Oh, you mean my *if and when* statement. This isn't the
best time to ask me that question,'' he said wryly. ''A
lady I thought might share parenting with me just broke
things off and disappeared into the sunset. But hey, I'm
not in any rush,'' he lied smoothly. In truth, he'd thought
a lot lately about having a houseful of kids.

Mabel looked stricken as he opened the station-wagon
door and settled her into the front seat. Cole wondered
why someone he barely knew cared whether or not he had
children. Then again, maybe the whole subject made her
nervous, considering how, according to Tibby, her own
daughter treated her. That was probably it.

''When we reach old Doc Carlyle's,'' Mabel announced, ''I'll move to the back seat and let you ride up
here.''

''Not necessary. Tibby'll be driving home from there.
I'll keep the dog company. By the way, *old* Doc Carlyle
is laid up. *Young* Carlyle's the one working on Tibby's
dog.''

''Oh? How young?''

'''Bout my age, I'd guess.''

''Did Ariel know that?'' Mabel muttered to herself.
Turning to him, she asked more loudly, ''Is he bald like
his father?''

Cole recalled the doctor's shock of curly hair and snorted. "Not so you'd notice."

"I see. And did he seem interested in our sweet Tibby?"

"That's an understatement. He was practically drooling on her when I left." Cole shook out his sunglasses and hid a scowl. Now why did he say that? Mabel would think he was a jerk, too.

"Oh, my. Should you have left them alone?"

"She's a big girl, Mrs. Sparks."

"Twenty-six. But Tibby is... I mean, she..." Mabel seemed at a loss for words.

"She's what?" Cole lowered his glasses, peering at her through narrowed eyes.

"Our Tibby has led a sheltered life."

Cole knew he'd been away from Yaqui Springs for a long time. Was he missing some vital piece of information here? "Was Tibby headed for a convent or something?"

"Goodness, no. But by today's standards, I think Tibby is quite innocent."

"Mrs. Sparks, by today's standards, *I'm* innocent." Cole flushed. He hadn't meant to say that. He didn't tell many people that he'd had a bad experience with a girl he'd met in college. One that had left him gun-shy of women until a couple of years ago when a friend had introduced him to Cicely. Still, Mabel came from an era that might disapprove of any bodily contact between unmarried persons of the opposite sex.

On the other hand, according to Tibby, Mabel thought he was nice-looking.

In any case, they shouldn't gossip. "Uh, this probably isn't a conversation we should be having," Cole said. "We're almost at the clinic. If Tibby gives the slightest hint that the doc got out of line, I'll pretend I'm her brother and set him straight.'' Cole actually found himself warming to the idea of playing Tibby's protector.

''Her brother?'' Mabel reared back to study him thoroughly. ''Brothers don't cut ice these days. Tell him you're her lover.''

The very suggestion slammed a hot fist into Cole's gut. Slack-jawed, he took the sharp right turn into the veterinarian's parking lot on two wheels, spewing gravel all over the place. Cole couldn't say why he was so relieved to see Tibby, her dog and the vet all standing calmly in the shade of a gnarled Joshua tree.

He leaped from the car, putting an end to his unsettling chat with Mabel. What if she was going bonkers? He'd read an article that said people in nursing homes occasionally developed a fixation on sex. Who was to say it couldn't happen in a retirement community?

Safely hidden behind his dark lenses, Cole examined Tibby for any sign of agitation as he made haste to join their little entourage. She seemed perfectly relaxed. In fact, she didn't notice him until he was right in front of her.

''Back so soon?'' Eyes showing surprise, Tibby sneaked a peek at her watch. ''Grant's been telling me about some of his funnier experiences with his patients and their owners. I guess time flew.''

''Great,'' Cole muttered. He petted the dog and inspected his nose. ''You're much improved, fella.'' Then he faced the couple and said coolly, ''If the pooch could talk, I'll bet he'd tell you he wasn't amused by cute stories about animals in pain.''

''They aren't all in pain,'' Tibby said as if Cole were a quart low on brains.

In answer he tossed her the keys. ''You drive. Exterminator and I'll share the back again. If you've squared your account with the doc, I suggest we take off. Mrs. Sparks is beat.''

Tibby's annoyance at his high-handed manner switched to concern. "I'm finished here." She clasped the young vet's hand. "Thanks so much, Grant. I'll put the salve on twice a day like you said. And I'll keep him on a leash whenever I take him out. I appreciate your tips on obedience training."

"Remember, you have to be firm. On the other hand, he's probably learned his lesson." The vet seemed unwilling to release her fingers.

Cole was on the verge of exploding when the man finally turned Tibby loose.

"Remember to watch for infection," the vet cautioned. "Any sign at all, day or night, call me. Otherwise I'll drop by the store when I go to Yaqui Springs to see Mildred's new dog. Soon," he promised around a toothy smile.

Mabel stopped in the process of swinging her feet outside the car. "Mildred has a new dog? Well, glory be."

"It wasn't her idea," Tibby said, extending a hand to stay the older woman. "I'll fill you in on the way home. Bye, Grant." She flashed him a dimpled smile and backed slowly away as if reluctant to depart.

"Bye, Grant," Cole mimicked in falsetto. He hadn't intended anyone to hear. But from the twinkle in Mabel's eye, Cole knew the former schoolteacher had. Damn. He hoped he hadn't given her the impression he was jealous of that ape. Promising himself he'd set her straight at the first opportunity, Cole hoisted the dog in and climbed in after him, taking care not to slam the door. Then he had to sit there like a lackey, holding Tibby's pet while she introduced Mabel to Grant Carlyle and vice versa.

By the time Tibby had settled behind the wheel and

they drove off, Cole decided he'd had quite a bellyful of veterinarians. But why? Why did he give a damn if Tibby Mack fawned over some hairy ape till the cows came home? All he wanted from her was one lousy piece of property. A piece that rightfully belonged to him, anyway.

Cole scratched Exterminator's ears and stayed discreetly out of Tibby and Mabel's conversation. His thoughts turned to the letter from Tibby's attorney—a letter threatening to close down his operation. Any delay was bound to cost him big bucks. Cole needed every cent he had to finish the course. Contrary to what the residents seemed to believe, Gramps had left him property but no cash. The only money in this venture came from his own dwindling savings.

Sunday or not, the minute he set foot in the house, he'd get on the horn to his lawyer. If sweet Tibby Mack thought he'd give up his dream of owning a golf course without a whimper, she had another think coming.

And if that sounded like sour grapes, so be it.

CHAPTER SIX

TIBBY CRUISED to the end of Mabel's driveway and stopped.

Cole grabbed the older woman's bag and hopped out, leaving behind a more rambunctious dog than the passive animal he'd consoled on the way to the clinic. "I'll be right back," he promised the Great Dane through the window's narrow opening.

Exterminator pressed his nose to the opening and howled. Nothing Tibby said made him quit. "Fine, be man's best friend," she muttered. "But remember who feeds you."

At her front door, Mabel thanked Cole profusely and patted his cheek. "I wish you'd spirit Tibby away for a fun afternoon. Otherwise she'll work twice as hard to make up for lost time. She used to golf with your grandfather on Sundays or explore the desert with Winnie's group. Lately all she does is work, work, work. There are a lot of nice places to picnic in the park off the old Truckhaven Trail."

Truth was, Cole couldn't wait to be shut of Tibby Mack. Except…he found one thing Mabel said of interest. "Tibby golfs? Then why is she so against my building a course here?"

Mabel shrugged. "I like amusement parks, but that doesn't mean I'd want one in my backyard."

"I see. I wish I had the resources to build a block wall between our properties, but I don't right now."

"Well, I'm sure you two will work it out. A person is so much more amenable to compromise in a relaxed setting, don't you agree?"

Cole nodded, grasping Mabel's implication. Making his way to the car, he mulled over her thinly veiled challenge. Exterminator barked happily when Cole opened the back door of the car to reclaim his former seat.

It irritated Tibby that Cole obviously expected her to drive through town acting as his chauffeur. "I see you made two conquests today," she grumbled. "You have Mabel and my dog eating out of your hand."

Cole patted the wriggling Great Dane. "I'm sure you'd rather they both took a nip out of my hide. It'd give you a hilarious story to tell Carlyle."

Tibby reddened. "At least Grant's a gentleman. Have the decency to leave him out of our petty disagreements."

"No problem."

Tibby put on her sunglasses so she wouldn't have to meet his mocking gaze in the mirror. "I can't wait to see what havoc your bulldozers have wreaked. From the dust cloud hanging over my house, it could double as a nuclear test site."

Cole didn't think this was the time to act on Mabel's suggestion. The woman in the driver's seat looked anything but amenable to a picnic—or a compromise.

"No smart comeback?" Tibby demanded, flooring her brakes at a crossroads.

Now that he'd been flung forward and back by her neck-breaking stop, Cole decided he needed a breath of fresh air. "Why don't I get out here? A walk will clear my head. First on my agenda when I get home is having my lawyer block your injunction.'' Leaping out of the car, Cole was careful to keep the dog inside.

Tibby watched him cross the street, her eyes glued to the hypnotic sway of his hip pockets. She sat there drumming her fingers on the steering wheel until he turned the corner by Ralph Hopple's mobile home and disappeared from sight. Hang it all, she thought peevishly, she'd let him bring out the shrew in her again.

Exterminator scrambled into the front seat and braced his big paws on the dash. Nose twitching, ears alert, he barked sharply at his mistress.

''Don't look at me like that. I say good riddance.'' Driving off, Tibby wondered why her heart refused to agree with that statement. At the next crossroads, the Great Dane bounced from window to window, obviously looking for Cole. But no matter how slowly Tibby drove, the streets remained stubbornly empty of humans. Sighing, she passed the store and parked beneath her kitchen window.

A bulldozer and a backhoe both labored nearby, belching columns of diesel smoke into a once cerulean sky. The big dog wagged his tail and woofed expectantly at the cluster of men who worked along with the machines. Cole, of course, wasn't among them. Idly she stroked the dog's ears. ''Come on, boy, give it up. He's gone. From here on, it's thee and me. You'd better get used to it. I have.''

Refusing to listen to the nagging voice that called her a bald-faced liar, Tibby urged the dog into the house.

Now that the noise had abated—while the door was closed, anyway—she sighed again. Comforted by familiar surroundings, she brewed a pot of strong blackberry-currant tea. Using her best yoga techniques, she soon blocked out everything that reminded her of Cole O'Donnell's intrusion into her well-ordered life. Or she did, that is, until Justine Banks showed up for the haircut and coloring Tibby had promised her in exchange for working at the store.

From the outset it was clear that Justine wanted to gossip. "I sat beside Ariel in chapel this morning. She said you had dinner with Cole O'Donnell last night. Candlelight and wine," the woman mused dreamily as Tibby warmed a sweet-smelling herbal shampoo between her palms. "So tell me, did he kiss you?" Justine whispered.

"Justine!" Tibby scrubbed a bit too hard and the older woman yelped. "Sorry," Tibby said, immediately lightening her touch. "No, he didn't kiss me. Make sure you spread that information around town." Tibby rinsed off the shampoo. As she applied a conditioner she'd developed from marigold petals and sunflower oil, she told her about Exterminator's grand finale with the raspberry torte.

"Honestly, Tibby, I agree with Mabel. The last thing you need is a dog." Justine's words rode up and down the scale as a result of Tibby's vigorous toweling.

Tibby led her friend to the chair where a new environmental colorant waited. "When did you see Mabel?" Tibby asked, her mind more on what the salesman had told her about the product than on Justine's gentle reproof.

"She was out watering her yard, and I stopped to chat for a minute on my way here. Mabel was full of your trip to the new veterinarian. She said he's a dish."

"Mm-mm." Tibby held a rat-tail comb between her teeth.

Justine clasped both hands to her breast. "It's so exciting, Tibby. You went from *no* young men in your life, to not one but *two* of them vying for your attention."

The comb fell from Tibby's mouth and clattered to the

floor. "The only thing Cole O'Donnell's vying for is the property I won from Yale fair and square."

"You've forgotten those lovely roses so soon?" Justine stole a sly peek at Tibby.

"That's another thing, Justine. Cole didn't send that bouquet."

Justine stiffened. "Nonsense, child. His name was on the card."

"About that card… It disappeared."

"Really? Well, I'm sure it'll turn up. Shall we get on with the color? The Moped Mavericks are going out to Ocotillo Wells today. Henrietta says there's a stand of rare elephant trees we should see. Join us. It'll be like old times."

"I wish I could. I read that desert tribes used the elephant tree for a wide range of medicinal purposes. I'd love to see if there're any twigs lying around. But my tomatoes and beans need picking. The garden's a mess from Cole's dust."

"Of course you can't sneak away, Ms. Workaholic. Silly me."

COLE, WHO'D TAKEN a shortcut home, saw Tibby drive in. Phone to his ear, he paced from window to window, listening as the ringing in Lane Davis's law office broke off and clicked to a recorder. He disconnected, then dialed his friend at home. This time Lane answered, and Cole heard the clink of glasses in the background. Male and female laughter and the splash of water.

"Yo, Lane. Cole here. When did you start throwing pool parties?" Lane and his brother were the only men Cole knew who disliked partying as much as he did. Or they used to. Cole listened to the corporate attorney's weak explanation and apology, realizing how long he'd been out of touch with the old crowd.

"I'm not mad because you didn't invite me, Lane. I'm in the desert building a golf course.... Oh, Cicely told you? Yeah, we split. Or rather, she split." Cole was surprised that the admission didn't cause him even the smallest twinge of regret. "She's there now...? No—why would I mind? She's a free agent, Lane. Hey, buddy, since we're on my dime, could we discuss why I called? I need some legal advice." Cole laughed. "Sure, I expect a bill." That settled, he launched into the problem, taking care not to make Tibby sound like an ogre.

Lane hemmed and hawed, saying he wasn't up on federal regulations. He said a few other things, among them that he'd do some digging and call Cole midweek.

"Dig fast, pal. My money's dwindling.... What do you mean, charm the lady? I tried nice.... No, dammit, I didn't send roses.... Poker?" Cole laughed. "She's not the type to gamble. If you suggest witchcraft, Lane, I'm finding myself a new lawyer.... Oh, go soak your head." Cole dropped the handset back into its base. He stood for a moment, feeling at loose ends. Not because he missed the Hollywood scene or because his best friend expressed an interest in dating Cicely. The yawning void in his gut had more to do with Lane's uncertainty regarding the post office. A shack, for God's sake.

Restless, he wandered out to check on the workmen's progress. After a few minutes it was evident he was in their way. The dust was so thick he found it hard to breathe, even with the disposable face mask the crew chief gave him.

Circling a huge brush pile, Cole stared straight at Tibby's orchards and her previously lush gardens. What a mess! He ripped off the mask and gazed guiltily toward her house. There was no way to clean up until after the dozers moved to another sector. Cole had to admit, though, if he were her, he'd be plenty p.o.'d.

Perhaps Mabel's suggestion had merit, after all. Cole squinted at the sun barely visible beyond the haze kicked up by the dozers. He guessed they had a good six hours of daylight left. A picnic might be the very thing to bury the hatchet and reach an amicable compromise.

The notion of luring Tibby into a setting where he could soften her up grew on Cole as he trekked home. In spite of spending summers here, he didn't know the area. He'd boated, and fished in a few derbies. He'd explored his grandfather's land. Mostly he'd played tennis and golfed with Yale at Bogey Wells.

Tibby lived here full-time. She probably knew a lot of interesting hideaways. And other facts that'd be good in brochures. Not that he'd ask for her help until she was in a better frame of mind.

Anticipation mounting, Cole picked up the phone and called her.

"A picnic?" she exclaimed suspiciously. "Lay in a supply of poison apples, did you, O'Donnell?"

"What is it with you? It's perfectly OK if you dash around playing the high priestess of benevolence. But when anyone tries to turn the tables, you throw their good intentions back in their face."

Denial died on Tibby's lips as she glanced at Justine, who mouthed that she should go. Tibby remembered the curious things the women of Yaqui Springs had said lately. Was that how they saw her efforts to repay some of their kindness—as a sort of self-righteous benevolence? Tibby swallowed a lump. "I'm sorry, Cole. I'd go, only...I can't keep Exterminator cooped up inside all afternoon."

"Forget the dog," Justine said, plopping down the hand mirror through which she'd viewed her brighter hair color.

Cole heard the exchange going on at the other end. "You have company?"

"Justine," Tibby replied. "She's on her way out."

"Oh...I guess we could take Exterminator," Cole said without a lot of enthusiasm. A too-recent memory of his ruined silk shirt persisted.

"Really? I take back what I said last night. I guess you're not a poor sport, O'Donnell. And I insist on fixing our lunch. Deal?"

"Sure. Wear hiking boots and bring the mutt's leash."

"Aye, aye, Captain," Tibby said softly, unable to stem the joy blazing a warm trail through her body. "Give me half an hour. Shall I walk over?" She made a face at Justine and shooing motions with her hands.

"All he's vying for is your land, huh?" Justine murmured near Tibby's ear before she swished out, a satisfied smile on her face.

"I'll pick you up," Cole said, oblivious to the women's byplay.

"All right. See you." Tibby clutched the phone a moment. Strangely euphoric, she gently replaced it, then raced into the store and filled a basket with fresh fruit, as well as tomatoes, sprouts, cream cheese and pita bread for pocket sandwiches. The fruit was for dessert. She certainly didn't want a repeat of the torte incident. On her way out, Tibby tossed in two tall bottles of springwater.

Though rushed and out of breath, Tibby managed to walk sedately out the door as Cole drove in.

"We're going picnicking in that?" she gasped, staring dumbfounded at Cole's spit-polished XJE.

"You expected a broomstick?"

She fought to hang on to the Great Dane, who wanted

to greet Cole with sloppy doggie kisses. "I figured you'd take Yale's Jeep. It has all-terrain tires and four-wheel drive."

"I would, but he willed the Jeep and the Mercedes to his doctor. Here, I'll take the basket. Stuff the dog in behind your seat where he'll have more room."

Tibby let the basket slide through her fingers. "You're teasing, right? Why would your grandfather leave cars to his doctor?"

"They were friends. Fraternity brothers. Are you going to debate this all afternoon?" Cole asked impatiently.

"No, of course not. I guess I shouldn't be surprised. He left something to nearly everyone in town. We were touched." She unsnapped the dog's leash, coiled it and slid in.

Cole wanted to ask if the land was what his grandfather had left Tibby. The thought flew out of his mind when he went to close her door. "You're hiking in a dress?"

"Is there a law against it?"

"Not that I know of." Cole shrugged and rounded the hood of the car. After stowing the picnic basket, he jumped in and stoked the engine to life. "Strikes me as being damned uncomfortable, is all."

Tibby fingered her gored boot-length denim skirt. She'd paired it with a white short-sleeved blouse tied loosely at the waist. Did he think she'd done it to entice him? "Gram didn't approve of women wearing pants. She said the ones who settled this land wore dresses, and that we—"

"Women won the right to make their own decisions a long time ago, Tibby. Isn't it time you pleased yourself?"

"I do. It's like I told Justine the other day. This is who I am." She swept a hand from her head to her knees. "I know men like women who look like your girlfriend, Cole. But miniskirts and bangles aren't me."

A tic that sometimes plagued Cole flared in his left eye. "I...we...Cicely. That is, we're not..."

Tibby read in his eyes what he couldn't seem to force past his tongue. She wrapped her fingers around his forearm. "Because of the roses, Cole? I'm so sorry."

Heat arced up his arm from her touch, yet he sensed the concern in her tone, in the warmth shimmering from her eyes. His first sighting of the *sweet* Tibby Mack lauded by the residents of Yaqui Springs. And he had to set her straight. Had to see all that sweetness fade away. "My falling out with Cicely goes much deeper than a misunderstanding over roses. We don't see eye to eye on my long-term commitment to the golf course—and other important things."

"Oh." Tibby withdrew her hand and faced the front. *How* long-term?

"Hey, enough sad face already," Cole said, brushing his knuckles lightly against her chin. "We're on our way to a picnic, and I have no idea which direction to take once we hit the highway."

Exterminator thrust his head between them and barked.

Cole flinched, making Tibby laugh. "Well, we could go south into the Jacumba Mountains. Or there's Smuggler's Cave. I love the honeycombed granite passageways. They look sort of otherworldly, which I suppose is why some people refer to it as the valley of the moon. But if you like, we can go west, to where the old town of Salton used to be before the flood. It's a maze of arroyos and washes. According to legend, there are Spanish galleons and pirate ships buried out there. I used to love tagging after the Moped Mavericks. I was positive I'd find buried treasure."

"Gramps bought a metal detector and a lot of prospecting paraphernalia. Years ago he spent weeks searching for Pegleg Smith's lost gold. He quit after it was rumored to have been found. I'd forgotten that." He smiled lopsidedly.

"I remember. And you went with him a couple of times. He sent you to the store to stock up on trail mix, beef jerky and those packets of dried foods. You hated them."

"They were disgusting. I was into hamburgers and french fries. The outings were great, though. Summers here helped me survive the rest of the year."

Tibby noticed that his hands had tensed around the steering wheel and that a moodiness had settled over him. "Didn't you like school?"

"School was my salvation. I didn't like going home. I spent as little time there as possible."

"You didn't get along with your mother?"

"You can't *not* get along with someone who's never there." He seemed about to say more, then hiked a careless shoulder. "Now I'm boring you. You choose where we go, OK?"

Tibby digested what he'd said and some of the facts he'd glossed over. She'd never have guessed that Cole had a less-than-perfect childhood. The boy she'd pestered had been supremely self-assured. She'd always been the timid one.

He'd pulled up at a four-way stop and gazed at her quizzically, so Tibby pretended to study the map. "Shall we visit the caves? They're closer than the mountains and cooler than the gold flats."

"Which direction?"

She pointed. Soon they fell into discussing the Salton Sea, whose marshy shore appeared on their right. "Joe

Toliver claims the sea is a true paradox,'' Tibby said. "It's the only place in the world where wood sinks, fish have gizzards like birds, rocks float and vapors of dry ice bubble up through the warm water.''

"What's the catch?''

"There isn't one. Wood from ironwood trees sinks. Volcanic pumice floats. The fish are saltwater mullets. The dry-ice vapor is really oxygen rising from a cold natural spring under the sea. Really,'' she added when he arched a skeptical brow.

"You must be pretty smart to retain all that trivia. If I ever learned those facts, they're long gone.''

Tibby felt her cheeks grow warm. "I was home-schooled by the residents. All that one-on-one attention works, I guess.''

Reaching out, he gave a teasing yank on her braid. "Poor kid. Bet you never got to skip school.''

"You'd lose. Mabel nearly always fell for an unscheduled trip to the library. And don't tell Justine, but I never painted one of the sunsets I tricked her into analyzing from the dock.''

"Well, well. You surprise me.'' Cole picked up the tail of her braid and dusted it over the tip of her nose. "I had you pegged as Ms. Goody Two-shoes.''

Laughing, she batted his hand away and nearly missed spotting the first turn.

The road climbed, weaving among a profusion of Joshua trees, some of them forty feet high. The air cooled noticeably, and the terrain changed, becoming more rugged.

"This is nice,'' Tibby said, ducking around the dog, who'd leaned over the front seat to investigate Cole's shirt pocket. "This is the perfect time to come. Have you noticed that we have the road to ourselves? When schools let out, the park will be overrun with campers and day hikers."

"You'll have to tell me where you want to stop."

"Up ahead is a forestry road that takes off to the left. A mile from there is the cave and the moon-looking rocks. There's shade and a stream. The road isn't paved, though. I've only ever gone on a moped—we can always park and hike in."

"If we did that, wouldn't we be too tired to explore the cave? No, I think we can risk driving. A forestry road must mean the park rangers use it."

"I sincerely doubt we're talking low-slung Jaguars."

"Don't sell this baby short." Cole patted the hand-polished dash. "She's built solid as a tank."

A small frown pleated Tibby's brow. "I guess you know your car best. There—just around that next curve is the turn."

Cole slowed to a crawl. The road, red cinder, was a bit rutted. But he'd seen worse.

The car climbed one rut and fell into another. Tibby clung to the seat to keep from being thrown from side to side. Even the dog growled with displeasure. Then, unexpectedly, the road opened on a panoramic vista. Above and below stretched endless catacombs of granite. "This is it," Tibby said. "Park anywhere."

Cole turned to her with a cocky grin. "See, oh, ye of little faith? My car did just fine. Gramps's Jeep would have bounced us all over creation. I know—that's what we used to take camping."

"Go ahead, rub it in. But we're not out of here yet. I have to admit I'd feel a lot better if we'd seen at least one other car. Although you do have a car phone."

"No cell sites up here. That means we're out of phone range."

"So, you can always fax for help," she drawled.

"How do you think a fax operates? It takes a phone line. Don't worry. We'll go back the way we came. No sweat." He crawled out and stretched. "Shall we explore first, or eat and then go for a hike?"

"I'd vote to eat, then walk off the calories, but Exterminator might be more willing to lie quietly under a tree while we eat if we run his legs off first."

"Who in hell named that dog?" Cole watched Tibby snap a leash to the Dane's collar. He lent a hand when the dog lunged for a chipmunk that skittered out from a rock and ran under a low-growing bush, cheeks puffed with spring bounty.

"Thanks," she said when they had the animal corralled again. "To answer your question—they said at the animal shelter that he'd belonged to a couple of boys."

"That explains it. Here, let me wrangle him. You lead the way to the cave."

Tibby didn't argue. In spite of her skirt, she climbed nimbly over a big boulder to a worn narrow path that opened up into a maze of pockmarked rocks.

Bringing up the rear, Cole certainly couldn't complain about the view. In fact, he wondered why he'd thought she should dress differently for their outing. Her skirt switched enticingly from side to side, every once in a while affording him a peek of the slender leg above her boots. And the blouse she'd tied in front parted from the skirt's waistband each time she reached up for the next handhold. He even found the long braid that slapped rhythmically against the small of her back erotic. *Damn!* When had she stopped being a skinny kid?

By the time the panting drooling dog had jerked Cole uphill to where Tibby stood beside a gaping black hole, he, too, was panting. Not entirely from exertion.

The purpose of this excursion was to introduce a possible compromise—but not the kind Cole found running rampant through his mind just now.

So get a handle on it, doofus.

"This is the main cavern of Smuggler's Cave," Tibby pointed out. "Smaller tunnels fan out inside. Stories range from old prospectors holed up in the caves with stolen gold to more recent tales that it's an interim cache for drugs coming in across the border. Do you want to go inside?"

"Sure. Will we be able to see?"

"Voilà!" She produced a small penlight from her skirt pocket.

After the bright sun outside, stepping into the cave was like hitting a black wall. Tibby's small light didn't really penetrate the darkness. Cole ran smack into her. As he put out a hand to steady both of them, his fingers slid beneath her blouse, leaving nothing between him and her soft damp flesh. Cole snatched his hand back, but not before he felt Tibby's quick intake of breath. And his own.

"Dammit, why did you stop like that?"

"I, ah, it's darker in here than I remembered. I should have brought a larger flashlight."

"Well, you didn't, so let's get the hell out of here. Find that stream and let's eat." God, but he wanted to weld their bodies together and kiss her senseless. Impossible. They'd hadn't even begun to settle the legal quandary that created a chasm as wide as all hell between them.

Reacting to his curt tone, a tone she didn't understand, Tibby brushed past him, out the mouth of the cave and raced down the path.

But Cole didn't budge from the spot where he was rooted until Exterminator bounded forward, nearly tearing his arm from the socket. Fearing he couldn't keep his hands to himself if he joined her too quickly, Cole took his own sweet time covering the same ground. When he did arrive at the clearing, Tibby had already spread a plaid blanket in the middle of a small stand of giant spruce trees and now sat assembling pocket sandwiches as if nothing was wrong.

Taking his cue from her, Cole led the dog to the creek for a drink. But it wasn't until he tried tying the leash to a branch that he realized his hands were unsteady.

"I made you two sandwiches," Tibby said the moment he sat down. "I've noticed that most of the men who stop by the coffee bar for lunch eat two."

"Is that the extent of your experience with men?" Cole froze as their hands met over the sandwich. What made him say that? "I mean… Forget it," he muttered. "I don't know what I mean."

Tibby stiffened. "I don't know what you mean, either. I have wonderful memories of my father. He influenced my early years. Joe, Fred, Pete and your grandfather all let me tag after them. But if you were asking have I cooked intimate dinners for a date, the answer is no." He should be able to see how few opportunities there were in Yaqui Springs for her to go out with anyone her own age, for pity's sake.

"It's none of my business. An ice-breaking comment, that's all. Hey, this sandwich is terrific."

"Another icebreaker? I haven't been cloistered, Cole. I read voraciously and I have a well-rounded education. I'm capable of carrying on a decent conversation."

Cole winced, recalling that just this morning he'd asked Mabel if Tibby had been slated for the convent. He washed the last bite down with bottled water. "It's your resentment toward me that I don't understand. We don't have conversations, we have shouting matches."

"You're saying that's all my fault?" Tibby swept back her braid as she slapped fruit on a plate and plunked it between them. "You don't believe a word I say."

Cole's eyes shot wide open. "I think I've been fairly reasonable, considering you built on land I clearly inherited."

"Reasonable?" Tibby bit into a crisp apple. "I explained nicely that your grandfather donated a place to build the post office." She crunched again, and apple filled her cheeks, like those of the chipmunk they'd seen earlier.

"I won't argue," he said tightly. "I suggested this outing because my lawyer said two sensible adults ought to be able to reach a congenial compromise."

Tibby snatched the cluster of grapes right out of his hand. "If by congenial compromise you mean that I scrap the post office and you get the property, we've wasted quite enough of this day." She had the leftovers packed and all but dumped Cole off the blanket in less time than it took him to discover his grapes were missing. He only needed one look at her face to know his plan had failed miserably.

"Fine," he said, turning to collect the dog. "I was only trying to save you the expense of lawyers' fees and court costs."

They climbed into the car and rode in silence. The distance to the asphalt road seemed interminable to Tibby. From the way the car bounced, she was positive he'd break an axle or something. To her surprise they made it to the end of the forestry road in one piece. From there to the main highway, Tibby thought he drove like a madman. Or maybe it just felt like he rounded those hairpin curves on a wing and a prayer.

Twice she sneaked a look at him. Such a perfectly sculpted profile it took her breath away. Not as acutely as when he'd touched her bare skin up there in the cave, but close. Tibby began to imagine what kissing him would be like. To kiss and be kissed in return. Not a friendly peck, but an intense kiss, man to woman. What would Cole have done had she grabbed him by the shirtfront and kissed him first?

The shoreline appeared a greenish blur out Cole's window. Tibby paid no attention. She had slipped into a private fantasy and was immersed in the really good part when Cole left the highway for the gravel road leading into Yaqui Springs. A beautiful fantasy that suddenly disintegrated in a burst of pain as Cole swerved to miss a rock in the street and Tibby's head struck the side window. Hard.

Cole might have saved her the pain and himself the effort. The swerve caused him to hit a second larger rock. A grating sound underneath the car brought Exterminator up out of a sound sleep.

"Are you all right?" Cole yelled at Tibby over the dog's earsplitting barks.

"Wh-what happened?"

Cole lifted her chin to check her pupils for signs of concussion. Seeing nothing amiss, he popped open his door and bent to peer under the car. "Must have been a rock slide since we left. We ripped the housing off the gears. If there's an ounce of transmission fluid left, it would surprise me. Feel up to a walk home?"

"*We* ripped?" Tibby climbed out, resolved to the distance they'd have to walk. She was amazed to see Cole's house off to the left, and beyond, the portico jutting out from her store. "Come on," she directed the Great Dane, taking care to attach his leash. "So, Cole," she said silkily, "now we know this baby isn't built like a tank, don't we?"

Head high, she marched off.

Exterminator's tail drooped. Lowering his head, he balked, waiting for Cole until Tibby firmly pulled him along.

Finding a whole new repertoire of swear words, Cole dug out the picnic basket and started after her, grousing, "If there's a worse ending to a horrible day, I can't imagine what it'd be."

Cole trailed behind Tibby, and when at last they reached the store's parking lot, the largest of the backhoes working on his property backed over the easement and dropped its power shovel very near Tibby's porch.

She charged ahead, waving and shouting.

Cole stared openmouthed at a seventy-foot geyser of water. "Dammit to hell! That fool hit her water line."

Tibby stopped, scrubbed at her suddenly wet face and gaped at her garden, afloat in muck. She turned on Cole. "I know you said they'd wet things down after they finished for the day. But did they have to *drown* them?"

CHAPTER SEVEN

AN APOLOGY SOURED on Cole's tongue. Any attempt to make amends came too late. Tibby's tough exterior was ready to crack. The lovely green eyes stared helplessly at her ruined gardens. His fault, and words weren't adequate.

He set the picnic basket down on her porch and wrapped her in his arms. "God, I'm sorry," he whispered, lips pressed to her wet hair.

Tibby stiffened briefly, then sagged against him, accepting the comfort he offered.

Exterminator shook vigorously, slinging water everywhere. His low growl and droopy tail showed what he thought of the wetting.

"I'll fix everything, Tibby." Cole smoothed a wide palm over her dripping braid. "Let me take you inside out of the mess. Then I'll help the men drain your garden before everything's destroyed."

"It l-looks like a r-rice paddy." Tibby clenched fistfuls of his soggy shirt. She was determined not to cry in front of Cole or his workmen. Accidents happened—like the rock that had rolled onto the road, tearing up his expensive car. She still shook from that scare, but Cole wasn't crying over the damage. Nor was it his fault that she'd built completely unrealistic expectations for the afternoon.

Cole motioned to the backhoe driver behind Tibby's head. "Fix this leak ASAP! I'll be back to give you a hand," he yelled, continuing to shelter Tibby in the crook of one arm. He gathered the basket and the dog's leash in his free hand and herded the bedraggled entourage up the steps.

"You don't have to baby-sit me," Tibby sniffed. "I'm f-fine. Really."

"Yeah, I can see you are." Paying no attention to her protests, Cole opened the kitchen door. "Damn, we'll muddy your clean floor."

"It's OK. This kitchen's seen worse." She slipped from his grasp and ducked into the laundry room, returning with three fluffy towels. Handing one to Cole, she slung another carelessly over her shoulder and knelt, vigorously rubbing the third towel over Exterminator's coat.

Cole gently gripped her shoulders and pulled her upright. "I'll do that," he said gruffly. "Why is it so impossible for you to accept help, Tibby?"

"You want to smell like wet dog fur? Fine!" She shoved the towel into his hand.

He let it fall to the floor between them and looped hers around the back of her neck. Ignoring her yelp of surprise, he brought her nose to within an inch of the shirt plastered wetly to his chest. The warning glitter in his eyes didn't give Tibby time to avoid the kiss he settled on her lips with unerring accuracy.

Her heart went beserk for a moment, and after that Tibby forgot why she was supposed to avoid the wonderfully clever mouth that sent sizzling heat devils from her toes to the top of her head. Somewhere beyond the heat, Cole's cool fingers massaged her scalp. Then, before she had fully focused on the delicious sensation, he released her.

As she struggled to breathe, it took Tibby several rollicking heartbeats to discover that he'd unwound her braid and had begun to gently towel-dry her hair. She closed her eyes, savoring the experience. But apparently he regretted his action, because he left the towel bunched around her ears and bent to pick up Exterminator's smelly towel, instead.

"Here," he said. "I'd hate to deprive you of a bonding experience with the mutt. But before you dry him, you should go change out of those clothes." Cole flicked her shirt collar. "I don't need doctor's bills added to the cost of plumbers and landscape architects."

That said, he jerked open the door and left.

Outside, Cole sucked in a lungful of the humid air. Truth was, he wanted her out of his sight—out of his reach—before he kissed her again. The idea of kissing Tibby Mack had been nagging at him since the day he hit town. Just now, he'd figured one simple kiss would take her mind off her troubles and put closure to his curiosity. Except...the kiss was far from simple, and as for closure, his plan had backfired with the force of Gramps's old twelve-gauge shotgun.

Damned if she didn't have the sweetest lips.

As Cole stood rubbing a thoughtful finger over his own, his gaze skimmed a ring of hard hats huddled around the spurting break in Tibby's water line. After a firm mental shake, he yelled at the crew chief, "Hey, Bates, clamp that pipe, or shut off the water! You've turned the lady's garden into a swimming pool." He stomped down the steps two at a time and broke through the circle of men.

"Can't," Bates said, cracking a big wad of gum.

"Why not?" Cole saw what looked like a clean break in the pipe where the backhoe's teeth had sliced through the metal.

"Union rules. You gotta have a plumber."

"Then call one. Your man screwed up."

Bates hooked a thumb in his belt and shook his head.

"Rick's wheels sat squarely on the easement. Shouldn't've been pipes there."

Cole shut his eyes and massaged the bridge of his nose. "It's your driver who shouldn't have been there. But while we're arguing fault, the lady's meter is ticking away. I don't need to tell you that Yaqui Springs has a water shortage. Get a plumber. I'll pay and take it up with your boss later."

Another man, a grizzled fellow who lazily chewed a toothpick, spat it out. "Used to be a union plumber down the road apiece, but he went out of biz. Closest one I know is forty miles from here. Independent old cuss. Won't work Saturdays, let alone the Lord's day."

Cole tamped down on his mounting anger. "Not even for double time? Which, by the way, is what I'm paying you to stand around."

Unmoved, the man dug out a new toothpick. "Weed— that's the old boy's name—he won't haul ass on weekends for love nor money. And accordin' to my watch, it's straight up five. In my book that's quittin' time."

The crew scattered, leaving Cole ankle-deep in mud.

Tibby stepped out on her porch in time to hear the workman's parting shot. She'd rebraided her hair and donned clean clothes, including a pair of knee-high rubber boots that were a few sizes too big. Her stomach still jumped abnormally. She was far from over the experience, and she hadn't intended to face Cole again this soon. What she'd overheard spurred her anger. "What a bunch of dingbats."

Turning, Cole tugged at one ear. "I have a more descriptive term, but yours'll do. I know Gramps did his own house repairs. I'll go see what kind of plumbing supplies I can find in his shed. I hope there's one of those pipe gadgets to shut the water off at your meter."

"Pete Banks is pretty handy. Or Fred Feeny." Tibby dragged a couple of bushel baskets out of a cabinet filled with fruit jars and manhandled them to the bottom of the steps.

"What are those for?" Cole eyed the baskets rather than look at her. Just the memory of how her lips felt under his dampened his palms with sweat.

"I'm going to try to salvage some of my tomatoes," she said. "The ripe ones I'll can. I should be able to save the beans, too. My poor potatoes are just starting to bloom, and the carrots are barely poking through. I hope it didn't wash them out."

"I'm sorry, Tibby. It's a loblolly and growing worse. We have to stop this leak before dark. If there's time later, I'll help you. What do you think those lamebrains would've done if we hadn't come home when we did?"

"Probably fill in the hole and deny straying over the line."

"How did you get so pessimistic?"

"It started when you drove into town, O'Donnell."

Cole knew when to advance and when to retreat. This was definitely retreat time. He hurried home. After a bit of rummaging, he found a coupling he thought would work. When a quick search of his grandfather's workshop failed to turn up a hacksaw, he called Pete Banks and asked to borrow one.

Pete, Fred, Joe Toliver and other townsmen had assembled by the time Cole returned. Fred was on his knees in the mud bailing water. Once he'd cleared the debris, Pete sawed the pipe, Cole fit the coupler and Joe clamped it tight. A cheer went up all around when no new leaks sprouted. A small victory relative to the mud hole in which they stood.

Cole had remembered to bring a shovel. He started filling the hole. "Thanks for helping. The jackass who did this claimed plumbing isn't in his union contract."

Fred clapped Cole on the shoulder. "We men in Yaqui Springs have learned to be jacks-of-all-trades. Between us, there's not much we can't handle. By the way, I saw that fancy car of yours parked up on the road. She losing oil?"

"A rock cracked the transmission housing. Figure I'll have it towed to Indio tomorrow."

"I've got a winch on the back of my pickup. I'll tow you at no charge."

Cole leaned on his shovel. "I can't let you do that."

Pete lowered his voice. "It's what neighbors do, Cole. Besides, we need to talk. Me and the boys, we've been studying your post-office predicament. Is it possible for you to keep Tibby occupied for a full day? Joe engineered a slick little plan to move that sucker."

"I don't know." Cole cast a quick glance at Tibby. "I called my lawyer. He's checking my legal recourse. Let's wait and see what he turns up. Said he'd call me next week."

Pete Banks stroked his mustache. "The way we've got it doped out, it'll actually be much handier for Tibby once the building's moved. Where it stands now there's no entrance from the store into the post office. She has to go outside in all types of weather to take care of the mail. Her office is on the opposite side of the store. It's simple. Remove the siding and cut a door. Jack up the post office. Six guys could swing it around easy. A couple more to move the pier blocks. Probably a seven-, eight-hour job at the most."

"Really?" Cole's skepticism remained. "Then tell her. If she agrees with your plan, I'll gladly lend muscle. Why sneak around?" He leveled a suspicious look at Pete.

Were the men trying to throw up roadblocks between him and Tibby?

"Son," began Joe, who'd remained silent throughout, "when you get to be our age, you'll realize it's a woman's nature to resist any and all change. A psychologist on Oprah's show the other day said it's a comfort-zone thing. Hell, anybody who's been married as long as me knows that's a fact." His wry grin produced a mumbled agreement from his sidekicks.

Cole managed another peek at Tibby. She was busy picking tomatoes. From the look on her face, it wasn't hard to tell her comfort zone had been breached. "Thing is," he said, "after today I don't know if she'd go anywhere with me for ten seconds, let alone a whole day. Besides, I have no idea how long it'll take to fix my car."

"There's no rush," Joe said calmly. "Let the dust settle. Or should I say mud?" He paused for another round of chuckles. "Tell you what, Cole. We've got some fine-tuning still to do on our plan. Can't afford a botch. Maybe it'd be better if you aren't involved. Or our wives. They'd spill the beans for sure." He clapped Cole on the shoulder.

Everyone agreed that was best. Everyone except Cole. But, for the moment anyway, he bowed to majority rule. Albeit reluctantly. At least they'd agreed to wait and see what Lane Davis discovered. In any event, that should be time enough for today's calamity to fade in Tibby's mind. No sense worrying about the future when they had the here and now to deal with.

"We still have an hour or so of daylight left, men. If we dig three or four trenches out from her garden, it might drain faster. I'm accepting volunteers."

Every man stepped forward, with the exception of Ralph Hopple, and he wasn't too steady on his feet. Cole was just as glad Ralph elected to wash the produce Tibby had picked, instead. All Cole needed was to feel responsible for the old boy's heart attack.

"Do you have extra shovels?" Cole asked Tibby. As she straightened and gazed at him in confusion, he explained what he and the men were going to do.

"You don't..." she started to dispute. But something in Cole's eyes stopped her. "Uh, thanks, everyone."

"Now that didn't hurt so much, did it?" Cole teased, brushing his knuckles lightly across her chin.

Tibby ducked. "You sound like my grandmother. She was forever telling me to swallow my pride. It's nonfattening, she'd say."

"I remember she had a quick wit. She and Gramps. They used to play off each other. Mm," he mused, "they were both widowed a long time. Do you think they ever...?"

"Absolutely not," Tibby blurted, and felt her ears grow hot.

"What's the matter? Don't you believe they had... urges?"

"Even if they did," Tibby said primly, "their values wouldn't have allowed Gram and Yale to *act* on them. But I doubt you'd understand. You grew up in Hollywood."

With Ralph Hopple ten feet away hosing off tomatoes, Cole decided it wasn't the time to correct her impression of his values. On the other hand, Ralph was half-deaf. What the hell, maybe it'd put color in her cheeks. Cole shackled Tibby's wrist and yanked her up against his chest. Eyes narrowed, lips a micrometer from hers, he whispered, "Oh, I understand. Like the Romans, we Hollywoodites are all shamelessly decadent." He winked and felt her stiffen. He also saw her pulse leap, and he ever so lightly stroked her throat with his thumb. When the right shade of excitement—or was it shock?—darkened her eyes, he released her and left her quivering in her oversize boots.

Cole's husky laugh fueled Tibby's reaction. Toy with her, would he? She crossed to one of the tomato-filled baskets, grabbed a soft ripe one, then wound up, hurled it and took great pleasure in the satisfying splat that reddened the crest of his collar.

"Bull's-eye!" Ralph Hopple bounced around gleefully. "That's a great arm you have. Hit 'im again, girl!"

Tibby stared cross-eyed at the plump red fruit Ralph dangled under her nose. Sorely tempted, she put her hands behind her back. Even in the waning light there was no mistaking the damage to Cole's shirt. Crimson pulp and pale seeds decorated his broad shoulders. Juice dripped from his right ear. She should apologize, but darn, it had sure provided relief from the tension knotting her stomach ever since that kiss.

Cole spun around, incredulity slowly evolving to admiration. "Feel better?" he drawled, slowly unbuttoning his shirt. "Counting the raspberry paw smears from last night, that's two ruined shirts. If this keeps up, Tibby, you'll owe me a whole wardrobe." He eased out of the sticky shirt and deliberately wiped his neck, smiling crookedly because her eyes were glued to his bare chest.

The full view of Cole's naked chest was definitely affecting her body's thermostat. What if he decided to retaliate the way he had earlier—with another kiss? A delicious shiver slid up Tibby's spine and down again.

But he didn't pursue her fantasy. He tossed the shirt over a tree branch, and ignored the men's good-natured ribbing. Instead, he grabbed a shovel and started digging a ditch.

Fun over, the others followed suit. When the last sliver of daylight shuddered out, Pete strung extension cords from the house and draped lightbulbs over the limbs of the apple tree. Soon after, more help materialized. And before they'd completed the last trench, Cole judged that three-fourths of the Yaqui Springs inhabitants had shown up and pitched in.

The prospect of living here—in a place with a real sense of community—gave him a good feeling. His golf course would be a positive addition. He envisioned permanent houses springing up nearby, as well—houses filled with families, whose 2.5 children would balance out the population of Yaqui Springs. Retirees, plus kids with golf-loving parents. All of them needing Tibby's store. Had she considered the advantages his golf course meant for her business?

It turned out that he wasn't given an opportunity to ask. She and the women scurried off to her kitchen to start freezing and canning the produce.

The men continued to toil outside, staking plants and washing leaves. Finally, when they'd done all they could, a small enclave headed by Joe Toliver collected flashlights and went to take another look at the post office. Cole declined. He made arrangements with Fred Feeny to tow the Jag into Indio first thing in the morning. After collecting his tools and his tomato-stained shirt, Cole went home to ponder the problem some more.

No matter how much he'd benefit from resolving the issue of that damned post office, he was strangely reluctant to participate in anything that wasn't square and aboveboard. He realized his views had changed the moment he felt Tibby trembling in his arms. Before that kiss, he'd paid scant heed to the thought of her vulnerability.

Now that he had, he was plagued by guilt—and disconcerting dreams.

Cole arose early from a fitful sleep and rushed out to survey the extent of the damage to her gardens in daylight. Already the muddy trenches were drying, and Tibby's carefully washed plants were beginning to turn their faces toward the morning sun. Thank goodness. One crisis averted.

Cole had no more than returned home when Fred Feeny arrived as promised to transport his Jag for repairs. Golf clubs protruded from the bed of Fred's pickup.

"Am I making you miss your standing game?" Cole eyed the bright blue club covers someone had painstakingly knit. Fred's wife, he supposed. Funny, but that small domestic touch reminded Cole of what he lacked in his life.

"If you have your clubs handy, Cole, I thought we might call for a twosome on the way home. It's been a while since you played the course at Bogey Wells, hasn't it?"

"Quite a few years. That'd be great. I've been meaning to check out the competition. The only thing I have to do today is call that bulldozer company and lodge a complaint."

"Call, but you can't fight union regulations."

"You're probably right. Still, their boss needs to know I'm not a happy camper."

"Right. So take care of the call, then grab your clubs. I'll go throw a line on your car and meet you there."

Cole gave a two-fingered salute before returning to his house. After getting the runaround from various executives in the heavy-equipment company, Cole fired the lot. He'd rent a Caterpillar and do his own clearing; it'd save him money, and he wouldn't have to put up with all this grief.

In a black mood, he collected his golf bag and slammed out of the house. First person he laid eyes on was Tibby—running to keep up with her dog. Her flowered dress billowed thigh-high, providing a tantalizing view that halted him in his tracks.

His sudden appearance halted Tibby, too. But not by choice. Exterminator veered off to greet Cole, almost jerking Tibby off her feet.

"Whoa, boy!" Cole's clubs slid off his shoulder as he dived for the dog's collar. Two muddy paws landed on his faded green T-shirt, leaving a row of grimy tracks all the way to his belt buckle.

Tibby hauled back on the leash, but the effort had little effect on the animal, who happily lapped Cole's face. "Sorry," she said once she'd caught her breath. "He likes you. Doggone it—now I owe you another shirt. At least this one's old."

She was so obviously miffed at the prospect of owing him anything Cole couldn't resist teasing her. "This is a vintage T-shirt. It might look old, but it's new."

"It's new, but it looks old?"

"Expensive process, trying to achieve the effect of age. The only place I know that carries them is a little shop in Rome."

"Rome, as in Italy?"

"The very same. A family-owned company. Each shirt is handmade. Nothing fussy, but I understand Mel Gibson buys them by the gross. This one nearly cost me a second mortgage on my Jag."

"But it looks old." Missing the glint in his eye, Tibby worriedly ran the tips of her fingers across the fabric.

Cole trapped her hand over his heart. He decided he'd

cornered himself with that bad move and released her hand, tightening his hold on the bag of clubs. "I was kidding, Tibby. You don't owe me any shirts. Fred's waiting up on the road," he muttered, "and I have to change clothes again."

"Sorry. I thought I'd take Exterminator out before your demolition crew starts."

"They aren't coming. Well, they are, but just to pick up their equipment. I'll be doing my own clearing from now on."

She glanced away. "Oh. So you were served with the injunction."

"No. The equipment company is unreliable. I terminated our contract."

Tibby lurched sideways as the dog gave chase to a low-flying mockingbird. "Whoa, darn it. You don't want to mess with that bird, pal. He'll take a nip out of your nose and we'll have to make another trip to the vet."

"And won't that be a hardship." Cole flopped his golf bag against the porch railing. The nine and six irons clanked. Damn, he was normally careful with his clubs.

"What's that supposed to mean—it won't be a hardship? You obviously didn't see his last vet bill!"

"Sure. The way old Grant was sniffing at your heels, he'd make a house call in a flash."

"He'd also charge me an arm and a leg. Why do I get the feeling you don't like Grant? What did he do to you?"

"Nothing. Watch yourself around him, that's all. I've seen a lot of his type."

Her eyes narrowed. "His type as opposed to whose type? Yours?" Tibby might have said more, but a car entered the east end of the access road and zoomed toward the store. She checked her watch. "A customer so early?"

Cole, standing taller on the porch, said, "Well, well.

Speak of the devil. It's your friend Carlyle. Drives a respectable black Beemer. Figures.''

"Grant's here?" Tibby shaded her eyes. "I hope there's nothing wrong with Peek-a-boo. That's Millie's dog," she added for Cole's benefit.

"You'd better go see," he said, unable to control his curt tone of voice. "Anyway, I have to change my shirt and hit the road." Cole almost stumbled over the Dane, who'd slunk between him and the door and lay heaped at his feet like a fur rug. But escape wasn't to be. Dr. Carlyle had spotted them.

"Morning," he said, joining them after a healthy jog across the parking lot. His eyes skipped briefly over Cole and settled warmly on Tibby. "Dad felt better today. He wanted a morning alone with the practice. And I wanted a morning alone with you," he told her, as his gaze slowly raked her from head to toe. "I've been to see Mildred. She mentioned some antique shops that are off the beaten path. I understand you enjoy antiquing."

"Oh, I do," Tibby said. "But unfortunately I have a business to run."

"That's right," Cole put in. "And the golf bunch will be there for coffee soon." He stuck his watch under Tibby's nose and tapped it.

"Not to worry," Grant said, reaching for Tibby's hand. "Mildred knew you'd say you were too busy. She called someone—Justine was the woman's name. She'll be here any second to keep an eye on your store."

Tibby blushed. "But, ah, Justine is more or less afraid of my dog. I can't go off and leave him unattended." Her eyes roamed to the animal lying very still at Cole's feet, then slowly lifted to the man himself.

"Don't look at me to dog-sit!" Cole exclaimed. "My

car's on its way to the shop, and I have a golf date with Fred Feeny.''

Grant Carlyle reclaimed Tibby's attention. ''I don't usually allow animals in my BMW. It's new,'' he said. ''However, when I worked on the Dane he seemed well behaved. And if that's the only way I can entice you to go,'' he said, again focusing on Tibby, ''then we'll take him.''

Well behaved? Cole thought about the dirty shirt he had on and the stained and shredded one he'd tossed in the garbage. Absently he petted the dog flopped at his feet. The day suddenly looked brighter. He had visions of muddy paw prints or even a nice warm puddle or two on Doc Carlyle's plush carpets. ''You two have fun,'' he said, disengaging his feet from Exterminator's leash. Stepping over the animal, Cole went back into his house.

Tibby tried coaxing the dog off Cole's front walk. She tried setting her feet and pulling. Nothing worked. Yet it bothered her when Grant grasped Exterminator's collar and by half choking the dog, forced him to follow. ''You need a firmer hand, Tibby.''

Cole, who'd stripped off his shirt and stood peering out his window, didn't like the way the Dane cowered. He almost intervened. Had his hand on the doorknob even, then reconsidered. Maybe he was only reacting to Exterminator's pathetic whimpers and drooping tail. After all, it wasn't his pet, and Carlyle made his living working with animals. Refusing to watch, he rummaged around for a clean shirt. When at last he left the house, the BMW no longer sat in the cluster of cars belonging to Tibby's regular customers.

TIBBY WONDERED why she wasn't more ecstatic about being handed a morning off as they drove out of the lot.

Next to gardening and quilting, poking about in musty antique stores was her favorite pastime. Still, it didn't feel right. Exterminator must think that, too. She glanced at him, flattened uncomfortably on a towel Grant had spread on the floor in back. The dog's eyes were sad and he whined. Tibby much preferred his lively bouncing from window to window as he'd done in her car and Cole's.

Once Grant turned onto the main road, she saw Fred Feeny's truck up ahead. He had Cole's car secured on his hoist. Passing him, she twisted in the seat to see if Cole was there yet. He wasn't.

"Somebody you know own that Jag?" Grant asked.

"Cole." Tibby briefly outlined the damage caused by the rock.

"I never thought to ask before—what *is* your relationship to O'Donnell?"

Tibby gnawed at her lower lip. Put so bluntly, it was a question she didn't know how to answer. After too long a silence during which Grant shot her quick dark looks, she said, "Our grandparents were longtime neighbors. When they died, we inherited their properties, making us neighbors, too." A simple version of a more complicated relationship, but she didn't know Grant well enough to share the details. Nor could she bring herself to rehash the ruckus she and Cole were having over one stupid section of land.

"Why do I have the feeling you're leaving something out?" He gave her a stiff smile.

"Nothing of the sort. If I'd known we were going to spend the morning discussing my neighbor, I would've stayed home."

"Ouch. OK, tell me something about yourself."

"There's not much to tell. Why don't you go first?

Why did you become a veterinarian? Because you love animals?''

"Because I love money." He chuckled. "It's a lucrative field." For the next fifteen minutes, Grant regaled her with a list of his expensive possessions.

Hepplewhite was the only name Tibby recognized. His voice, however, was hypnotic. She found herself nodding off when all of a sudden he asked, "What do you collect?"

"Huh?" She stifled a yawn. "Not much. I have a house full of things that belonged to my grandmother and great-grandmother."

His eyes gleamed. "You may be sitting on a treasure chest. I'll be happy to check the place over and help you catalog things. I warn you, though, if I find a piece to die for, I'll drive a hard bargain."

"Sell the things I grew up with? I couldn't, Grant. And I don't care what they're worth. To me old things have sentimental value."

He looked down his nose. "Mildred told me you antiqued."

"I poke." She laughed. "I like unicorns. Plus old kitchen gadgets and cranberry glass."

"Well, that's more like it." He proceeded to give her a lecture on how easy it was to buy fake cranberry glass if you weren't careful.

Tibby was extremely glad when he pulled up outside a barn spilling over with dusty furniture. "Did you roll the window down a little?" she asked as he opened her door. "I know it's shady under this tree, but Exterminator needs air."

"I'd feel better if you'd give that animal a new name. Did you bring water and some doggie treats to keep him occupied?"

"I did." She pointed to a compact zippered case that sat at her feet.

Grant glanced at the dog. "He'll probably sleep the whole time, but why don't you leave him a little something just in case?"

As Tibby poured some water into a bowl and arranged a few pretzel treats on the towel that covered the floor, she thought the dog looked more cowed by Grant's presence than sleepy. But she supposed Exterminator might still associate the vet with the pain of having those quills pulled from his nose. "Be a good dog," she murmured, scratching the dark muzzle and between his soft ears. "We won't be gone long."

But she hadn't reckoned on the fact that the barn was multilevels of discarded relics. Or that Grant seemed determined not to miss a single one. Everything she picked up to look at he flatly told her was junk. He said it with such a sneer, Tibby was determined to buy something just to show him she was her own boss. Preferably something ghastly.

Some two hours later, on a table near the back of the top floor, she found the perfect piece. A dish for serving deviled eggs—and made out of carnival glass. Not the popular rosy sherbet color, but the hobnailed, iridescent purple, green and magenta hues that looked like an oil slick. Truly hideous.

Grant saw her pick it up and turn it over. He snatched it out of her hand. "That's horrid. It's garbage. Why waste time looking at it?"

"I've been wanting one. I always take deviled eggs to the Fourth of July potluck. I'm going to buy it." She yanked it back and cradled it against her breast.

"I see antiquing isn't as serious a hobby for you as it is for me. Get your trinket and we'll go. Their stuff is more popular-culture collectibles than true antiques. Not what I'm looking for.''

Tibby paid for her purchase and chatted with the white-haired proprietor while Grant fidgeted with his car keys.

''Why don't I go open the car and let the dog out for a minute to do his thing?''

Tibby smiled and nodded to Grant, but just then the woman handed her the sales slip and her dish, so they walked out together.

A good thing, too. Grant's BMW looked like the aftermath of a war zone. He let out a muffled roar, and Tibby thought that if she hadn't stepped between him and the car door, he might have killed her dog.

Exterminator's water dish was overturned. His treats were ground to dust in the thick carpet. The side pocket holding maps was torn off and the maps themselves were confetti. As was the entire back seat. Buttery caramel leather shredded. Chewed. In the middle of the debris sat Exterminator, bits of foam rubber stuck to his nose—smirking.

''I thought you said this dog was civilized!'' Grant raged.

''He is…mostly. Did you leave candy in here someplace?'' Tibby asked, sifting through the mess.

''No, but still, that animal should be better trained.''

''Sorry.'' Tibby climbed into the back and looped a shaking arm around her pet. ''I haven't had him long. I plan to start training him soon. I'll pay damages of course.''

Livid, Grant slid behind the wheel. He started the car and tore out of the lot, spraying gravel.

The Dane licked Tibby's face, then meekly laid his head in her lap. She wanted to scream to break the heavy silence. But the way Grant's brows tunneled over the bridge of his nose, she was afraid to even speak. "Bad dog," she whispered.

No words passed between her and Grant until he roared to a stop outside Mack's General Store. This time he didn't come around to open her door. He did rummage in the glove box and hand her a business card. "Mindi Carlyle," it read. "Canine Behavioral Consultant and Holistic Veterinarian." Tibby blinked, raised her head and met Grant's cold glare.

"My ex-wife," he said. "I suggest you take that dog in for counseling."

Clutching the card, Tibby scooted across what was left of the seat. She expected Grant to wait for information on her insurance. But the minute she and Exterminator's feet hit the ground, Grant slammed her door and drove off.

"Fine," Tibby muttered half under her breath. She deposited the ex-wife's business card in the garbage can beside the entrance to her store and muscled Exterminator inside. Was the dog smiling? She eyed him dubiously.

"Oh, sure. Cozy up to Cole so I owe him more shirts. Eat the car of the only other man who's ever given me a second look." By now she was thoroughly exasperated with the male of both human and canine species.

Suddenly, though, the humor in the situation struck her. And the truth. Grant Carlyle was a pompous ass. She didn't want him asking her out again.

She'd mail him the information on her insurance—and she'd find another vet.

CHAPTER EIGHT

JUSTINE WAS SITTING behind the counter reading a book. At Tibby's laughter, she closed it and hopped up. "Back so soon? The doc said you'd be having lunch out."

"Exterminator ate." Unable to keep a straight face, Tibby told the story in fits and spurts. "And Grant's not the only loser. I spent hard-earned cash on this white elephant." She displayed the ugly plate.

Justine wiped tears of laughter from her eyes. "My lands, Tibby. Will you ever have tales to tell your grandchildren!"

Tibby sobered. "Grand-dogs, maybe. I'm never getting married. I have my career, my garden, my hobbies and all of you to care for."

"Surely you don't mean that, dear." Justine peered at the dog over her glasses with quite a bit of misgiving.

"I do. Oh, look—the mail truck. If you don't mind staying a few extra minutes, I'll sort the mail and put it in the boxes early."

"I don't mind. Say, Tibby, why didn't Lara connect the post office to her office? This morning Pete said it's a shame you have to dash out in all kinds of weather."

"Forget it, Justine. This sounds like some harebrained strategy of Cole's."

"Why are you being so stubborn, Tibby? Your grandmother, rest her soul, would have bent over backward to work out an agreeable compromise with that boy."

Tibby looked away. She knew Justine was right. And if it'd been anybody but Cole asking, she'd have done the same thing. But of course the residents had no idea how she'd felt the first time he left. And he would leave again. She'd sooner he did it now than later—after he'd well and truly stolen her heart. Tibby recalled the feel of his hands in her hair last night and the taste of his lips on hers. She refused to admit that it might already be too late.

"I intended to surprise everyone at the Fourth of July potluck, but I'll tell you now, Justine, if you promise to keep it a secret. I've ordered a dedication plaque for our post office in Grandmother's name. I'd like Pete to make the presentation."

Justine bit her lip worriedly. "How…how long has this been in the works, Tibby?"

She shrugged. "Awhile."

Justine folded her apron and dropped it on the counter. "Since before or after you learned about Cole's golf course?"

"What difference does it make?" Tibby unhooked Exterminator's leash and filled his bowl with water. Lingering, she fondled his ears.

"Because it wouldn't honor Lara if the idea was born of a mean spirit," Justine said quietly. "She believed first and foremost in being a good neighbor to everyone."

Tibby's stomach tensed as she left the store. Justine was right. Grandmother used to say that kindness was the oil that took the friction out of life. Tibby wrestled with her conscience as she quickly sorted the mail. Maybe she should stop fighting Cole and really sit down with him and try to hammer out a compromise. Hadn't he said yesterday that was the course his lawyer suggested they take?

But Gram's attorney said to get a ruling from the postmaster general's office. Tibby had planned to, then been sidetracked by Grant Carlyle. Checking her watch, she calculated the time difference between California and Washington, D.C. Yikes. If she hoped to obtain an answer today, she'd better get cracking.

Half an hour after sitting down to make the call, getting transferred to the fifth department secretary and for the fifth time telling her story anew, Tibby understood the frustration her grandmother must have felt when she'd set up the post office.

By quitting time in D.C., she was ready to scream—and had yet to hear an educated guess, let alone a ruling, from anyone. A couple of people she talked to said she needed to put her request in writing. Two others promised to send her a form—for what she had no idea. One woman said the postmaster general was on vacation. She suggested Tibby give him two weeks after he returned to deal with important issues, and then try calling again.

Did the residents realize it was a miracle they even had postal service in Yaqui Springs? Tibby thought not.

A series of customers trickled into the store, taking her mind off the problem for the time being. About four-thirty Fred and Cole dropped in for some cold bottled water. Both men were invigorated from playing eighteen holes of golf. Cole's hair, darkened by sweat, was held off his forehead by a colorfully banded kerchief that lent him a decidedly rakish air.

"Who won?" she asked, handing them their change.

Neither man answered. Both had their heads tipped back, each doing his best to drain his water in one chug. Cole gave up first and blotted his mouth on his sleeve. "That was good." He grinned at Tibby. "Do you know that all they serve from their carts at Bogey Wells is beer? Twenty kinds, but still beer."

"They sell bottled water in the clubhouse bar."

"We were late for tee off. It took forever to find an auto shop equipped to work on the Jag. Besides," he said with a shade of irony, "I didn't feel particularly welcome at the clubhouse. It seems their directors read your newsletter. I don't suppose you're aware that they refer to my enterprise as Cole's folly?"

Tibby knew the color must have drained from her face. "I, uh, we may have discussed whether or not the area could support two golf courses." She fiddled with her braid, then slung it over her shoulder. "They have a right to worry. You'll siphon off a third of their revenue the day you open."

"My sources tell me Bogey Wells has a waiting list for memberships and no room for weekend golfers. Golf is the fastest-growing sport around. To keep it affordable, we need five times more public courses."

"More courses wouldn't be so bad," Tibby agreed, "if they didn't automatically bring real-estate development. First condos, then hotels. Before you know it, a marina and a landing strip."

"People also want to shop where they golf. You're in on the ground floor in that department, Tibby. Add a few souvenirs, a trendy boutique and you'd increase your profits enough to hire full-time help. Maybe get back into playing a little golf yourself."

Tibby's head shot up. "Who says I play?"

Cole glanced at Fred, but he'd gone to dump his water bottle in the recycling bin. "I think Mabel Sparks mentioned it first. Today I got the impression you used to knock a few balls around Bogey Wells."

Winnie and Joe Toliver strolled through the front door. The tinkling bell blocked out Tibby's mumbled reply.

"Joe taught Tibby to play golf when she was just a tyke," Winnie said candidly. "Lara bought her a good set of clubs for her thirteenth birthday. They're probably gathering dust.'' She nudged Tibby. ''All work and no play makes for a dull girl.''

Cole grinned. ''I've seen her clubs. And her bag. The mice may have moved in.''

Uncomfortable with the direction of the conversation, Tibby asked if the Tolivers needed help.

Winnie inspected her pale pink fingernails. ''Justine stopped by all in a dither over your morning excursion. It sounded like the script from a bad comedy. Sometimes the artist in Justine causes her to exaggerate,'' Winnie said, chuckling. ''I came to hear this tale for myself.''

Cole's ears perked up. ''Did Mr. BMW get a flat? Or better yet, did Exterminator leave paw prints down the front of his Gianni Versace shirt?''

Tibby shrank as all eyes turned expectantly on her.

''According to Justine,'' Joe put in, ''Tibby's dog thought the doctor's backseat was a juicy bone. Goodbye, leather. If it'd been my car, he'd be a goner.''

Cole might have laughed. He surely would have smiled if Tibby hadn't looked so bleak. ''I think Tibby feels a little like you would if your child misbehaved. Being a vet and all, maybe Carlyle was more forgiving than I was when Exterminator ground raspberry sauce into my silk shirt,'' Cole said sheepishly. ''I hope so, anyway.''

Surprised at Cole's intuitiveness, Tibby sighed. ''Grant was majorly ticked off. Said my dog needs to go in for counseling.''

This time Cole laughed.

''It's not funny, Cole. I'm afraid Exterminator tore up Grant's car on purpose. He acted like he expected me to be pleased.''

Cole reined in his laughter. ''Maybe the pup is jealous.''

Winnie looked perplexed. "You mean that dog will run off all of Tibby's suitors?"

"Pul-leeze! Like I have so many."

Though Winnie's question had been aimed at him, Cole didn't answer. The rosy flush creeping up Tibby's graceful neck spoke of her embarrassment. The bruised look in her eyes carried a different message. Longing? Loneliness? Both?

Their eyes met. Tibby reflected that she'd always been successful in hiding the chink in her armor—until yesterday, when Cole O'Donnell had kissed her. And today. Right now. Yet she couldn't tear her gaze away.

Conversation swirled around them. Suggestions for suppressing Exterminator's territorial impulses floated through the electrically charged air. Gooseflesh peppered Cole's still sweating skin; he stripped off his bandanna and wiped his face. Thank goodness that broke the connection between him and Tibby. With a shaking hand, he drained the last swallow of water from the bottle and immediately felt better. *Ah. What a relief. Just too much sun.*

He joined the men. "Well, Fred." Cole clasped the older man's hand. "Thanks for the tow and the game. I see the construction company picked up their machines, so I'm off to do some calling around for a rental dozer. Any ideas?"

"I know someone," Joe piped up. "Swing by my place. I have the guy's business card."

"Appreciate it." The three walked out together.

Tibby followed Cole's departure with her eyes. The room tilted precariously, and she rubbed her suddenly queasy stomach.

"Tibby?" Winnie reached out a hand. "Don't you feel well?"

"I...feel wobbly. Probably because I missed breakfast

and lunch. I see that fresh bananas came in today. Care to join me in a healthy shake?''

"A banana shake is hardly a substantial meal. You're always lecturing us to eat right,'' Winnie said sternly. "How often do you skip meals? You're thin as a dime. If you turned sideways, no one would see you.''

Tibby selected a banana and peeled it carefully. "It's a bother to cook for one. And I have to admit, I've been a bit lax about meals since Gram died. She enjoyed cooking and she always made mealtimes special. We'd talk about books we'd read. Crafts in progress. Funny things that happened at the store.'' Glumly she bit into the banana, not bothering with a shake. "At first I tried to cook. I shared casseroles with Yale and Mildred. Now he's gone, and Millie claims her freezer is stuffed.''

"There's Cole. I'll bet he'd enjoy home cooking.''

Tibby rolled her eyes. "The one time we shared a dinner turned out a disaster. You heard him. My dog ruined his shirt and Cole all but tossed us out of his house.''

"That dog.'' Winnie cast a glance at the Great Dane, who lay stretched out flat, sleeping. "Couldn't you have adopted something smaller? Like maybe a nice cocker spaniel? Anything not quite so inclined to chase the men out of your life?''

Tibby ate the rest of her banana and dropped the peel into her compost bucket. "Dr. Carlyle isn't a great loss. And Cole O'Donnell's a city slicker at heart. I'm betting he gets antsy or bored and doesn't stick out a summer here. Five dollars says he'll take up with Ms. Centerfold again.'' Her lungs constricted at the mere suggestion.

"I've got ten dollars that says not.'' Winnie pulled a bill from her purse and waved it under Tibby's nose. "Double or nothing.'' She drew it back. "But you can't do anything to deliberately drive him away.''

Tibby gazed a moment at the bill. "All right. Just don't plan on taking your winnings to Vegas. I know you and Joe are going there next October."

"I can't lose. Cole told Joe it'll take six months to finish the course. That boy's like Yale—once he makes a commitment, he hangs in."

"Yes, but he needs the land I won from his grandfather. I can't turn it over after everything Gram went through to authorize setting up a post office. I expect Cole to scrap the whole deal, sell out and go back to Hollywood."

"Care to bet another ten?" Winnie rubbed thumb and forefinger together.

"Yes. No! Do you have inside information?" Tibby asked suspiciously. "If so, that's not fair. Has Cole decided to relocate his clubhouse?"

"Not that I know of." Winnie returned the ten to her purse and covered the distance to the door. "We'll stick with one bet. I hate to take your money, Tibby."

The door slammed in her wake. Tibby jumped and Exterminator whined, in sympathy, she thought. "Am I so transparent, boy?" she murmured, patting his head. "Does Winnie know that's a bet I wouldn't mind losing?" Moments later a chill walked up Tibby's spine. Winnie seemed awfully confident. Were they up to something again?

The big dog began to pace in front of the door. Needing some air, anyway, Tibby snapped on his leash and took him outside. They walked along the easement between her property and Cole's. Across the field a coyote slunk out from behind a pile of rubble the dozer had pushed aside. The dog's head shot up. Barking, he took off, and Tibby, caught unawares, tripped along behind like a rag doll.

"Stop!" she shouted, double-looping the leather strap around her wrist. At the same time she tried to dig her heels into the ruts. The sandals she'd put on that morning flipped and flopped until she lost first one, then the other. The dog slowed as she fell to her knees but he kept on going, dragging her along. He continued even when she toppled to her stomach. "Oof! Stop, you son of a hyena!" She felt her dress rip somewhere in the vicinity of her knee. "Ow!" she yelled when he swung left and her arm connected with a half-buried cactus. At last she managed to clasp her right hand over her left, exerting enough pressure to bring him to a standstill.

Unwilling to give up the chase, Exterminator dug furrows with his hind feet, throwing pebbles and sand in Tibby's face. Spitting and cursing, she heard Exterminator's barks shift to delighted yelps and deduced someone was coming. Probably Cole, she thought dismally, considering her run of bad luck today. She didn't want Cole, or anyone, to find her spread-eagled like buzzard bait. Scrambling to her knees, she managed to stand before he arrived.

"Tibby, what in hell happened?" Cole supported her a moment, but when it still looked as if she'd crumple, he braced a hand at her back and an arm beneath her knees, then swung her high and held her close.

Her eyes zeroed in on Cole's stony face. "Coyote," she finally rasped, in spite of lungs that refused to contract around a deep breath and a heart galloping at the speed of a runaway train.

"Why didn't you let go of the damned leash?"

"At first I hung on because I thought the coyote might be rabid. Then when the dog didn't stop, I was too wound up in the leash."

"You'd better consider obedience school for that mutt. Those are some nasty scrapes. Let's get you home and scrubbed."

She made a face and drew in a shaky breath. "I can take care of a few scratches. Ariel lent me a book and some videos to help with training. Put me down. I'll walk. My legs don't feel so spongy now."

"Not on your life. You were hurt on my property. I'll see to your injuries."

"I figured you'd yell at me for trespassing." Her self-deprecating laugh wasn't quite steady. "Must have been quite a sight, me bumping along like a runnerless dog-sled."

"It scared the hell out of me." Cole loosened the leash from her bleeding hand. Leading the now docile Great Dane, Cole strode across the clearing. "I don't even know why I walked out to check the work that'd been done, except I'd just called the fellow Joe recommended about renting a dozer."

"I'm glad you did. You scared off the coyote. Otherwise I might have been dragged to kingdom come."

"How much do you weigh?" Cole tightened the arm under her thighs.

"What a thing to ask a lady." She pushed at his shoulders. "Put me down. Why are you taking me to your place? I said I wanted to go home."

"Hush." He juggled her as he pried open the screen door. "If I let you go home, you wouldn't tell me if you needed to see a doctor." Setting her on her feet for a moment, he unclasped Exterminator's leash. "Stay," he told the dog firmly, pointing to a corner of the screened porch. "And no more monkeyshines, you hear?"

The dog hung his head and flopped down next to a chair, his dark eyes huge with remorse.

Tibby, who'd hobbled to the doorway leading into the kitchen, watched with interest. "He minds you, O'Donnell. What's the secret?"

"Beats me. I've never owned a dog. Must be something in the tone of voice." He joined her at the door, took her elbow and gently guided her through the living room and down the hall to the master bathroom, where he eased her down on the closed toilet seat.

Embarrassed by the intimacy of being in the close quarters of his private bathroom, Tibby gazed everywhere but at Cole. She noted an accumulation of masculine toiletries lining the shelf above the pedestal sink, like soldiers awaiting inspection. The whole room sparkled, and there were no wet towels lying about. Hmm.

Henrietta Feeny said men only got married when they could no longer see over the top of the dirty towels in their bathrooms or around the dirty dishes in their sinks. If that was true in Cole's case, he'd *never* get married. Both rooms were spotless.

Articles in Tibby's favorite women's magazines referred to marriages as partnerships. Which implied sharing. She liked that version of marriage a lot better. If and when she ever married, she'd want someone to share not only chores, but child rearing. And laughter along with the hardships.

Cole rummaged in the closet and returned with a fluffy burgundy washcloth and towel.

"Good choice. Those won't show the blood," Tibby joked as Cole tested the water for temperature before soaping and dousing the cloth.

"They're soft. That's why I chose them," he said, kneeling on the plush navy rug. Ignoring her attempt to take the cloth from his hands, Cole washed the obvious places first. Her hands, elbows and even her chin. Then he rinsed the cloth and returned to cleanse her scratched feet. "I'm sorry," he said two or three times when she winced or sucked in a breath. "We don't want these to get infected."

"*You're* sorry? I'm sorry to be such a baby." All the same she jerked away as he parted the lower half of her torn skirt and a piece of material plastered to a bloody gash stuck tight. "Ow, that smarts." She fanned it with the towel and tried to smile.

Cole slid his hand lightly up and down her bare leg.

Tibby gasped from the startling current that seized her abdomen.

Cole's pained gaze rose hesitantly. "Your left knee took the brunt of the ride. If you can stand, just climb in the shower and soak the material off."

"Whose shower? Not yours."

He looked puzzled. "Is something wrong with my shower? Oh—would you rather use the tub? The guest bath has a tub. I thought you might want to wash your hair. It's full of dirt and twigs. Sage, I think."

"It's not that. What'll people say? The neighbors." She drew her knees to her chest. But the three buttons hanging by threads popped off, leaving the full length of her legs exposed to Cole. She quickly yanked the edges of her skirt together.

Cole stood, then opened the shower door, leaned in and turned on the water. When it was adjusted to his satisfaction, he pulled two towels off the rack. Thrusting them into her hands, he turned and walked into the hallway. "When I decide to scrub your back, Tibby, you won't be bleeding all over my floor. Robe's on a hook behind the door—lock it if you want. The door, I mean. I was going to suggest you leave it open in case you faint or slip. Now, if you aren't out in twenty minutes, I'll call the paramedics."

Tibby flinched as the door banged shut. She stared at

it, wondering why she always seemed to put her foot in her mouth around Cole. Little by little the steam clouded her vision. Mindful of what he'd said, she loosened her braid and stepped under the warm spray. Her cuts stung, especially the ones on her knees as she peeled the dress down. A few bruises were beginning to show up here and there. She'd be lucky to crawl out of bed tomorrow.

The scent of the soap reminded her of Cole. It hinted at patchouli, a musky intimate oil. She'd learned in working with herbs that scent was an individual preference—and often seductive. Men were drawn to women whose scent they found pleasing and vice versa. Now that she knew what he liked...

Feeling a little guilty for using her olfactory talent to spy on him, she stuck her head under the faucet and reached for the bottle of shampoo that sat on the corner shelf. Lemongrass and a softer elusive scent that was quite refreshing. "Mm, nice," she murmured as she lathered her thick hair. But she wasn't altogether surprised by his choice. Her book on aromatherapy said men liked basil, cinnamon, jasmine and lemongrass.

At last she turned off the faucets, then wrapped herself in one towel and squeezed her hair in the other. Cole must be quite familiar with women to automatically hand her two towels. But of course. He'd invited Cicely for the weekend. It was naive to think they had a just-friends relationship. And Cicely sure hadn't cared what the neighbors thought.

Annoyed at her own reactions, Tibby slipped gingerly into Cole's maroon velour robe. His scent rose up around her, creating an ache that had nothing to do with her recent ride over the rough ground. She closed her eyes and buried her nose in the cowl collar. A sharp rap on the door startled her.

"Tibby?" Cole's voice was worried. "Are you all right?" He rattled the knob and to his surprise, the door wasn't locked. For a moment there was silence on both sides. Finally Tibby poked her head around the corner.

"Has it been twenty minutes already?"

"Yes. I kept an ear tuned to the water. It's been a while since it shut off. You...didn't lock the door."

"I, ah, no." She let the door swing wider as she reached up and ran a hand through her hair. "Heavens, I didn't want the paramedics to break your door down." Her lips curved in a smile, but Cole's eyes flashed to the raw scrapes he could see now that her sleeve had fallen back.

"These look bad." His fingers circled her wrist as he turned her to the light to assess the damage. "I have bandages and salve out in the kitchen. But maybe I'd better go find you something to wear and drive you to an emergency room. Where's the closest one?"

"Brawley." She craned her neck to see the part of her arm he was looking at, and their foreheads bumped. Tibby rubbed a thumb over his frown, erasing it. "I must be accident-prone today. Did that hurt?"

He leaned a shoulder negligently against the doorjamb. "I have a hard head." They grinned dopily at each other for a moment.

Finally Tibby sobered and said, "My cuts look worse than they are. Most are superficial. I like to try holistic methods of treatment first. If you have my shoes handy, I'll scoot on home and dab the worst scrapes with aloe vera and comfrey."

"Before we eat? While you were showering, I fixed a pasta salad."

"You did?" Her smile widened, then faded. "It's getting late. I need to feed Exterminator. Lord knows I can't afford any more disasters. One of Ariel's books says training begins with consistency.''

"I fed him. Two leftover hamburger patties crumbled with a slice of bacon.''

She crossed her arms, then let them fall limp at her sides. "Bacon? No wonder he's taken a shine to you. Just don't let it become a habit, O'Donnell. You should watch your cholesterol, and I don't want an overweight dog.''

"Yes, ma'am.'' Cole stepped back and motioned for her to precede him into the kitchen. The lightweight velour clung to her curves. Trailing her through the house shot his pulse up a notch or two. And when she sat across from him and the front gaped, revealing a shadowy cleft between her breasts, he tried awfully hard to concentrate on his salad.

"This is good,'' she exclaimed, closing her eyes to savor the tasty dressing. "If your mom was never around, who taught you to cook?''

"Gramps. He started me out when I was twelve. Cooking is the last thing a twelve-year-old boy wants to do. We almost came to blows over it the year I turned sixteen. Now I actually find it relaxing.''

She leaned an elbow, the uninjured one, on the table, then rested her chin in her palm. She gazed at him, smiling softly. "Little things about you surprise me, O'Donnell. You're thoughtful, gentle, good with animals and you cook. Why hasn't some lucky lady snapped you up?''

Cole gulped down a curled spinach noodle whole. "I beg your pardon?''

"Married, O'Donnell. Why haven't you tied the knot?'' She waved a fork, speared with a black olive.

"Why haven't you?'' he asked, sounding a bit testy.

Tibby laid her fork aside. She steepled her fingers in her lap and lowered her eyes. "Too pushy a question, huh?'' She looked up at him again, her huge eyes a soft shimmering green.

Hunger raced through Cole, heating his blood. Critically aware of the fact that Tibby wore nothing but his robe, he recalled, with some part of his brain, what Mabel Sparks had said about Tibby's innocence. That was why she assumed he was thoughtful and gentle. Only he wasn't having thoughtful or gentle feelings. They were crazy and completely mixed-up where Tibby Mack was concerned. Cole tore his gaze away. He had no right to kiss her, to touch her. Because out there—beyond the window, cloaked in darkness—lay a triangle of land that came between them more surely than a lover.

She'd asked him a simple enough question. Too bad it came with complicated answers. ''What kind of life have I been able to offer a woman?'' he asked, his fingers unconsciously shredding a roll. ''Me, living out of hotels like a nomad. I'd be sticking her in an iron-gated condo for months on end. I can't…won't do that to someone I love. If this golf course pans out—if I don't lose my shirt—I plan to start a family.''

Someone he loved! Cicely. Tibby's throat constricted. Naturally he viewed *her*, Tibby, as the person standing in his way. His kindness, his show of concern for her injuries, the shower, the robe, the pasta salad—all calculated to weaken her resolve and gain him what he wanted. *The land.* And ultimately Cicely Brock. No matter how precipitously the woman had left Yaqui Springs, she fit into Cole's plans for the future.

Cole and Cicely—their names even matched. They probably phoned each other every night and…

Almost sick, Tibby bunched her napkin and climbed awkwardly to her feet, ignoring Cole's baffled expression. It took more effort to snatch up her shoes and limp, head held high, to the bathroom, where she'd left her grungy clothes.

A minute later Cole followed. "Tibby, what are you doing?" He rattled the knob. This time she *had* locked the door. "Tibby!" He pounded with the flat of his hand, not liking the rustling noises inside, punctuated now and again by a tiny yelp of pain. He was totally unprepared for her to fling the door open as wildly as she did, mashing him against the wall.

In spite of her scrapes and bruises, she moved fast. It took a few moments for Cole to gather his wits. Long enough for her to have leashed a sleepy dog and dragged him out the back door.

A few seconds behind her, Cole burst outside in time to see the moonlight gilding her long straight hair. "Tibby, dammit, *now* what'd I say to set you off?"

She didn't answer.

He smacked the door hard, his voice rising, then muffled by the trees that swallowed her. "You're deaf when it comes to that blasted post office, Tibby Mack. I'm building this golf course, come hell or high water, so you might as well get it through your stubborn head."

"Go fly a kite, O'Donnell." Her strained words floated eerily from somewhere up the trail. "I won that land from your grandfather in a golf match. Ask anyone. Ask the old-timers at Bogey Wells."

The news staggered Cole. *Golf? She won it playing golf? But his grandfather was no slouch at the game. In fact, he was good.* His thoughts jumbled, Cole raced after Tibby. He wanted all the details. Every last one. He'd no more than reached the store's parking lot when he heard the door to her house shut decisively.

Tomorrow. Tomorrow he'd find out the truth, dammit.

CHAPTER NINE

COLE SKIPPED breakfast and waited by the window for the golf regulars to pile into Tibby's coffee bar. Not long ago Fred, Joe, Pete and the others had given him the impression that they didn't know anything about the passing of his grandfather's land into Tibby's hands, or her grandmother's, as the case might be. Tibby insisted that they did. Today Cole planned to confront the whole group and ferret out who was blowing smoke.

"Ah, there they are." He charged out the front door and made a beeline for Mack's General Store.

Through the side window he saw the men milling around pouring coffee and helping themselves to muffins, which Tibby carried in on a tray. As Cole stepped inside, the enticing odor of fresh baked goods surrounded him. His stomach growled loudly.

Talk stopped and everyone turned.

It wasn't quite the entrance Cole had in mind. He stuffed his hands in his pockets and did his best to appear nonchalant.

"If that isn't the sound of a forlorn bachelor, I don't know what is," Fred teased jovially. "Come on in here, boy. Tibby, bring that tray. Put Cole out of his misery."

Cole glanced at her, realizing she hadn't joined in the camaraderie. She brought him the tray reluctantly, probably out of deference to Fred. Her eyes weren't just unfriendly, they looked right through him. Cole figured the minute he made his selection she'd bolt. If he hoped to keep this group together for answers, it was now or never.

"Joe," he said as he pretended to inspect each row of muffins, "last night Tibby told me she won the property for the post office in a golf match with Gramps. I remember Winnie said you taught Tibby to play golf. Since my grandfather normally shot par, you must be some heck of a teacher, you sly dog."

No one said a word while Cole deliberated between the zucchini and the carrot-raisin muffins. As soon as he picked one up, Tibby turned to leave. Circling her wrist, he smiled. "Don't run off, ace. I might sample both kinds." He found it interesting that the men had formed a protective semicircle around Joe.

"Behold, the fine golfers you said would back you to the hilt, Tibby. They aren't exactly rushing to your defense." Cole's fingers slid up to her elbow. He loosened his hold when he encountered the bruises from last evening's tumble.

She wrenched her arm away. Angry color fired her cheeks as she waded into the group. "Tell him the truth. He thinks I ripped off that land, for goodness' sake."

The men shifted and rolled their eyes. "Now, Tibby," Fred chided. "We didn't see any need to embarrass a man to his grandson over some fluke."

"Yeah," Pete muttered. "Everybody has an off day. Cole's building this course as a tribute to Yale. Why sully his good name...well, you know what I mean."

Tibby smacked the tray down on the table closest to Cole. "No, I don't know what you mean. I know Yale never spoke of it after that day, but the fact is, we bet on an eighteen-hole game and I won." With a withering glance at the others, she turned to Cole. "My friends— and I use the term loosely—will go to great lengths to see that you build a golf course in Yaqui Springs. You'll just have to take my word on this land business."

"Really?" Cole sniffed his muffin. Carrot, with nutmeg. No, cardamon, he decided. The spicy scent left his mouth watering. "You know," he said after tasting the muffin, "I told my attorney you weren't a gambler, Tibby. Now I find out you are. I'm intrigued. So make me the same bet you made Gramps. If you win, I choose a new location for my clubhouse. You lose, we relocate the post office." A Cheshire-cat grin played at the corners of his mouth as he bit into the muffin again.

"Go soak your head, O'Donnell."

Pete stepped between the two. Fingers thrust between his lips, he whistled and held out his arms like a referee. "Time." Drawing Cole aside, he whispered, "Last night at Joe's we worked out all the particulars for moving the you-know-what to you-know-where. Don't back Tibby into a corner when it's not necessary."

"Wait a minute. Move the post office without telling her? That's pulling a fast one—not my style. Besides," he murmured, "are you saying she can beat me?" He poked Pete in the shoulder. "I've been known to give Curtis Strange and Cory Pavin a run for their money."

"I'm not saying she *can* beat you. But somebody wins and somebody loses. Any way you look at it, there'll be hard feelings."

Cole peeped around the taller man's blocky shoulders, taking in Tibby's scowl. He frowned. No one spoke. After a moment had passed he whispered, "Tibby obviously sets great store by the wager process. If she lost, she'd be honor-bound to move the post office, right?"

Pete gave an unhappy nod.

Cole tossed his muffin paper in the trash. "You know as well as I do that she hasn't touched her clubs in months.

But I'm not out to humiliate her, Pete. Just seems to me a match would solve a lot of problems once and for all.''

All the men looked unsure as Cole wove his way back to Tibby. Helping himself to another muffin, he said, ''Tell you what I'm gonna do. My deal stands. If you go for it, I'll spot you five or six strokes overall. What do you say? It's a fair proposal.''

''I say take a flying leap off the nearest dock, buster. I already played eighteen holes for that property and won.''

Fred snatched Cole's second muffin. He balanced it carefully by its yellow paper cup. Joe and Pete caught Cole beneath each arm and hustled him toward the entry. ''We hafta run, Tibby, or we'll be late to tee off. Come on, Cole. She won't budge.''

Cole twisted in their grip. ''One stroke per hole,'' he called to Tibby. ''That's my final offer. You won't get any better odds.''

The men groaned. ''Are you nuts?'' Pete gasped. ''Nobody gives that big a handicap.''

''You said it was a fluke that she beat Gramps.''

Joe threw up his hands. ''Yes, but—''

''Well, I'm a better player than Gramps was.'' Cole wriggled loose when he saw Tibby's eyes light. He sauntered over to the coffeepot and poured a cup. Pulling a few bills from his pocket, he dropped the money into her honor jar. ''Don't let me hold you men up. I'll catch you later,'' he said, plucking his muffin out of Fred's hand.

Just then Ralph Hopple tottered through the door. Scratching his head, he eyed the regulars. ''You guys still here? Taking a holiday from golf or something?'' As he headed for the coffeepot, he bumped into Cole. ''Surprised to see you, young fella. There's a couple of old boys off-loading a Caterpillar at your place. Figured you'd be there protecting Tibby's water pipes." He laughed heartily at his own joke.

"Already?" Cole set his cup aside and ran to the side window. "They are. I need your answer ASAP, Tibby. Do we have a bet or not?"

"It's not a decision I care to rush." As if to prove a point, she began filling the glass case with the leftover muffins. Maybe Cole banked on her not being any good. Or he might be another Jack Nicklaus, for all she knew. In any event he'd have to play scratch golf or better to be offering her eighteen strokes. Or else he was a fool. And she didn't believe that for a minute. "Give me until tomorrow to make up my mind?"

Cole's grin spread from ear to ear. "You got it. If you decide to play, I'll even spot you time to bone up on your game."

"That's decent of you. So tomorrow. Same time?"

"Works for me. That way we'll have plenty of witnesses."

"You mean *you'll* have witnesses. The men seem to have developed selective memories where I'm concerned. Do you mind if I invite their wives to listen in?"

"Why make a federal case out of it?"

"It *is* a federal case, O'Donnell. That's a federal post office."

"OK, whatever. Hey, I need to hit the road. I want to make sure that dozer works before the guys who delivered it take off. Those yahoos yesterday cost me time. By next week I'll be laying a sprinkler system." Cole capped his coffee, said goodbye to Ralph, and took off across the parking lot at a run.

Ralph caught the door to keep it from slamming. He drained his cup, then turned to Tibby. "You gonna take his bet, girl?"

"I don't know. He seems terribly confident."

"Young pup sees himself as a golf guru. If he was that good, he'd be playing with the big guys, not building courses."

"Maybe. You take several golf magazines. Do you recall ever seeing his name listed as playing in any pro-am tournaments?"

"Nope."

"Do you mind if I borrow a stack of back issues and look for myself?"

"I'll go get 'em. You can do some research between waiting on customers."

"Thanks, Ralph. This post office was a big deal to Gram. I'd feel like I'd really let her down if I foolishly let it slip from our hands."

"Wouldn't moving the blasted building make life easier on you?"

"Easier, how? The mailman honks. I meet him and collect the bag with the incoming mail and give him the outgoing. If I'm busy, we do the exchange in the metal collection box. The parking lot remains free for my customers."

"What about when it rains? You run outside and get wet."

She laughed. "Sprinting now and then is good for the heart."

"I know you'd never complain. But Joe and Pete claim the builder should've hooked the post office up to the store and cut a door into it from Lara's office."

"Mm. That would be nicer. But Gram planned to add a Laundromat in that corner. Two things she hoped to provide someday were laundry facilities and a gas pump. Gram had an eye to attracting winter travelers, if not more full-time residents."

"So you're saying Lara was more in tune with young O'Donnell's plans, eh?"

Tibby's eyebrows rose. "Weren't you going after a stack of magazines?"

A slight frown settled between Ralph's faded blue eyes. "Yep. That I was."

Tibby fussed with shelves and straightened already perfect rows of stock after he'd left. Was Ralph insinuating she should give in to Cole? It was darned sneaky of him, bringing up Gram that way. Especially when he knew she'd invested and lost money with would-be developers who'd claimed they'd clean up the pollutants and the brine and make the Salton Sea a haven for winter travelers.

Tibby, for one, liked things as they were. Small towns had charm. And Gram's aim hadn't been to turn the place into another Palm Springs—like Cole's was.

Ralph returned with the magazines. "Saw a county sheriff pull up at Cole's," he wheezed. "Don't suppose that's your handiwork is it, missy? Won't take too many strikes before that boy's outta the game. I hear he's pressed for cash. Hear he's earmarked every penny he has to his name. Guess I'll mosey over and eavesdrop."

Once Ralph had left a second time, Tibby wandered outside. She heard the idle chug of the dozer, but neither Cole nor the sheriff was in sight. Yes, there was the man's car. But why should she feel guilty? *Because you've juggled a business on a shoestring,* her conscience nagged. *You know what it's like. And because maybe he'd stay if you gave him a break.*

Blessedly, two carloads of travelers drove in to buy camping supplies and get directions to Anza-Borrego Desert State Park. Their arrival coincided with a rush that lasted well past lunch. Tibby was too busy to give Cole a passing thought until late afternoon. During a lull she took Exterminator out for a short walk. He'd heel fine for all of about ten seconds, then he'd discover something to chase and yank her down the road.

The third time this occurred it dawned on Tibby that Cole's dozer still growled in the background. From the stacks of brush dotting the landscape, it appeared he'd been working steadily all morning. Was he ignoring a court order?

She loped with the dog to the edge of her property and shaded her eyes. Yes, there he sat atop the big yellow monster. He was clad only in shorts, and sweat glistened across his sunburned torso. A folded red bandanna kept his overlong dark curls out of his eyes. Each time he worked the pedals or the levers that raised and lowered the blade, the muscles in his arms and legs bunched and flexed. His limbs looked bright as boiled lobsters in the grueling heat of the midday sun. The fool. Where was his umbrella canopy? Had he never heard of heatstroke?

Tibby's stomach clenched. She waved, trying to get his attention. He gave no indication that he'd seen her.

"Is he trying to kill himself?" Disgusted, she back-tracked to the store where she grabbed a jar of aloe cream she'd blended with red clover to take away the sting of sunburn. She tore open a packet of men's white T-shirts and soaked one in cool water. Armed with those things, plus a gallon jug of bottled water and a buckaroo hat, she raced out again. Topping the rise beyond her garden, she gazed down on Cole's handiwork. There seemed to be a pattern to his clearing. A series of figure eights with strips of desert plants and an occasional arroyo between the leveled patches.

Nerves strung tight began to flutter. She imagined velvet greens in the clearings, and pathways winding through the desert to tee boxes placed at the lower edge of each eight. If that was what Cole had planned, it was a unique concept. An entire golf course taking advantage of the desert's natural beauty. Eager to ask him about it, she picked her way over to the dozer.

She was standing practically under his blade when Cole saw her. His heart constricted and slammed against his breastbone. Every aching muscle in his body screamed in protest as he put on all the stops to keep the tracks from moving forward and the blade suspended. "Dammit, woman, get back! Are you nuts?" He stripped off the earplugs that blocked out the engine's noise and wiped sweat away with a shaking arm.

Her smile dissolved and the light winked out of her eyes.

"I'm sorry," he shouted above the low rumble of the motor, "but what if I hadn't seen you and dropped the blade?" Fear still thrummed in his stomach as he went blindly through the steps to silence the engine. He slid down and was surprised to find that his legs refused to support him. If Tibby hadn't been close enough to grab him, he would have fallen on his face.

"Are you dizzy?"

Cole blinked at the three Tibby's all bearing a worried expression. Suddenly surrounded by her cool sweet scent, he decided dizzy was the least of what he was. He thought he nodded, but nothing tilted, so he could have been dreaming. Then she eased him against the dozer's track and tugged a cold wet shirt over his head. That brought a dose of reality. "St-stop." His teeth chattered.

"Cole, you're overheated. I want you to drink a small amount of this water and stay in the shade. Have you been out here all day without water?"

He gulped a few welcome swallows from the jug she

held before she jerked it away. "I had a bottle of water. When I finish roughing out nine holes, I'll stop for lunch."

"It's hours past lunch and you're burned to a cinder. Where's your watch?"

"Guess I went off without it. I was hell-bent on confronting the men to see why they hadn't backed your story." He ripped the water jug out of her hand and poured it over his burned arms and legs.

She snatched it back and urged him to sip some. "The *why* is easy. They want your golf course. Their wives are the ones who confuse me," she said, recapping the container. "A few play golf, but not that many. I can't figure why they signed the petition. I guess the only way to settle this is for us to play that grudge match."

He put out a hand and smoothed it over the taut lines bracketing her lips. "It's not a grudge match, Tibby. I want us to get along. But…things keep happening."

As always, his touch sent a deluge of heat into the pit of her stomach. Weakness overtook her limbs, and as always she found herself softening. Found herself willing to compromise—to meet him more than halfway. Did he know that? Was it why he made excuses to touch her? If so, she should stay the heck away from him.

Only not yet. Plunking the hat rakishly on his head, she slung one of his arms around her shoulders. "Come on," she said gruffly. "I'll help you home. You've had quite enough sun. I brought some cream that'll take the fire out of those burns. Even then, you may not sleep a wink tonight."

"If I can't, will you come nurse me, sweet Tibby?"

"Tease away, Cole. Burned as you are, you may *need* nursing. And yes, if you start throwing up or feeling faint, call me."

Cole slowed his steps. "You'd do that—come over in the middle of the night?"

"It's no big deal, O'Donnell. Winnie, Henrietta, Mabel, anyone in town would do the same. What's so odd about lending a helping hand?"

"Nothing. Everything. I've always taken care of myself."

"Ha! Someone took care of you as a child." Tibby struggled to balance him. "And you weren't nearly this heavy, either."

He attempted to relieve her of his weight. "I did take care of myself as a kid. Just leave me, Tibby. Don't put yourself out."

She paused in her efforts to guide him up the porch steps, ignoring his order. "Then you must not have had things like chicken pox or earaches or flu."

He gazed at her steadily. "I had all of those, and tonsillitis so bad that one night—I guess I was in sixth grade—I called a cab and took myself to the emergency room. Gramps carried the insurance on me. I didn't want them to call him, but they did. He drove all night to be there for my surgery and brought me here to recuperate. I guess he kept Anna informed."

"Cole, that's child abuse." Tibby led him to the wicker settee on the screened porch. "Yale should have reported her. I don't care if she *was* your mother."

"He did once when she went to Chicago with friends and left me to fend for myself." Cole shrugged. "The apartment was clean and I had food to eat. I knew I was capable, so I sort of resented the authorities poking around."

"How old were you?" She peeled off the damp shirt and smoothed cream over his magenta skin.

"Probably seven or so. Second grade. I knew my phone

number and my way around the kitchen. There's a difference between abuse and neglect."

"Not in my book," Tibby said huffily.

Cole shivered at the light slathering of cool cream she gently patted on the exposed flesh above his knee. "Does Tibby, translated, mean little earth mother?"

She paused in her ministrations. "I've never seen it in any book of names. My parents were missionaries in Brazil when I was born. I don't know if they heard it there or not. Why do you ask?"

"I can see you with a whole houseful of kids. Like that nursery rhyme—the one about the woman who lived in a shoe. Kids and dogs and cats, all chasing around those apple trees of yours." He grinned.

Blushing, Tibby put the jar of cream into his hand and straightened. "And I do this all on my own without a Mr. Shoe? Keep the hat, O'Donnell. If you ask me, the sun fried your brains."

Cole's comeback was squelched by a pounding at his door. Tibby motioned for him to stay seated while she crossed the room to answer the knock.

Justine Banks opened the screen and stepped past Tibby. "Hi, Cole. Oh, my stars, what happened to you, you poor boy?"

Tibby telegraphed him a knowing smile, as if to say, *See? All the ladies in town will fuss over you.*

"Guess I didn't know my own limitations, Justine. I wanted to rough out nine holes today. Tibby dropped by with a drink of water and convinced me it was smarter to stop at eight. I got sort of sunburned."

"Sort of?" Tibby snorted. "Like a boiled lobster."

Justine darted a glance between the two. "I can come back another time. I noticed the dozer had quit, so I thought you might show me what paperwork you need done, Cole.''

That got Tibby's attention. "You're doing his book-keeping? I was going to ask if you'd watch the store for a few hours every day."

"Oh, Tibby." Justine's face fell. "I already volunteered to help Cole. Do you need time to practice golf? Pete told me about the match."

Tibby shrugged. "I'm not a hundred percent decided."

Cole glanced up sharply. "I thought you were, from the way you sounded."

"Maybe I can do both jobs," Justine said, obviously trying to promote peace.

Cole shook his head. "What I have in mind is pretty involved, Justine. Ordering a computer-controlled sprinkler system is time-consuming. I'm counting on you to buy the fertilizers, too. To do that, you have to take classes at the agricultural college in El Centro. The California EPA requires a chemical applicator's license to sterilize the greens with methyl bromide before I apply seed. My California license expired, and since I'm clearing the land, I won't have time to take renewal classes. In addition, there'll be a hundred little trips back and forth to the planning commission. Your days will be full."

"Sounds exciting." Justine's eyes sparkled with interest.

Tibby crossed her arms. "Speaking of the planning commission, Cole—Ralph said you had a visit from the county sheriff today. I'm surprised you continued grading."

"Oh, that." Cole waved a hand expansively. "He agreed that as owner of the property, I have a right to clean out some of the underbrush. The injunction stated I wasn't to clear-cut all two hundred acres or lay a blade to the portion you claim. I told him we were working that out. We are, aren't we?" He grinned appealingly.

"Oh, you bet we are. You have all the angles figured, don't you? This morning when you offered me time to bone up on my game, you knew darned well that you had *my* part-time help in *your* pocket."

"Honestly, Tibby, it didn't enter my mind. Does this mean the match is off?"

"To the contrary, O'Donnell. It's definitely on." With that, she stormed from the house.

"Oh, dear." Justine wrung her hands. "Tibby sounds upset. I wish you two had hit it off better. Our sweet Tibby never raises her voice."

"She tends to with me," Cole said. "But I'm more than willing to look for her sweet side. Tell me, Justine, how well does she play golf?"

"Your grandfather never told you about their game?"

"No. Did she actually beat him or did he let her win?"

"Tibby wouldn't lie."

"But Gramps was good."

She smiled agreeably. "And he did like to win."

"I know, Justine. That's why I find the whole thing so absurd."

"Absurd? Tibby cared for your grandfather. Like she does for everyone in Yaqui Springs. To an older lonely person, caring means a lot."

A wistful expression darkened Cole's eyes. "What's that got to do with age? Don't we all want someone to care?"

"Appears to me she cared enough to bring you in out of the blistering sun and slather you with one of her special lotions to take your pain away."

Cole was jolted out of his fog. "You wouldn't be trying to sell me on Tibby Mack, would you, Justine?"

"Oh, my." Guilt spread across the wrinkled face.

"If it's matchmaking you're about, you're working on the wrong person."

Justine clapped her hands lightly. "So you'll call off this silly match?"

"Unfortunately, no. After paying taxes, I've got barely enough money to build this course." He leaned forward and clasped his hands between his knees. "I need that property for my clubhouse. And if I can't use the General Store's left-turn lane and give my customers access over the easement between our properties, I'll have to come up with a hundred grand to pay the county to build a second turn lane at the north end. It's highway robbery, but that's how the planning commission works." He paused, shrugging lightly. "If I can't reserve some operating capital, I'm sunk."

"Does Tibby know?"

"That I need her road? I gave her a copy of the plans."

"Sweet-talking wouldn't hurt. A big box of chocolates, that sort of thing."

Cole scratched his chin. "Like roses, Justine? A huge bouquet, let's say?"

She dropped into the closest chair. "It was Winnie's idea. We didn't know there was a Cicely when we placed the order, I swear. Our aim was for you and Tibby to kiss and make up."

"A man likes to win or lose by his own efforts. Did it ever occur to you that I might have made headway with Tibby if every man, woman and dog in town would quit butting in?"

"So you're saying I shouldn't have offered to do your paperwork?"

"Yes. I mean…no. I mean, no more interfering between Tibby and me in any way, shape or form, Justine."

She looked properly chastised. "Gotcha, boss. Shall we talk sprinklers?"

"Yes. I can't tell you what a relief it is to have that cleared up. Thank God Tibby doesn't know. She doesn't, does she?"

Justine shook her head until her newly tinted curls bounced.

Taking her at her word, Cole gathered up all his information and they poured over sprinkler brochures, finally settling on a good yet affordable system. He pulled out reams of forms that needed to be filled out and filed with the county. They dealt with wiring, certified seed, sand samples and humus. Plus triplicate copies to say he wasn't using reclaimed water and therefore had no need to build a desalinization plant.

"Forms for the fire department?" Justine asked after he piled on five new sets.

"County policy for the aid car in case someone has a heart attack. Hey, you're beginning to look a little overwhelmed. Start with this batch. We'll touch base again when you're done."

"Good idea." She started for the door, juggling the load. "By the way, Cole, I'll need to use the typewriter in Tibby's office. You might invite her to breakfast at the Bogey Wells clubhouse tomorrow morning. She used to love going there with Yale."

Cole's brows met over the bridge of his nose. "Justine, you just agreed not to meddle."

"Sorry." She shrugged and dropped a stack of forms.

Cole retrieved them and found her a basket. "I'll forgive your lapse this time," he said, seeing her to the door. "Hmm," he murmured, half to himself, "maybe breakfast is not such a bad idea. It'd give Tibby and me a chance to relax and talk without interruption."

"Exactly my point. Oh—" she stopped on the walkway "—did you know Tibby collects unicorns? Winnie mentioned seeing a crystal one in the gift shop at the resort. If you called ahead, I'll bet they'd wrap it."

"Enough, Justine. No unicorns."

"All right." Her lip protruded a bit. "Men are so obtuse when it comes to courting a woman. I trust you'll tell Tibby I'm free to open up for her in the morning?"

"That I'll do. And, Justine, not all men are obtuse. I'll think about the unicorn." He carried her smile back inside with him. Wasting no time in case the rumor mill beat him to the punch, he walked stiffly to the phone. His burned skin felt tight, and he found himself wishing Tibby would apply another coat of aloe tonight. Now, in fact...

"Tibby? Cole, here." He chuckled at the lengthy silence. "You always sound wary when I call—like I'm the big bad wolf. Repeat after me—'Hi, Cole. Glad you called.'"

A smile curved her lips at that, but of course he couldn't see it. "I thought I might hear from you," she said sweetly, as if they hadn't parted badly. "I suppose the cream's worn off. I recommend a cool shower, a vinegar rinse if you have some in your cupboard, and then apply more cream. Do that two or three times before you go to bed. It'll take out the fire and keep your skin moist." The memory of how his skin felt under her hand affected Tibby's speech—made her words come out jerky.

"You OK? You're not catching a cold from the drenching you took the other day, are you?"

"I'm fine. Y-you caught me just as I'd swallowed hot tea."

"You drink a lot of tea. Do you have it for breakfast, too?"

"I've never developed a taste for coffee. Don't tell me

this trivia concerning my dietary habits really interests you.''

"Sure it does, Tibby. I want to know everything about you." His voice deepened appreciably. "Another reason I called is to invite you out for breakfast tomorrow. I thought maybe we'd go to the club at Bogey Wells. I mentioned the possibility to Justine. She'll be happy to watch the store."

Tibby swallowed twice and hoped he didn't hear. It stood to reason that Cole would be as curious about her golfing skills as she was about his. What better place to get answers than at the clubhouse where she used to play? "Tell you what," she said, deciding to scotch his plans. "I'll fix ginger griddle scones and ham-and-cheese toasties, and save us both a drive. I may even throw in apple-date muffins."

Winnie barged into Tibby's office in time to hear her side of the conversation. Smiling broadly, she rubbed her stomach and grinned. "The way to a man's heart is still through his stomach," she mouthed, then winked.

Tibby rolled her eyes. "Cole? Are you with me? Now who's wary? I promise no hemlock—and no dog trying to steal your food. Ariel's husband ran a steel cable between those two apple trees, so Exterminator can run to his heart's content in the shade. Ariel claims he'll be easier to train If he's worn-out."

Cole's thoughts were still on the scones. Everyone in town said how great they were. And the last time he'd eaten toasties was when Tibby's grandmother had brought a batch to Gramps. They were…incredible. "No man in his right mind would turn down an offer for a home-cooked meal. If I hesitated, it was because I, uh, hate putting you to extra work."

"It's no trouble, Cole. I love to cook."

"And I love to eat. That makes us a perfect team, doesn't it?"

"Is six OK?" Tibby squeaked, unable to manage more as his gravelly innuendo laid a row of goose bumps along her skin.

"Six is good, Tibby. I'm an early riser, too. Another thing we have in common."

She didn't trust herself to respond. "Bring an appetite," she murmured, and hung up fast.

Cole listened to the buzz. It was as if he felt her frustration humming along the wire. Slowly he cradled his receiver and hauled in a ragged breath. If he left now, he might just make it to Bogey Wells in time to buy that damned unicorn.

CHAPTER TEN

COLE LAY NAKED on his bed watching rainbows spin off the cut crystal of the little unicorn. It was smaller than he'd expected; sack and all, it had fit easily in his shirt pocket. The attractive clerk who'd waited on him had flirted shamelessly, but he'd felt no response. She'd been aggressive enough that he'd admitted he was buying the unicorn for "a special lady." A second clerk, a kid with dreamy eyes magnified by oval glasses, suggested he let them gift wrap it. A nice gesture, but he'd declined. He didn't want Tibby to feel pressured by a wrapped gift— as if it represented a bribe.

He ran a fingertip over the gently swirled horn. If Tibby knew how he'd agonized between this one that stood alone, regally pawing the air, and another joined to a tiny castle, she'd probably laugh. But he'd rarely bought women gifts. And he'd never gone to this much trouble or given it this much thought.

Feeling the lamp's heat against his sunburned arm, Cole let his fingers slide away. Tibby had been right about the vinegar and the aloe mixture. The red was already fading. At nine o'clock he'd felt compelled to call and thank her; he'd been worried when she didn't answer. Not five minutes later Tibby had stopped by to see how he was doing. Cole wished she'd been able to come in, but she said she had yeast rolls rising. And Exterminator was impatient to be off.

He yawned. It was midnight and he still had a stack of brochures to peruse. He needed an eight-thousand-gallon holding tank set an equal distance between his two wells. The only way to keep it from being an eyesore would be to bury it, and that meant renting a backhoe.

Flipping through his ledger, he penciled in an amount. The figure made him cringe, but it couldn't be helped. Twice he reworked the column and shuffled funds. As an architect, he'd worked primarily on building private courses; going public was a whole different show. The county stuck its nose into everything. Yet the people he planned to serve couldn't afford the outrageous membership fees private courses charged. He had to keep costs within his budget.

The clock hands crept up on two before Cole closed the ledger with a sigh and snapped off the light. Nothing like cutting it close. He half expected to be chased all night by bold black numbers. Instead, he dreamed of unicorns and Tibby Mack.

DAYLIGHT SPLASHED across the bed, waking him. He jumped up, refreshed in spite of having had only three hours' sleep. And he looked forward to the day, something he hadn't done in a while. Yesterday's sunburn felt neither tight nor hot as he stepped beneath a stinging shower and washed away the last vestiges of Tibby's special cream. After toweling off, he dressed casually in gray cotton slacks and a comfortable well-washed cotton-knit pullover. Then he promptly changed into a regular shirt with a breast pocket. He didn't want to give Tibby the unicorn first thing when he walked through the door, nor did he want to risk breaking the delicate horn by stuffing it into his pants pocket.

As he ran a comb through his hair, he grimaced. If he

didn't make an appointment with a barber soon, he'd have to tie it in a ponytail. Since he'd returned stateside, days never seemed to have enough hours. Right now his desk groaned under three days' worth of mail. Mail he'd collected yesterday from Tibby's post office. Mail he wouldn't have yet if he'd had to drive to Brawley, he admitted reluctantly, pausing to strap on his watch. But then, he wasn't asking her to close the post office, only to move it.

In his eagerness Cole realized he had gotten ready too early. He sat at his desk and began to sort the mail. Mostly advertisements. The ones touting seed and fertilizers he set aside. He must have received twenty-five sand samples in all. Justine had her work cut out for her as soon as she completed the course on chemicals.

He slit open a letter bearing a farming-association seal. Some co-op asking if he'd sell his acreage. They wanted to expand their goat-and-pig-farming operation. Oh, wouldn't Tibby love that? Smiling, Cole tucked the sheet aside to show her the next time she got testy over his golf course. Ah, here was a letter from Lane Davis—in his guise of attorney rather than friend. High time, too. Although he'd actually promised to call. A crisp one-page note on formal letterhead didn't bode well for Cole's case. "Hmm. Maybe not." Cole reread the passage. Lane said if Tibby lacked proof that Yale had freely and willingly donated the land for the post office, then Cole's recorded deed would stand up in court.

Rocking back in the swivel chair, Cole tapped the letter against his lips. If his dreams last night, and for the past several nights, were any indication, his feelings for Tibby had changed drastically from when he'd first contacted Lane. Cole had seen guys fall suddenly for a particular woman. Men who the week before wouldn't have even considered marriage. The ones who came to mind were still head over heels in love with their wives. Cole had never really known what love meant; did he know now?

Bringing the chair forward with a snap, he tossed Lane's letter on a pile of correspondence needing further attention. Time for breakfast. Hunger he understood. From college psychology he'd learned that hunger fell on the lowest rung of Maslow's ladder to self-actualization. The need for love sat on rung number three, if memory served. Cole did remember because he'd been a smart-ass who'd argued that love wasn't a basic need, based on his own lack thereof. And the prof had assigned him a load of extra reading and said to the class that obviously Mr. O'Donnell had a long way to go to self-fulfillment.

God, he'd hated to admit some twit of a professor knew Cole Patrick O'Donnell better than he did himself. Almost as much as he hated falling into these damned philosophical moods. Who cared? If he didn't get his butt in gear and hightail it over to Tibby's on time, he was liable to be flat on his back looking up at rung one.

He was halfway out the door when he remembered the unicorn and a good-size bone he'd brought home in a doggie bag last night from the steakhouse in Bogey Wells where he'd eaten dinner. After hearing the fate of Grant Carlyle's BMW, Cole decided he was darned well going to stay on Exterminator's good side.

If left to Tibby, the dog would probably never get meat. Mack's General Store stocked every grain, fruit and vegetable known to man; however, Cole had noticed Tibby's meat selection was pretty anemic. Although it probably wouldn't hurt him to think along those lines, considering his family history. He needed someone like Tibby looking out for him. *Whoa! A big jump from one breakfast.*

Exterminator barked from the minute Cole set foot on

the easement to when he reached Tibby's yard. Already the Dane had worn a path between the two trees. He lunged against the wire as Cole drew close and seemed frustrated when the heavy cable dragged him back. Damn, Cole disliked hearing the dog's surprised yelp at being brought up short. One of these days he'd build a proper pen. *Whoa, again!*

The dog reared up on his hind legs and placed his paws on Cole's shoulders, lapping his face. Cole petted the sleek coat. Next thing he knew, the dog had sniffed out the sack with the bone. He lifted it right out of Cole's side pocket and big as you please, nosed it open.

"What a pooch." Cole laughed aloud as the dog plopped down and began contentedly gnawing at the bone. "Now if Tibby had taught you to fold the sack and deposit it in the garbage, we'd be in fat city," he said, snatching it from a gust of wind.

Still laughing, he turned and saw Tibby leaning negligently against the screen door, arms crossed, a smile on her face as she watched his antics. The laughter clogged his throat, or maybe it was the whiff of cinnamon and apples floating on the air. He was loath to admit it was the welcome sight of her standing there in a bright blue-checked jumper spattered with white-and-yellow daisies. Lace ruffles edged a petticoat that peeked out below the skirt, affording Cole the tiniest glimpse of narrow ankles. There wasn't one thing provocative about the damned Pollyanna garb. Yet Cole thought if sunshine and smiles could be woven in a fabric to capture a man's heart, the outfit Tibby had on would do the job.

"Are you spoiling my dog?" she teased. Her words washed over Cole like the summer breeze that'd whisked away the sack. He nodded, feeling sixteen again.

"He adores you and I forgive you," she said with a

saucy toss of her waist-long hair, which today hung loose. Waves shimmered like gold in the morning sun.

All at once Tibby separated herself from the door. "Are you planning to come inside, O'Donnell? Or must I bring your food out?" A tiny dimple winked in her left cheek. "I'm afraid I only have one doggie dish."

Unlike other women he'd met, Cole didn't think Tibby had the vaguest notion that her new look had knocked him for a loop. Or maybe she did, and she was toying with him.

Two could play those games. Cole bounded up the steps, swept her into his arms and planted an open-mouthed kiss full on her lips. The instant she went limp in his arms, he threaded one hand through her hair and tipped her head back till the ends brushed the porch. She clutched his shoulders—in passion? Or panic? He'd resolved to let her go, but couldn't resist taking a last nibble of her moist lower lip. Deliberately provocative, he growled near her ear, "Didn't you invite me to this private rendezvous to lick powdered sugar from your lips and sample…other delights?"

Cole felt, more than heard, the shaky breath she drew. They clung together, from chest to knee, and with her tilted slightly off balance, he had the advantage. If he hadn't begun to feel so affected himself, he might have teased her a bit longer. And now a buzzer bleated insistently in the kitchen, rivaling the primitive drums pounding through his blood. Cole knew the wisest course was to release her quickly and laugh it off as a joke.

So that was what he did. He unwound their limbs, making no remark at all when she tripped in her mad rush to reach the stove. Carefully blanketing his desire, he gallantly handed her the quilted oven mitts. She looked pos-

itively shell-shocked. Not that he'd bargained on being so shaken up himself.

Striving to act as normal as possible—difficult, considering that he was in a state impossible to hide—Cole turned to the fridge and yanked open the door. The icy rush of air brought a measure of relief. ''I see you have empty glasses on the table. Shall I fill them with juice, milk or water?'' he asked evenly, determined to emerge the victor against out-of-control hormones.

Even though they were back-to-back, because they stood so close, Cole knew how long Tibby grappled with her own self-restraint before her breathing leveled enough for her to answer his simple question.

''The apple juice is homemade and fresh. Or I've got milk if you prefer. Skim,'' she added, the last word sounding strained.

Cole took a firm grip on the pitcher of juice. Damn, but this was going to be a long breakfast. And he had no one to blame but himself. He'd had too little sleep to be playing with fire like this. Back to bed was where he wanted to go—taking Tibby with him.

Shocked by that revelation, he needed both hands to steady the pitcher while he poured. He supposed he should have been prepared. But he wasn't. The raw passion she unleashed in him had taken him by surprise. The first time he'd kissed her had been half out of annoyance and half out of curiosity. Today's kiss had started out in jest. An impulse. Between then and now, though, the stakes of the game had changed. He wanted her fiercely and on every level. His complacent world suddenly shifted on its axis. The stakes might have changed, but the rules hadn't. He wouldn't have her—or anyone—thinking he'd slept with her just to get that damned property.

"Cole!" Tibby's voice jerked him from a blinding weakness that seemed to suspend time and him.

"Stop! You're pouring apple juice on my new table-cloth."

"What?"

She snatched the pitcher from his hands and frantically mopped the spill from the sunflower-print cloth, using matching napkins she ripped from bright yellow rings. When he tried to help and knocked a fork on the floor, which he bent sluggishly to retrieve, Tibby caught him by the arm and pulled out a chair. "Sit," she ordered. "Cole, are you feeling all right?" She felt his cheek with the back of her hand. "First that…kiss, and now this." She made a sweeping gesture with her hand. "I knew it. You had too much sun yesterday. Are you disoriented? Oh, Cole, you need a doctor."

"I don't need a doctor, Tibby. I need breakfast." Lame, but the best he could do on short notice. She'd run for her life if she had any idea of his real problem.

She clutched the juice pitcher to her breast. "Are you diabetic? Ralph Hopple is. He's seeing a holistic healer who's helped him a lot. If you'd told me, I'd have made a drink of goat's rue and bilberry leaves. Do you use plenty of garlic in cooking? It's a natural blood cleanser."

Fascinated, Cole studied the earnest expression that darkened her eyes as she talked. "I'm not diabetic. I'm starved, is all." He did his best to sound truthful. "Will you still take pity on me?" he joked, clutching her hand.

"No heatstroke and no diabetes?" Her brows inched together. "There wasn't a full moon last night or any-thing. So why did you kiss me?"

Cole reached up and ran a thumb over her lips, slightly swollen from his kiss. "It wasn't moon madness, Tibby.

I find you extremely kissable. And if you don't occupy our mouths with food, I'll probably kiss you again.''

''F-food it is.'' Darn, why did she always stutter and stammer in Cole's presence? Especially when he seemed bent on teasing her. Gathering her wits, she slapped his hand away, set the pitcher over the sticky spill and marched to the stove where the scones and ham toasties cooled. ''Someday you're going to tease the wrong woman, Cole O'Donnell. And she's going to punch your lights out—or chase you all the way to the altar. Mark my words,'' she said, plunking scones and fresh strawberries on the table.

''What gave you the idea I'm avoiding marriage?'' he asked as he filled his plate and then did the same with hers.

She made room for the second platter. ''Yale said you were too busy building your career to get married. But I thought you were too busy being a playboy.''

''Being a playboy is highly overrated. In this day and age most men are all talk when it comes to sleeping around. Something we do to save face with other guys. Who wants to admit he's waiting for Ms. Right? Or worse, that his daddy-clock is ticking?''

Tibby rested her elbow on the table and her chin in the palm of her hand. ''Do men do that, too? Long for a family, I mean. I thought it was only women.''

Her ''too'' was telling. Cole shifted uncomfortably in his seat. ''Hey, that's a heavy duty topic for a first date.''

''Sorry. I thought this was a business meeting. Didn't you invite me to the club to find out how well I play golf?''

''When a man asks a woman to share a meal, it normally constitutes a date. However, since you brought it up, how well *do* you play?'' He waggled his brows.

She missed that and crushed her scone to smithereens. Darned if he didn't evoke a case of the guilts faster than a marauding rabbit sneaked carrots from her garden. As she gazed into his guileless gray eyes, her conscience nagged at her. She should at least warn him that she had a knack for the game.

"I beat Joe Toliver so often he turned me over to Yale. Your grandfather claimed I had a natural swing. He called me the queen of the greens."

Cole wiped his mouth with his napkin and laughed. "Gramps was a big kidder. Sure he wasn't referring to the fact that you want to turn everyone in town into vegetarians?" His grin settled with cocky assurance after he'd glanced behind him; sure enough, her clubs sat in the same corner, still covered with dust. "I'll wager the only birdies you see during our match are the feathered kind, Tibby."

She helped herself to the strawberries. Well, she *had* given him fair warning. "Have another toastie, Cole. In fact, have the rest. I'll find a calendar so we can firm up a date for our match." She was all business now.

Watching her glide away from the table, Cole was again struck by her easy grace. What, he wondered, did she wear to play golf? The long flared dresses she preferred would billow in the slightest wind. Yet he'd never seen her in anything else. More than ever, he was sure his grandfather, being a true gentleman, had let Tibby win. She had an air of fragility about her. The kind that had men knocking themselves out to open car doors or carry her packages.

Speaking of fragility...Cole fingered the gift he carried in his breast pocket. He removed the bag with the unicorn as she came back with an appointment calendar.

"Is a Sunday morning good? It's easier to set a tee-off

time on Sunday. A lot of the regular golfers go to church in Palm Springs. I'll call and confirm all this if you'd like. Say in three weeks?''

"Sure. Great." Feeling especially magnanimous, Cole said expansively, "Make it six." Heck, he'd give her lots of time to practice. "That'll put it after the Fourth of July. We don't need stray firecrackers interfering with our game.''

Tibby chewed her lip a moment. He was being awfully accommodating. Either that or he was sure of winning. "If you're comfortable with that, I'll pencil the date on my calendar. I'll write it down for you, too." The extra weeks gave her time to set up her indoor putting green and also spend time at the driving range. With any luck Cole wouldn't even know she was practicing.

"Here," he said as he traded the note she handed him for the bag with the gift.

"What's this?" Eyes cautious, she avoided taking what he thrust at her in a closed hand. "If you think I'm gullible enough to fall for one of those trick golf balls, think again, O'Donnell.''

"If you don't beat all when it comes to suspicious women. It's a gift. Take it. Justine mentioned you had a collection. You don't even have to thank me." He removed the small figure from the sack and set it beside her plate. The sun streaming in over the top of the café curtains shot the crystal through with fire.

Affected by Cole's unexpected thoughtfulness and the carving's simple beauty, Tibby's heart sped up. Joy tangled with ineffectual words of gratitude.

Based on the tears that slipped silently down her cheeks as she traced a finger over the mythical creature and the way she kept repeating his name, Cole surmised she liked the gift.

"I'm glad it pleases you. I had to choose between two, and since I've never seen your collection…" He shrugged self-consciously.

She jumped to her feet, clasping the unicorn in one hand and Cole's broad sun-bronzed hand in the other. "You must see it. My grandmother started the collection when I was born. At first I only received unicorns on my birthday. Then the residents started bringing them back from their travels. I've almost outgrown the corner cabinet."

She tugged him through the dining room. Cole had the impression of lightly sprigged wallpaper and polished mahogany furniture. A table with ten chairs. He envisioned a family of six, with room for company. Where that vivid image sprang from, he had no idea. But it was clear. Two girls. Miniatures of Tibby. And two boys—both gray-eyed with dark curls.

Cole hardly knew when they'd stepped into a smaller room. A sunroom with a redbrick floor and white wicker furniture. Two walls were lined with overflowing bookshelves. A comfortable welcoming room. He missed what Tibby said regarding the unicorns on the top shelf.

"Wow," he exclaimed as she rattled off where each had come from and who had given it to her. A delicate delft unicorn Ariel had brought from Holland. A cinnabar one from Winnie and Joe's trip to China. A light lavender one that Tibby said was venetian glass. Cole was shaking his head in astonishment before she reached the third shelf. And yet it pleased him to see that, in her entire collection, she had no other crystal piece. He beamed like a kid when she moved some around on the top shelf and set his gift on a small velvet dias where it caught the sun.

"It's beautiful, Cole. I love it. Love it. *Love it!*" She clasped her hands and spun in a circle.

He bent and brushed the tip of her nose with his. "Of course you're so shy and reserved I could never tell."

"I am shy." Unable to explain her giddy feelings, she broke from his gaze and pushed at his solid chest. Even then, she had to make a concerted effort to keep from flinging out her arms and dancing around the room like a frisky colt. Rising on tiptoe, she kissed him impulsively on the cheek, instead.

Cole's hand immediately flew to cover the spot. "What was that for?"

"I hadn't thanked you properly."

"Careful, or I'll be showing up here every night with unicorns."

Tibby shrugged. "They aren't so easy to find. I've looked in Brawley, Indio and Palm Springs. Last year a jewelry store in Palm Springs had one carved from jade. Needless to say, it was out of my price range."

Cole made a mental note to check out the jewelry stores in Palm Springs the next time he had reason to go there. He knew Tibby's birthday was in February and had already passed. But Christmas wasn't so far away. With luck his golf course should be up and running by then.

On second thought, maybe he ought to wait and see if she was still speaking to him by Christmas. She might not take kindly to being beaten in their golf match. Tempted as he was to explore a relationship with Tibby, he wouldn't risk going soft on her the way Gramps had. It made sense to keep his distance until after they played. Hadn't he learned to separate business from pleasure?

"Breakfast was good, Tibby. I'm sorry I ruined your tablecloth. I'll do the dishes while you soak out the stain."

She paused when they were halfway through the dining room. "You do dishes?"

"I learned early in life that if I wanted to eat and didn't

want food poisoning, the dishes had to be washed. Yes, I do dishes. What do you think—that I have a maid?''

"I guess I *didn't* think—or I'd have offered to help at your house the other night.''

"That night deserves forgetting. My apologies, Tibby. It's a sorry excuse, but things went from bad to worse for me that day.''

"Ah. Cicely. Did I tell you the florist refused to say who sent the flowers? He said the customer has a right to privacy—unless the flowers end up at a crime scene.''

Well, he supposed the Mavericks' crime was a pretty minor one in the scheme of things. Deception, interference, attempted matchmaking. Cole wondered how she'd react if she knew her friends had been to blame. Better keep that knowledge to himself for the moment.

"How is Cicely?'' Tibby asked casually as she cleared the table.

"Fine. She's dating my attorney, Lane Davis. I don't know if they're serious.''

She turned from the sink in time to catch his frown. Her heart pitched wildly. So she'd been right; Cicely was still number one. "I'd be glad to write and explain that the flowers must have been a joke or something.''

"No need, but thanks for offering.'' He began rinsing their plates in the sink.

She took them from his hands. "Gram put in a commercial-grade dishwasher a few years ago. It takes a week to fill. But I know exactly how everything fits. I'm sure you have other things on your agenda.''

"OK. Well,'' he muttered, "if I can't help, guess I'll go. I have ten greens to clear today. I'd better hop to it.''

"You shouldn't go out in the hot sun again today, Cole.''

"I have a hat some nice lady gave me. I plan to wear

long pants and a long-sleeved shirt. I'll take frequent water breaks, I promise.''

"Go ahead, say it. I'm not your mother.''

His eyes softened immediately. ''You're not, thank
goodness. Or I'd probably be in the hospital with heatstroke.''

"I'm sorry you don't get on well with your mother.
Rarely a day goes by that I don't wish mine was still
around. And Gram. Life is so short and family so pre-
cious.'' She paused. ''Is there any hope of you two ever
mending fences?''

"Not all fences are worth mending, Tibby.'' His eyes
glittered darkly.

Wishing that pertained to his feelings for Cicely, as
well, Tibby said nothing as Cole strode to the door. Exterminator barked the instant his hand touched the knob.

"Oh, I didn't thank you for Exterminator's treat. I was
joking earlier when I said you were spoiling him. Most
people wouldn't think of bringing a treat for someone's
pet. That was a nice thing to do, Cole.''

"After the course is up and running, I'd like to build
the mutt a pen. A big dog needs lots of room.''

"I know. I considered asking one of the men to tackle
that project. It breaks my heart to see him confined on
that cable. How high a fence will I need? I imagine he
could clear six feet with room to spare.''

"I expect that's right. Most kennels go up eight feet
with wire, then they cap toward the enclosure with another
foot or so.''

"What a good idea. I knew I didn't want to run the
risk of him breaking loose and tangling with another cactus. Or a coyote. Or even a skunk, glory be.''

"You mean you wouldn't like another chance to visit
Dr. Carlyle?''

"That bore? Really, Cole." Tibby saw mischief tugging at the corners of his mouth. "Oh, you. You were yanking my chain again. I'm sure everyone in town—and maybe in Bogey Wells—has heard what Exterminator did to Grant's car." Her eyes widened. "Sometime I'll have to tell you about my afternoon antiquing with Dr. Carlyle."

"Tonight?" Cole forgot completely that he'd been planning to avoid her company until after the match.

Tibby would have liked nothing better than to spend more time getting to know Cole. However, she had work to do—and she'd earmarked tonight to assemble her electronic greens. "Maybe another time, Cole. I'm behind at the store. I've got inventory and ordering to finish before Monday."

"You still have to eat. I've been told I make a mean chili relleno. How about it? My place at six?"

A warm tingly feeling started at Tibby's toes and worked its way out in a generous smile. "I might have been able to resist anything else. I warn you, O'Donnell, you'd better not be fooling. I'm an expert chili relleno tester."

"Good." Cole started walking toward his place—and hoped he didn't look goofy when he punched a fist at the sky. He couldn't help it; he felt like a man just given a million dollars. Stopping to pat the Great Dane's sleek sides, he babbled as much to the dog. Straightening abruptly, Cole turned back to Tibby. "Hey, bring the mutt," he called. "I'm not serving dessert."

Tibby nodded and waved to let him know she'd heard. His long lithe strides carried him out of sight before she quit grinning like a fool and hurried back into the house. *Darn, how self-destructive could one woman be?* Cole O'Donnell had wormed his way into her heart again. No

matter how often she reminded herself that she was now
mature enough to accept whatever he willingly offered,
on whatever terms he offered it, she couldn't shake the
fear that he'd leave again.

This time his leaving would be different, and so much
worse. Because what she felt for him now was *real*, not
like the fantasy and teenage infatuation it'd been ten years
ago. And if he left this time, she wasn't sure her heart
would get over it.

CHAPTER ELEVEN

COLE'S SPICY Mexican dish was a delight. Tibby ballooned out her cheeks and fell back in her chair. "I'm stuffed. I haven't eaten so much at one sitting in years. Cole, you're incredible."

Her remark drew a laugh from Cole. "Ordinarily men prefer to hear that statement later in the evening." Smiling benignly, he topped off his wineglass, but respected her wish when she covered hers and shook her head. He'd been crazy to ever consider staying away from Tibby. "Tomorrow night it's your turn to cook, Ms. Mack. What heart-smart cuisine might I expect?"

"I've enjoyed tonight, Cole. Dinner and our conversation, too. I'm glad we like a lot of the same music, books and movies. *But* I don't recall inviting you to eat at my place tomorrow night. Surely you don't mean to make a habit of this." She froze for a moment, envisioning the mock fairways she'd woven throughout her house. She'd still have to sneak some time at a driving range to be ready for their match. Her nights from now on were reserved. However, it was impossible to ignore Cole's expression.

"Why not?" He sounded disgruntled. "If you like my company and I like yours? I've had enough solitary meals to last a lifetime, Tibby. If it's cooking that bothers you, I still have a few recipes up my sleeve. Same time, same station tomorrow night?"

"Cole..."

"Humor me, Tibby. I'll even serve iced raspberry tea in place of wine."

"OK," she agreed hesitantly, because she *had* enjoyed the evening. "Let's take a picnic out on the sea. I have Gram's sixteen-foot runabout."

"I hiked along the dock last night around dusk. The no-see-ums practically ate me alive."

"Oh." She hadn't been thinking straight. "Once the valley farms start their summer irrigation schedules, it lowers the water level. The bugs multiply by hordes. Sometimes the stench of rotting marsh grasses reaches us, as well. The sea has changed since we were kids. For the worse."

"Isn't someone regulating the amount of water farmers siphon from the sea?"

"That's not the problem. It's their backwash. Polluted dregs leaching chemicals out of their fertilizers. The state looks the other way because what's more important—revenue produced from feeding the hungry masses or one below-sea-level sink that by all geological calculations should have dried up eons ago?"

"Isn't there a committee studying the problem? When I was going through my grandfather's files, I stumbled across notes from past meetings."

"Yale served as our representative. But the committee didn't accomplish much. Nobody agreed. I probably have their meeting schedule, if you want to go."

"Perhaps I should. I'm trying to build a business here that depends on year-round participation. I can't have my customers battling bugs or obnoxious odors. Bring the schedule when you come for dinner tomorrow night."

"Cole," she groaned, "I didn't *exactly* say yes."

"Pretty clever, huh?" Appearing properly contrite, he

reached across the table and captured her hand. His thumb made lazy circles on her palm. "So you'll come for dinner."

Tibby felt the flow of blood change direction midstream and congeal in places it ought not to congeal. "All right, all right." She reclaimed her hand. "I should g-go now. Inventory." Her voice slipped so low on the scale that Exterminator opened one eye and growled.

Cole lifted her hand and placed a row of kisses from her wrist to her elbow. "You'll run out of paperwork sooner or later, Tibby. I, on the other hand, have lots of cookbooks."

Tibby snatched back her fingers. "Did I tell you that Justine made a fine mess of ordering your sprinkler system? I found her in a puddle of tears today. She'd figured a hundred too many left elbow joints, all male connectors and no female receivers. It took two hours to straighten things out. You owe me, Cole."

"Really? Being in your debt sounds promising. You know I have no money. But my body is yours for the taking." He slid his chair closer.

"Yeah, right," she drawled, her heart thudding a warning. "Maybe I'll accept the payment you offered earlier. You fix dinner every night between now and our golf match, and I'll call things square."

"Deal."

"You don't want to dicker?"

"Nope. Playing house suits me," he said, leaning toward her with a lazy smile.

She hastily started stacking their plates. "Sure you aren't planning to poison me before the match?"

He raked his hair forward until it stood on end. Rising, he curled his fingers into claws and laughed evilly. "Only the Shadow knows."

"You nut. It's tough to scare a devout romantic-suspense reader. So give me a break, O'Donnell. For that poor rendition, you get to do dishes by yourself. Come on, Exterminator, time to go."

Cole slicked his hair into place. "Stay. No more high jinks, I promise."

In spite of his wholesome boyish appeal, the jumping nerves in her stomach prompted Tibby to prod her sleepy dog into leaving.

Partway down the lane, she slowed and glanced back at Cole's house. She was surprised to find him standing at the kitchen window watching her. Once again he was seeing to her safety. She, with the killer dog. Of course, her killer dog looked at Cole with cow eyes. Some killer. Some dog.

Tibby was confused by Cole's recent actions toward her. Maybe she should just move the darned post office. But if she did, there'd be no reason for the golf match. *Poof* would go his interest. Oh, he might tease and make innuendos about them playing house, but she suspected that the minute he laid hands on the property, he'd finish the course, hire a manager and then light out for the coast to be with Cicely.

Lord only knew why Tibby was trying to stave off the inevitable. She should have more pride in herself. But she'd found she had no pride when it came to Cole.

Puppy love. A crush. That was what Gram had termed Tibby's feelings for Cole all those years ago. But the way she felt today was far more complicated.

If Gram knew the truth, surely she'd forgive Tibby for using the post office so shamelessly. Didn't Lara always say, "Tibby, girl, you don't plan your future by looking in the rearview mirror. Get out there and make things happen."

And that was precisely what Tibby had in mind when she stayed up half the night practicing chip shots and putts. She was going to make something happen if she could. She would do her best to delay Cole's leaving. With time, there was a slim possibility he might realize this was where he belonged—in Yaqui Springs and with her. But in that case, shouldn't she let him see *more* of her rather than try to avoid him?

IN THE MORNING, Tibby's primary thought was to smash her alarm clock. But the sound of Cole's dozer roaring to life in the distance transformed her attitude. Hiding the ravages of a sleepless night, she took Exterminator for a run, blithely tossing Cole a carefree wave as she dodged the cloud of dust he'd kicked up. Twice she jogged past. Did he see how well Exterminator was learning to heel? No. He didn't look. Well, what did she expect? She'd probably been kidding herself.

On the dot of eight she opened the store. Not two minutes later, in the midst of a jaw-breaking yawn, Tibby found her place invaded by Moped Mavericks, excluding Justine Banks.

Winnie stepped forward. "We're here to help, Tibby."

"Help with what?" Tibby's bleary eyes refused to focus.

"Give you time to practice. What else? The men are backing Cole to the hilt. Someone's started a pool at Bogey Wells."

"Aren't you backing Cole, too? Your names were on that petition, if I recall. Don't switch allegiance on my account."

"It's not a matter of allegiance. Those men seem to think we women don't have a clue. It's time we fixed their wagons."

Tibby glanced from one lined eager face to the next. "I can't let this turn into a town feud. It's one simple game between Cole and me. No need for either you or your husbands to get involved. Regardless of how things work out, Yaqui Springs will gain a golf course and keep the post office."

"But *nothing's* working out!" cried Henrietta. "Everybody's grouchy."

Tibby crossed her arms. "And you didn't think about that earlier?"

"Why, what do you mean?" Winnie asked nervously.

"I mean the way you went around me to invite Cole here."

"Oh, that." Winnie looked relieved. "We expected you two to hit it off. Since you don't like him—"

"I never said that!" Tibby burst out.

"You do like him?" Winnie's ears perked up. "Then why don't you throw in the towel, dear?"

Tibby's chin tilted stubbornly. "It's his attitude. Oh, there's more. I can't begin to explain."

Rosamond hugged her. "We know you'll do what's fair, Tibby."

"This is getting us nowhere." Tibby threw up her hands. "Why don't you all try some of my new decaf coffee? Almond cream." Did they think it was fair for Cole to divide the town and make her life topsy-turvy? She ignored the small voice inside that said it wasn't Cole's fault, either.

Amid grumbles and protests, she led everyone from her office. She'd no more than filled the last cup and poured water for her own tea when the door swung open and Cole dashed in. He was shirtless. A fine layer of dust coated his chest and his old blue jeans. He cradled both arms low to his waist. For a moment Tibby thought he'd been hurt. She stood, unable to move, her heart in her throat.

He rushed up to her, barely seeing the others. "I found this little guy cowering under a mesquite. He's half-starved and dehydrated." In his arms he held a scrawny black-and-white kitten. "What should I do?"

"Oh, poor thing," she crooned. "He's not very big. I wonder if he can drink by himself or if we'll need to feed him with an eyedropper."

All the women crowded around. "Someone probably just dropped him off on the highway," exclaimed Ariel. "It makes me so mad when people do that."

Tibby hurried into the storeroom and out again, carrying a box and a fair-size jar lid. She filled the lid with cool water. "Here, try him on this. Let's put a towel in the box. Winnie, they're in aisle two. Would you get me one, please?"

The cat could barely stand on his bony legs, but he buried his nose in the water and lapped the lid dry. "Well, look at him." Beaming, Cole ran the knuckle of his first finger between the kitten's ears. A rumble erupted somewhere below his hand.

"Looks like you've got yourself a pet," Tibby mused. "Jars of baby food are in aisle six. Try him on strained lamb, and not very much."

"Me? I left my dozer running."

"So go turn it off. I can't take him. Exterminator—"

Ariel patted Cole's arm. "Around here, it's finders, keepers. Beachcomber sounds like a good name. Or Motorboat from the size of that purr."

"Too unwieldy for such a little dude," Cole murmured as he parked the kitten on his chest and went in search of aisle six.

"Hobo," ventured Winnie. "The symbol hoboes used

to carve on the fence post of a house that gave handouts was a smiley cat face.''

"Try Bum," Tibby said. "It's shorter and more up-to-date."

Cole came back with the jar of baby food. He popped the lid and scooped out a fingerful. The cat closed his blue eyes and licked the puréed meat. "Bum." Cole let the name roll off his tongue. "It fits. OK, little buddy. Let's go take a look at your new home. I'll pay for this stuff when I come to stock up," he told Tibby, heading for the door. Gathering the cat close, he nudged the door open and called over his shoulder, "We'll see how he and Exterminator hit it off tonight when you come to dinner. But it's Bum's house, remember."

Tibby picked up her teacup and laughed. It took a minute before she was aware that all other eyes in the room were gazing at her curiously. "What?" she asked.

"Dinner?" Winnie's tone demanded answers.

Rosamond gazed at Tibby over her half glasses. "We thought you fixed him breakfast yesterday."

"I did—" Tibby caught herself a second too late.

"And there's a rumor you had dinner with him *last* night," Ariel said smugly.

The ladies pounced. "Breakfast yesterday, now dinner twice in a row. Ooh, do I hear wedding bells?"

"Don't start, Winnie," Tibby warned, hands on hips. "Out, all of you. Scram. I've got inventory to finish, and I'm in no mood for idle gossip," she said as they laughed and trooped out, meeting Justine on her way in.

She looked harried and carried a stack of books. "Oh, Tibby," she wailed. "You've got to help me study for this class. Obtaining a chemical applicator's license is no easy feat. I took a gazillion notes."

"You're the one who volunteered to help Cole. Not me," Tibby said.

Justine pouted. "Tibby, don't be mean."

"All right," she sighed. "I guess my inventory can wait."

"Leave time to shower and change clothes before you go to Cole's for dinner tonight," advised Ariel, peeking back around the door frame.

"Dinner?" Justine said sharply. "At his house? Didn't he take you to breakfast at Bogey Wells yesterday?"

"Tibby made him breakfast at her house," Winnie announced, as if Tibby wasn't capable of answering for herself.

Justine's lips turned down. "That's a shame."

Ariel swooped into the room. "A shame? They had dinner together last night and another date tonight. Not too shabby if you ask me."

"Pul-leeze." Tibby grabbed Justine's arm and urged her toward the office. The last thing she needed was them ganging up on her and Cole. Group matchmaking—scary thought.

Justine balked. "I wanted him to take you to Bogey Wells. As well as breakfast, I sort of thought he'd give you a present."

Tibby snapped her fingers. "That's right, he mentioned that you told him about my unicorn collection. Well, Mrs. Buttinski, you can pat yourself on the back. He brought me a beautiful crystal unicorn," she said softly.

A collective "ah" went up from the women.

Tibby glanced around the circle of beatific smiles. "If the lot of you are meddling, please stop. Cole and I have enough problems."

"We just want you both to stay in Yaqui Springs,"

said Henrietta. "We didn't mean to cause problems with those darned roses."

"You sent them? But why?" More confused than ever, Tibby took it as an affront. "Then I think you owe Cole an apology. You made him lose his girlfriend."

"No," Mabel interjected. "She didn't leave over the roses. We—"

"Mabel." Winnie caught her friend's plump arm. "You heard Tibby say she was swamped."

"Wait," Tibby commanded. "You did what, Mabel?"

"We tried to welcome her with a meal," Winnie said, signaling the others with a jerk of her head. "Don't worry, Tibby. Everything happens for a reason."

Tibby gazed around a suddenly empty room. Even Justine had left with the others. Normally Tibby didn't mind peace and quiet, but she was more than a little rattled by their admission. If Cole ever found out what they'd done, he'd be furious. Not only that, he'd think she was in on it.

Frustrated, she completed her inventory. When it came time to close, she gave serious thought to canceling dinner with Cole.

In the end she went.

At dinner he remarked on her distractedness. "You look tired, Tibby. Much as I'd like you to stick around, you should probably go home to bed."

"I'm not tired," she lied, thinking these late-night practices were going to be the death of her. "I discovered by accident that our Moped Mavericks sent those roses," she blurted.

"I know." Cole trailed her to the door. "They're as subtle as a freight train, but they're nice ladies."

From his perspective, maybe, she thought irritably.

What did he mean, he knew? She leaned around him to call her dog.

"You're nicer, though," Cole murmured, settling a soft kiss on her mouth. He nipped at her lips until he felt her tremble in his arms. Fearing it could easily turn into more than kisses, he set her gently aside. If he talked her into sharing his bed before the match, she'd have reason to think he might go easy on her during their game. He had no intention of doing that; he'd be playing to win. But he'd begun to picture her in his bed—and not just for a night or two. A slip now could ruin everything.

Whenever Cole kissed her, Tibby lost her ability to think. But when he stopped, she wanted him to continue. She had to get out of here—away from him to clear her head. Her earlier resolution not to avoid him wasn't going to work, after all. Too risky, too confusing. Blindly she searched for her dog. When she spotted him, the scene brought an unexpected smile. Cole's cat was snuggled on the Great Dane's back, his small head pillowed between the pointed ears as both animals snoozed. "Look, will you? Isn't that cute?"

Cole sprinted across the room and grabbed the kitten. "Cute, maybe, but not very bright. Bum wouldn't even make much of an appetizer for that beast of yours."

"Oh, now he's a beast. Yesterday you plied him with steak bones."

"Are you trying to pick a fight, Tibby? Take your mutt home. Get some rest. I'll see you tomorrow night."

"I don't think so. The stuffed eggplant was delicious. But I think it'd be best if we didn't meet again until it's time to tee off for our match." She snapped on Exterminator's leash and tugged him out the door. He yawned, looking unhappy about being rousted from a warm bed.

"Sharing a meal isn't a conflict of interest," Cole ob-

jected. Although he'd thought so yesterday at breakfast.
"The guys on the pro circuit eat and drink together all
the time." Stretching out his arm, he blocked her flight.

"Bully for them. Step aside, unless you want Exterminator to flatten you again."

Cole glanced down as the Dane's lips peeled back in a
second yawn. Two rows of sharp teeth gleamed white.
When had the evening gone sour? And why? He saw from
Tibby's eyes that it had. Removing his hand from the
casing, Cole let her pass. It troubled him more that she
never once looked back.

THE NEXT DAY, shortly after Tibby opened her store, Cole
took a crack at trying to reason with her again. She sold
him a case of cat food, a litter box and the works. And
politely but firmly showed him the door.

She was avoiding him, no question. This went on for a
week. And another.

Tired of being rebuffed, Cole was ready to admit defeat.
From where he sat atop a mound covering the water tank
that'd been installed, he observed a steady stream of customers at her store. Travelers in vans, campers, cars and
motorcycles stopped in droves. School was already out in
some states. Half the country seemed to vacation in California.

Cole hated seeing the dark circles under Tibby's eyes.
The pressure of that damned golf match didn't help when
she was obviously too busy to catch a single practice ses-
sion. That concerned him, too.

By the end of the third week, Cole attempted to pull
Justine off his paperwork and send her back to help Tibby.
"She deserves practice time," he said.

"I can't do it, Cole. I've got two more days of class.

If I quit now, there goes my certification. Who'll buy your fertilizer?"

"To hell with the fertilizer. Tibby's ready to drop. I want to win, but not if it's wholesale slaughter."

Justine shrugged. "I'll talk to Winnie. She's worked at the store in a pinch. I'd do it once the class ends, but your sprinkler system is due to arrive any day. Tibby said I have to check each piece and let the company know right away if the count is off or anything's broken."

"True enough." Cole sighed. "A golf course is only as good as its sprinkler system. I've got a wad of cash tied up in this one, plus a timetable for inspections. So, you'll talk to Winnie?"

Justine petted the kitten, who'd finally begun to fill out and grow into his feet. "It's good of you to worry about her, Cole, but Tibby usually knows what she's doing."

"Normally I'd agree. However, golf is a game of skill."

"She meditates on things that bother her. Well, I've gotta run, Cole."

He massaged his neck as he watched Justine climb into her car. Lingering on the porch, he stared at Tibby's brightly lit house. Come to think of it, her lights had been on late every night. Meditation? Maybe. But surely not this far in advance. The only practice she could get at night would be if she was watching video-instruction tapes. The golfers he knew considered tapes a laugh. Golfers learned by doing, not from watching someone else play.

By Sunday of the fifth week, Tibby came home after attending morning service at the chapel in Bogey Wells, and instead of opening the store, she got back in her old woody and drove off. Cole peered over the four-inch pipe he'd run into the water tank from both his wells, trying to see if she'd changed clothes. Was she practicing at last? Just when he'd begun to relax and whistle tunelessly, she returned. Cole checked his watch. She'd been gone less than three hours. Not long enough to play even nine holes.

It crossed his mind that she might be trying to make him feel guilty. If so, she'd succeeded. He'd fretted so much over her lack of practice, he'd neglected his own. Standing, he wrenched the last clamp tight and headed home to take a shower. He refused to take any blame for her poor performance. They'd had equal opportunities; it wasn't his fault if she chose not to use hers.

Two phone calls later, he'd hooked up with the golf pro at Bogey Wells. After a bracing shower, Cole loaded his clubs and left.

The big hand on his luminous watch stretched toward midnight by the time he rolled down his lane again. The golf pro, Vic, had started out a little know-it-all, but in the end turned out to be a fair guy. As it happened, Vic had played a course that Cole had designed in Hong Kong, and he'd had some insightful comments on how to make a course better. After the game they'd eaten dinner together at the club. Then they'd taken their conversation to the bar. Vic had claimed not to know anything about Tibby Mack's golfing abilities. Even so, Cole had enjoyed the outing, and he drove home feeling pleasantly relaxed. The first thing he noticed was that Tibby's house was dark. Wresting his clubs out of the Jag, Cole noticed that every light in the store was on. What the hell? Was she stocking shelves? He'd seen several trucks pull in and unload over the past few days.

He set his clubs in the house, expecting the store lights to go out as he fed Bum, then poured himself a generous nightcap of Yale's brandy—and a second. The lights stayed on. He finished a third brandy before his curiosity got the better of him. He slammed out of the house and weaved across the parking lot. Didn't she have sense enough to know she couldn't continue indefinitely without sleep? For someone who claimed to be promoting good health, she wasn't practicing what she preached.

He grabbed the door handle and raised a hand to knock. The door gave way. For a moment fear punched him in the gut. Uncaring of his own safety, he lunged into the room. Thankfully Tibby's body wasn't floating in a pool of blood. She sat calmly on the floor near the counter, the dress she'd worn earlier billowing around her like a parachute. Justine, clad in jeans, was almost hidden behind stacks of long and short lengths of PVC, sprinkler heads, springs and gaskets galore. Plastic elbows and T-connectors ringed the room like a mountain range.

Cole had consumed just enough brandy to see things through a fog.

"Hail, the prodigal son," quipped Tibby. "So nice of you to drop in, since this is your stupid sprinkler system. I hope you know how to assemble the control panel. We've spent four hours sorting diodes and computer chips."

"You mean it didn't come assembled?" His words seemed to flow a shade more slowly than his thoughts.

"Do Great Danes fly?"

Cole grasped the corner of the soft-drink case to try to steady the room.

Tibby popped a spring on one sprinkler head, followed by a gasket, then she screwed it into a T-connector before laying it aside. "O'Donnell, are you drunk?"

He shook his head, realizing immediately it was the wrong thing to do as his stomach pitched and rolled.

"You are," Tibby flared, rising gracefully as she spoke. "Justine, will you help me get him home? I'll be darned if I'm staying up all night assembling his toys when he's been out painting the town red.''

Cole managed to stand upright. "I'm quite capable of taking myself home, thank you. I don't recall asking for your help. Tomorrow I'll cart the whole mess to my place. Oh, and don't expect me to go easy on you next Sunday because you choose to play martyr, instead of practice. My grandfather may have held back. But *I'm* playing to win." Taking careful steps, he made his way out.

Tibby ran to the window. Her body tensed as he swayed to the left. She scrunched her face when he righted himself and didn't breathe as he navigated his front steps. A sigh escaped the minute she saw he'd made it safely into the house.

Justine shook out her leg kinks and joined Tibby at the window. "He's a proud stubborn man like his grandfather. Does he know you love him?"

Tibby gripped the sill a moment before she turned, a nervous laugh shuddering through her body. "I didn't realize I was that easy to read. If he had a clue how I felt, he'd be on the first stagecoach east. And you mustn't tell him, Justine. He'd use it to his advantage. Fortunately he's obsessed with building his golf course and beating me in the match."

"Every man in town is obsessed. Cole was the only one not in their huddle this morning. I heard Pete ask Joe how long he thought it would take Cole to beat you. I assure you, Tibby, we women will be in your corner with bells on."

"No bells, Justine. Win or lose, I'll be glad when this ordeal is over. Partly I'm just plain tired of sparring with Cole. Even more, I detest having you and the men bickering. Will you help me carry these pieces to Cole's house? It's better if I don't lay eyes on him again until we tee off next week.''

Though she did see him daily from a distance, Cole had apparently reached the same conclusion. He rarely came into the store. All he did was work on his sprinkler system. Tibby noticed how nice the network of pipes looked each time she ran her dog. Exterminator whined and tugged on the leash, begging to visit Cole—who studiously averted his gaze.

Tibby reined in the lunging Dane with a firm hand. If nothing else, her standoff with Cole had furthered Exterminator's obedience training.

Each day bled into the next, and each day the tension mounted.

Friday morning Ralph Hopple scurried into Tibby's store after the regulars drove off to play golf. ''Hee-hee. You want a good laugh, gal?'' Ralph loaded his coffee with three teaspoons of sugar, drawing out his story the way he always did.

''Watching your diabetes flare up doesn't make me laugh.'' Tibby scooped the cup out of his hand. ''On the far table is your sugar substitute.''

''Dang it, Tibby. You know how to spoil a good tale. Or did Pete and Joe already tell you about the coyotes chewing half the sprinkler heads off O'Donnell's fancy system—afore he even got it hooked to his control panel? The way Cole was carrying on, you'd think they were made outta solid gold.'' He chortled again.

''Ralph, that's not funny! Do you know how much that system cost?''

''Bah! He can afford it. Yale was a fat cat.''

''That may be, but Cole didn't get Yale's money. It was left to research or something. The only fat cat in that house is Bum.'' Worried, she gnawed her lip. ''I hope his insurance is going to cover the damage.''

''You don't sound like somebody who's gonna go out and whip that boy's butt. Did I put my money on the wrong horse, girlie?'' He giggled hoarsely. ''All the other guys're bettin' on O'Donnell, but I...''

Tibby stared him down. ''I'm not a horse and neither is Cole. And you shouldn't bet if you can't afford to lose.''

''Huh, you saying you're gonna let that city dude clean your clock?''

''You know me better than that, Ralph. I'll play to win. Cole may just be a better golfer than me.'' It was a thought that made her restless at night.

''Bah,'' Ralph muttered again. He left minus any coffee. The next time Tibby saw him she'd gone out to empty the trash. He and several other men were gathered near the front of the post office. Hmm, curious. Tibby took her time. Joe gestured to the building. Ralph stabbed a finger in the direction of the store. Tibby wished for the bionic woman's ears. She didn't watch much TV, but growing up, she'd always liked that show. She wasn't Jaime Sommers, though, and the men were too faraway to hear. They'd apparently convinced themselves her first win was accidental, so they were probably arguing over where to relocate the post office.

The thought was depressing.

Saturday night she played a last round at the house. Earlier in the day, Winnie had watched the store while Tibby spent two hours at the driving range. Now, ready as she'd ever be, she elected to get a good night's sleep. As she crawled into bed, one hand idly stroking Exterminator between his silky ears, she almost prayed they'd be hit by a freak thunderstorm.

Morning, however, dawned clear and bright. Tibby purposely waited until Cole had loaded his clubs into the Jag and driven off before she left the house.

When she joined him at the first tee, Tibby decided his reaction was worth the wait.

A murmur rising from the ladies of Yaqui Springs, gathered around to watch, caused Cole to turn from his last-minute inspection of his clubs. The women, yes, but where were the men? It was then, quite by chance, that his eyes encountered Tibby. Doing a double take, he felt his jaw drop. His gaze skidded back; he still wasn't sure it was her. She had on shorts. Black—a good three inches above her knees. Damn, but she had *legs!* Had saliva frothed from his mouth? He wiped a hand across his face.

"Cole. I trust you're well." Tibby sauntered over to where he stood. Casually raising her arms, she donned a black visor to shade her eyes. It fit snugly over her hair, which she wore in a tight French braid.

Cole's eyes drifted over her sleeveless cotton top, crimped at the waist by a plain black canvas belt. His gaze flicked up again, resting momentarily on full breasts faintly separated and outlined beneath the dazzling white shirt. Blood rushed to his head, and to other regions.

"You look a little peaked, Cole. Another rough night with brandy? Or were you out chasing coyotes?" Her voice sent ripples of unease along his exposed flesh.

He gnashed his teeth as an official stepped up and asked who planned to tee off first. "The lady, by all means," Cole managed, floundering for a sense of normalcy. He heard a tinkling of approval, again from Winnie and the other Mavericks. The men, darn their scruffy hides, still hadn't shown up. They'd picked a fine time to dawdle.

Tibby turned her attention momentarily to the official. Her gaze shifted again, idly traveling from Cole's shoes, up his muscled legs, to the white shorts and shirt and past that to a sexy Aussie hat. Smiling, she gave the barest tip of her visor before she pulled on her leather gloves and selected a driver.

Moments later Cole found himself staring at the gentle sway of her butt. Heat pooled in his groin. He wanted to close his eyes, but they remained transfixed as Tibby tipped her left knee ever so slightly into the right and connected with the ball.

A loud thwack yanked him right out of his trance. Automatically his eyes were drawn to the white sphere arcing through the sky. Higher and higher it rose, and at first Cole thought it was going to break to the right. A tiny smile flickered on his lips. Suddenly, as if some unseen hand had reached out and plucked it from its course, it landed like a bullet on the green and rolled to within two feet of the cup.

Cole's breakfast did a 360-degree turn and settled like a knot of lead at the bottom of his stomach. He silenced the crowd with a dark look. "Good shot," he murmured as Tibby swept past.

"Lucky shot," he muttered to his caddy moments before he stepped up to address the ball. Taking less than two seconds to contemplate, Cole smacked it with all the power he could muster. It rose even higher than Tibby's. He, along with the bystanders, sucked in his breath. Just when it seemed that his ball, too, would land on the green and maybe outdistance Tibby's, it angled to the left and landed in the rough.

There was no sound for long moments. Then the tittering of the women began. Cole shoved his club toward his caddy and strode off with the squared shoulders of a man walking to his doom.

CHAPTER TWELVE

TIBBY AMBLED ALONG with a loose-limbed stride. She hoped that if Grandmother Mack gazed down from above today, she'd forgive the purchase of this outfit. The freedom it gave her golf swing made it worth every penny she'd spent. As did the triple-A look of shock on Cole's face. Amazement, admiration and anxiety. His swing was decidedly off, even though he'd used a pitching wedge to knock his second attempt to within a foot of the cup.

Tibby chose her putter and gently tapped her ball in. Scooping it up, she graciously accepted the smattering of applause. As she passed Cole, who stood slack-jawed, an imp urged her to say quietly in a singsong, "Bir-die!"

Expression closed, Cole knelt and studied his ball. Rising, he gave a quick wrist-action tap that broke just a bit to the left. Luckily for him it caught the rim of the cup and made three revolutions before finally dropping in. His sigh blended with the clapping of a few bystanders. He tried not to think about the difference in their scores. Already he knew he shouldn't have spotted her so many strokes.

Tibby had won that hole, so she was the first to tee again—on a 480-yard par four with a dogleg left. Not wanting to overshoot the fairway, she picked out a number-two wood and hit a long beautiful rise that landed just short of where she'd hoped it would. Her fans gave a round of applause.

Eyeing her silently, Cole stepped to the tee. His ball flew straight and true, landing a good yard in front of Tibby's. Again only one or two people applauded. He glanced around before setting off. The men of Yaqui Springs still hadn't shown up.

Tibby noticed their absence, too. She hoped nothing had happened to them. If they hadn't caught up by the fourth hole, she'd ask Winnie. For the moment she needed to concentrate on her game. Using a three iron, she sailed the ball over the hole and down the far slope. Not a bad spot, but Tibby had never done well hitting uphill.

Cole laid his shot to within a yard of the hole. If it had rolled, very likely it would have gone in. He smirked a bit as Tibby and her entourage passed.

She took her time and viewed her ball from every angle. She talked it over with her caddy, a contemporary of Yale's whose advice she respected. Her ball seemed to climb the rise in slow motion, then it crossed the rim of the cup and slid out of sight. Proudly she collected her ball and sauntered past Cole. "Bir-die," she trilled.

He ignored her. At the tee he rocked from side to side, settling in to sink his putt. The ball sped straight for the cup. A whisper away, it veered to the left, as though drawn by a magnet, and rolled beyond. Cole groaned. He'd had a birdie within his grasp and lost it. Almost in a trance, he sank the putt for par.

"Too bad," Tibby said, and meant it. She hated to see anyone have bad luck.

"Them's the breaks," he snapped, striding past her.

Yes, and it was still early in the game, she thought, striking out for the third tee. Par five, down a narrow chute with a sand trap on one side and water on the other. A hole, Yale said, that separated the men from the boys. Tibby set her tee, gripped her club and blocked out everything but the green platter in the distance. She watched with bated breath as the ball curved left and came to rest in a clump of weeds between the sand and the fairway. It could have been worse. A lot worse.

"Helluva nice shot," Cole said, his gray eyes running over the slender curve of her arm. "I'm beginning to think the wrong person is carrying the handicap here."

Instead of making her feel good, his words made her feel guilty. No one had been square with him when it came to her playing abilities. He hadn't believed *her*, but Joe should have told him she'd always shown a natural ability. Or Pete or Fred. She scanned the growing number of spectators. No wonder they hadn't shown their faces.

When Cole's ball buried itself in sand with the thud of a military warhead, a hush fell over the crowd. He chose an eight iron on the way to the site. With a careless lazybones swing, he chipped the ball out and onto the green. No one was more surprised than he at ending up eight feet from the cup.

Tibby's ball rested on weeds, which gave it a slight elevation. Luckily she got a backspin on the ball. It floated over the cup and snaked back to within two feet of the opening. A rolling "ah" went up from the onlookers. She was afraid to even glance at Cole.

He wanted this eagle so bad he could taste it. He'd have it, by damn, if luck was with him. He stroked the ball with the finesse of a lover. Six inches from the cup, it curved right and gathered speed. When it stopped, he'd lost ground.

Tense, Tibby opened and closed her hands around the club's grip several times. Her ball rolled to the edge of the cup and stopped.

So, I'll birdie. Cole resigned himself. He focused on the task before him. He did everything correctly, but his ball had a mind of its own. Its path was almost a repeat of Tibby's shot, except that it came to a halt a couple of inches away from her marker.

Shaking her head, Tibby nudged her ball in. Near Cole, she did a little pirouette, and warbled, "Bir-die."

He wasn't by nature a violent man, but if she taunted him one more time in that obnoxious twang, Cole thought he'd strangle her on the spot, regardless of witnesses. He had to close his eyes and let the red haze settle before he trusted himself to make the easy three-quarter-inch putt without blowing it.

Hole four had to be shot through a stand of pine, and number five mocked them from the other side of a bridged gully that might as well have been the Grand Canyon. Tibby and Cole both eagled on four, saving Cole the indignity of hearing her gloat. The band of followers, sensing the grimness of the players, dropped back a few paces as Cole stalked to the fifth tee.

"I don't know how or when," he accused Tibby, "but you practiced. Not even Nicklaus or Player can return from a six-month hiatus and sink 'em like you've been doing. Well, maybe the pros do. Come on, Tibby, tell me the truth."

"If you're going to whine, O'Donnell, take back your darn handicap. You had the same number of weeks to practice that I did. But I sure don't want you and your cronies saying I snookered you. Where are they, by the way?"

He gazed around, perplexed, shrugging as she continued, "I'm willing to scratch the points you spotted me and play you square. Is that better?"

Removing his hat, Cole toyed with the leather-plaited band a moment. "Ordinarily I wouldn't welch on a deal, understand. But frankly you're damned good. I'd like to know if I can beat you in a no-holds-barred.''

"Done.'' Tibby stuck out her hand and they shook on it. "I'll tell the scorekeeper.''

Cole crushed the hat on his head and pulled the brim low over his eyes. But not before Tibby caught his Cheshire-cat grin. She wondered if he'd been playing conservatively on purpose and if she'd been had. Was that why Joe, Fred, Pete and the others had stayed away? Had they told Cole the way to get her was by appealing to her sense of fair play? Wiping the sweat from her brow, Tibby stepped up to the fifth tee, determined to show them all. She hit a fine shot over the gully. At the height of its arc, her ball suddenly windmilled and came to rest in the rough. Impossible to tell if Cole smiled, but she was sure he had. Grimly she moved aside.

He whacked a beauty; his next stroke was guaranteed to put him on the green. The tide had turned. Tibby read the message in his swagger as he crossed the bridge—and on the faces of her friends, some of whom knew next to nothing about golf.

For all her concentration, Tibby's turn only got her to the fairway, ten or so feet behind Cole. It earned her the right to shoot first, but that old devil crosswind did it to her again. Her ball sliced sideways, landing several feet short of the green.

Confidence oozed from Cole's every pore. His seven iron flashed in the sun. The ball fishtailed off the lower edge of Cole's club and sped thirty or so yards along the grass.

"He hit a worm-burner.'' Tibby hadn't meant for anyone to hear. But in the crowd's silence, her statement was all the more glaring. Ariel snickered, then Winnie, although they tried valiantly to smother the sound.

Cole thumbed back his hat. He didn't say a word. He didn't have to. His face said it all.

Number five, a par five, turned out to be disaster for both players. If there were two feasible ways to hit the ball, each chose the wrong one. It took eight strokes apiece to land in the bucket.

"Let's take a drink break," Tibby suggested. "A bottle of ice-cold guava juice sounds like the perfect pick-me-up. I told them no beer today."

Cole glanced around for the cart and some shade. "Gatorade for me."

"Potassium a little low, O'Donnell?" Tibby twisted the blade a little as she cracked the lid on her juice.

"Among other things." He laughed, then took a swig of his drink. "Ah, that hits the spot." Walking side by side, they headed for the sixth tee. "Actually, after that last shot, I'm wondering if I can build a course without a damn clubhouse."

Tibby smiled sweetly. "I realize I know nothing about the perfect layout for a golf course—" she lowered her eyelashes "—but have you thought of using Yale's house? The bar's already in, and when he remodeled his kitchen he bought brand-new top-quality appliances. Take out the furniture and voilà—a clubhouse."

Cole paused and stared at her over the neck of his bottle. "Then where would I live? Are you offering to rent Bum and me a room?" He waggled his brows.

"Well, I…" Flustered, Tibby gulped her juice. "Why couldn't y-you build a cabin closer to the main highway? They come prefab."

Something in Tibby's fluttery hands and her erratic speech drew Cole's attention. His remark had made her nervous. *Well, well, well.* Leaning close, he purred near her ear, "A lonely cabin in the desert isn't nearly as appealing as the thought of moving in with you, sweet-heart.''

"Stop it, Cole. We're at the tee.'' She handed her bottle to her caddy and marched off to place her ball. She swayed right and left several times, each time stopping short of a swing. Twice she glanced back. Cole's half-shuttered eyes studied her boldly, creating a flutter in her stomach. "Stop it,'' she ordered again.

He gave her one of those slow smiles intended to thicken her blood. "Pity,'' he murmured, "the term 'roommate' has such a nice ring.''

She pulled up short again. For a moment there was murder in her eyes. Cole judged he was in danger of having a number-one driver rammed down his throat. Instead, she stepped aside and took three whistling practice swings, then without looking at him, returned to the ball and drove a straight-arrow shot to kingdom come.

Cole and his caddy both shaded their eyes and gawked as the small white dot hung in the air. What seemed like hours later, it hit the fairway, pretty damn close to the green. Cole closed his mouth and yelped when he bit his tongue. His caddy muttered, "Zowie! Wish I'd had hang-time money on that baby.''

"Whose side are you on?'' grumbled Cole.

"Yours, my man. You're paying my freight today. But that doesn't mean I can't appreciate a sky ball, especially when you tried to make the lady whiff it.''

"I didn't,'' Cole denied as he met his caddy's wise brown eyes. "A closer assessment would be that I'm try-ing to get under the lady's skin.'' With a self-deprecating shrug, Cole accepted the driver the caddy handed him.

The fellow chuckled. "That's a switch. Most guys I know who golf with their ladies end up gettin' a divorce. Not t'other way around.''

"Well, I'm not recommending this method, mind you," said Cole. "So don't be too quick to write a book on it."

"Roger." The stocky gent tipped his cap and waited for Cole's shot.

Tibby avoided looking at Cole as he started for the tee. She was surprised into doing so when, halfway there, he switched directions and jogged over to her.

"I'm sorry for baiting you while you were playing. In most circles it'd get me tossed out of the game. I honestly wasn't trying to throw you off."

He seemed sincere. "Forget it, O'Donnell. I can't complain too loudly. It was one of my better shots." She blew on curved fingers and dusted them across her shirt above her left breast.

His eyes locked there for a moment, then made a slow cruise of her body. "Go ahead, brag. You play this course like you own it, champ."

"I forgot how much fun golf is. Your grandfather rarely played a standard eighteen holes. He said the same-old same-old was boring."

"Yeah. I remember. He taught me Low Ball and Go For It Gorilla."

Tibby smiled as she remembered playing these versions of the game with Yale—versions that required a great deal of skill.

"I lost a lot of my allowance to him," Cole went on, "until I learned to stay out of sand traps and focus on my playing style. He was great, wasn't he?"

"Yes." Unexpectedly the course before her eyes shimmered. "He also believed in playing fast to get on to other things. Quit stalling, Cole. It's your turn."

He'd throw in the towel and call it quits if he thought she'd let him take her in his arms to console her. Damn, but she'd genuinely cared for his grandfather. He supposed he'd known that for some time, but it really hit him now. He grimaced, reflecting that she loved every resident of Yaqui Springs—except him. Maybe he'd work on that after he got his golf course up and running in the black. No maybe about it. He would!

Staring down the fairway, Cole let his mind transport him to the green. That was how Gramps had taught him to play. To imagine each step in advance. It probably would have worked if his mind hadn't wandered off the second before his club connected with the ball. He'd been distracted by thoughts of Tibby, wondering whether Yale's technique worked when it came to women, too. His ball sliced to the right.

Not horribly, but enough so that Tibby parred the hole and he shot one over.

On seven they both bagged a bird.

On the eighth hole, no one was more shocked than Cole when he birdied and Tibby double bogied. She lost it in the rough and took two strokes over par to make it up.

Aware of Tibby's tension, Winnie and the other ladies stayed carefully in the background, clustered in the shade of a big old mesquite. Tibby sent her caddy on ahead. She took her bottle of juice and joined them.

"You're doing fine, dear," Winnie assured her. "With a one-stroke-per-hole handicap, you'll win hands down."

"We agreed to eliminate the handicap."

"Why?"

"It's better this way. No loopholes for anyone to say I'd taken unfair advantage."

"Who would? Fred, Joe, Pete, everyone heard Cole's offer."

"Exactly. Where are those old reprobates, by the way?"

"Oh, Tibby, that's a fitting description for the way

they've been acting." Winnie hooked an arm companion-
ably around Tibby's waist and led the group toward the
next hole. "We'd hear if they'd been in a wreck. Either
they're making themselves scarce to worry you, hoping
to throw you off, or they've cooked up some celebration
for the nineteenth hole." A common nickname for the
clubhouse bar. "We all agree they were acting secretive
this morning. My best guess is a party for their favorite
son."

"Yes," interjected Henrietta. "The way to outfox those
old goats is to go out there and beat that boy's pants off."

Tibby wrinkled her nose. "I'm trying. Cole's found his
range in the last two holes. That double bogey cost me."

"Land sakes, child, you haven't practiced."

Lowering her voice, Tibby said, "Yale left me his indoor electronic course, remember? I've been practicing
chips and putts every night. I probably should've told
Cole." Her gaze strayed to where he waited on the ninth
tee.

"Nonsense," Rosamond declared. "Some things are
better kept among us girls."

Tibby made up her mind that she would confess all if
she won. If she lost, there wouldn't be any need.

In Tibby's estimation, the ninth fairway was the pret-
tiest of the entire course. It was long, shaded by blooming
jacaranda trees and tall silver-dollar eucalypti. It wasn't a
snap by any means. The trees provided obstacles for errant
shots, and there were residential homes lining both sides
of the fairway. Even at that, it was preferable to number
ten, which was heavily bunkered and mounded, 425 yards
and uphill all the way.

Cole's shot on nine fell far short of what he needed to
gain the green. Tibby's was much better. She expected

him to take his second shot immediately—but, in fact, he moved in beside her.

"I saw you talking to the ladies. Any word on what happened to their husbands?"

"Winnie seems to think they're preparing a 'hail the conquering hero' party at the club. As if you didn't know."

"I swear I expected them to tag along giving me hot tips."

"I'll give you a hot tip. Play these next two holes conservatively."

He guffawed. "You expect me to take advice from the competition?"

"Suit yourself."

She looked so pretty and so earnest Cole had a hard time turning away. And an even harder time keeping his mind on the game. Which was probably why he did so poorly. Tibby birdied. He was lucky to make par.

They reversed the order at ten. What he desperately needed now was a hole in one. Not bloody likely with as little practice as he'd had.

Eleven was a green with subtle undulations, but Cole had found out the hard way the other day just how much havoc it dealt a putt.

Wonder of wonders, they both birdied.

"Nice playing, Mr. O," Tibby murmured as she toweled perspiration off her face and forearms.

"Same to you, Ms. M. Ready for another pit stop? I'm spitting cotton."

"Anytime. The course is ours till four."

He signaled the drink cart. "I meant to ask how you managed that feat."

"In case you hadn't noticed, the golf business falls off here once it gets hot. Are you sure you can make a living with a public course? You can't get away with charging as much.''

''My aim is affordable golf for people who don't retire with a golden handshake. Private courses are pricing a person with an average income out of the game.''

Tibby paused, her juice bottle an inch from her lips. ''That's very commendable, Cole. I didn't realize your motivations were so...altruistic.''

He arched a brow. ''Would you have moved the post office if you'd known?''

''Tear out my gardens, you mean? This conversation is pointless. You won't even try to understand. Establishing a post office for the residents was only Gram's first step. When she died, she was working to set up a public library.''

''Where? Maybe we could relocate the post office temporarily to that site.''

''In my fourth bedroom,'' she drawled.

''Oh.'' His eyes lit, but he passed on the opportunity. ''Shall we get on with the game? Some of *your* fans are beginning to wilt in this heat.''

''They're more loyal than your supporters, who're probably lounging in an air-conditioned bar. You know the women dote on you, too. They'd like us both to win.''

From the way her eyebrows gathered, Cole decided not to step into that trap. ''What's your opinion of the twelfth hole? It's the one that first gave me the idea of maintaining a desert landscape for my course.''

''You know very well it's a bear. You have to clear the first desert wash from the tee and the next one guards the green. If you don't make it in a single stroke, you're buried in sand.''

''Yeah. I love it.'' He brushed her chin with his knuckles and strode away feeling satisfied that his touch, no matter how slight, affected Tibby more than she'd like.

She still felt the faint scrape of his skin against hers well after he'd picked out a short-range wood and sent his ball spinning over the first wash. She had to ask her caddy where Cole's shot had landed, that was how off balance he'd left her.

"In a sweet position, Ms. Mack. To do as well, you'll need a little lift. Rein in the power this time."

She nodded absently, accepting the iron he handed her. Her back swing was smooth; so was her follow-through. Where the ball landed was out of her hands now, she realized, shading her eyes as it curved high into the afternoon sun. The murmurs of approval from the crowd and their muted applause told her it was good, which was more than she could see with her naked eye. Once they crossed the wash to the clipped Bermuda grass lying between the two traps, Tibby discovered what a feat she'd pulled off. Her ball and Cole's lay neck and neck, a foot apart. On closer inspection, it appeared his might be a scant half inch behind hers. She was content to let him go first. It'd make the shot easier for her.

The result was another bird each. Tibby had to sweat for hers. Hanging on to her one-point lead seemed like asking for a miracle. The heat was wearing on her.

The thirteenth green lived up to its name, requiring a two-hundred-yard drive over water to a postage-stamp-size lawn guarded by front bunkers. No hit-and-roll option on this one. And Tibby knew the next five holes were equally grueling. She was too shocked about collecting a bird to Cole's tough-won par to even brag.

"You don't play like a woman who hasn't practiced," Cole accused faintly.

Tibby made no comment, just saved her energy for the

hike to the next tee. They had to climb a long slope to a knoll. She worried about Mabel and Henrietta, who were overweight.

The caddies were puffing like steam engines by the time they reached the top. Tibby gazed down on the green; it was 160 yards away but gave the appearance of being farther. The drive wasn't so difficult as tricky—a matter of perception. When she used to play here with Yale, she'd seen many a seasoned golfer overshoot the green. Maybe that was the reason she hit a hop-skip-and-jump ball that rolled less than halfway down the hill.

She quit beating herself up when Cole overdrove the green by several yards. As a result they were both lucky to come in at par.

"I'll bet if this hole could talk," Cole said, shaking his head, "it'd be a dictionary of four-letter words."

"Don't I know it. I hate it when I screw up the easy ones."

"Well, the term 'easy' doesn't apply to the fifteenth and sixteenth, does it?"

"Afraid of a little water, O'Donnell?"

"A little?" He snorted. "On fifteen last week, I tried to drive for the green off the tee."

"Ah, and you found out golf balls don't float, right?"

"It pains me to admit it. And since sixteen crosses water twice, I considered chartering a boat for today."

"At least you're laughing about it. See that old iron-wood tree to the right of the tee? I hear men tend to wrap their clubs around it."

Cole birdied fifteen and squeaked by with par on sixteen. Tibby parred each.

"You said men wrap their clubs around the tree," Cole teased. "What about women?"

"We profit from our mistakes."

A deep grin creased his cheeks. "Good. Does that mean you'll let the winner buy you a drink when this is all over?"

"The fat lady's only singing in your dreams, O'Donnell." Tibby brushed past him, leading the way to hole number seventeen. A tough par four, requiring a tee shot to the right side of the fairway. If her second shot fell short of the green, it would land in a slippery sand trap.

A hush settled over the crowd. Although there was only one hole after this, the score was so close that a bogey here for either player would surely mean the game.

Cole's drive barely landed on the fairway. Tibby, who had a tendency to hook left, took careful aim. Her ball rose into the sun and swooped down several feet to the right of Cole's. There was no chitchat between them on the trek down the fairway. The crowd, sensing the mood, fanned out, allowing them plenty of room.

Cole desperately wanted a bird. The minute he saw the spin on the ball, he knew he was in trouble. When things shook out, however, the balance of power had shifted again. Tibby caged the bird and Cole had to be content with par.

The air grew more humid as everyone trudged toward the last hole. Tibby felt her energy ebbing. And she needed every speck for this final stretch. Number eighteen was a long, 585 yards with an itty-bitty green. To the novice it might look like a simple matter of drive, chip and putt. But dramatic elevation changes made this par five a real sleeper.

Tibby expected the absent men to join them for the finale and had used the long walk to psych herself up for their good-natured heckling. She was thrown off balance when they didn't show. Oh, well, she thought, soaking up last-minute advice from her caddy, win or lose, she, for one, intended to be a good sport regardless of the outcome.

Her swing wasn't as strong as it had been throughout the match. Two hundred yards, but she needed more.

After two false starts, Cole slammed his ball 280 yards if he hit it an inch. The muscles in his arms bulged from the tension created by the gorgeous 360-degree arc of his driver. Tibby fought to release the breath trapped in her lungs. From crown to toe he was beautiful.

Briefly closing her eyes, she positioned herself. She flanked her ball and took careful aim with an eight iron. A honey of a shot, blessedly regaining lost yardage.

Cole's awkward slice to the right pretty much ruined his opportunity for a birdie. To win now, he had to hope that Tibby bogied.

Indeed, on her next turn, she overshot the green.

They were both so intent on sinking tough putts that once they'd each dropped the ball into the cup, they gaped at the officials, not knowing who'd actually won.

According to the judges' tally, Tibby's score came in at sixty-seven and Cole one over at sixty-eight.

The women crowded close. "You did it," breathed Winnie, giving Tibby a hug. "Let's find our men and do some crowing."

Tibby craned her neck to locate Cole. Their eyes met over Winnie's shoulder. For a heartbeat his resigned gray eyes met her hesitant green ones. Then a smile lightened Cole's features and he gave Tibby a thumbs-up.

Relieved, she broke away from Winnie's loose grasp. "I need to go thank Cole for a good game," Tibby whispered. "I'll meet you in the clubhouse. Do me a favor, please. Don't rub the guys' noses in it. The match was far too close for that."

"Oh, Tibby. This is wonderful. We hoped you'd extend

the olive branch." Mabel patted her cheek. "That's why we love you, dear. You're so sweet. Always thinking about someone else's feelings."

"No. I'm not." She blushed. "I have to tell Cole about my practice sessions." She backed away, pausing only to ask her caddy to drop off her clubs. Then she hurried to catch up with Cole.

"Sixty-seven on a par seventy-two course is top golf in anyone's book, Tibby." Cole lifted her hand and placed a sizzling kiss in the center of her palm.

She shivered, but left her hand in his as she plunged into the task of explaining the elaborate indoor setup Yale had bequeathed her.

"Well, whaddaya know." Grinning, Cole flung an arm around her shoulder. "To think I actually felt sorry for you. This tale is one to tell our grandkids. Except that you'll have to promise me a rematch."

His talk of grandchildren—as if his and hers would be the same—threw Tibby off stride, and as a result she swallowed her reply.

"Don't think of weaseling out." Cole wagged a finger under her nose. "You know I'll never live this down among the guys. Only way to redeem myself is to beat you one of these days."

"Where *are* your partners in crime?" Tibby blinked away the sunlight as arm in arm they entered the club's darkened bar. Two lazy fans circled overhead, but the room was empty except for a couple of guests. Strangers.

Cole left Tibby long enough to ask the bartender if he'd seen Joe Toliver or Pete Banks. The young man shook his head.

"I know I promised we'd have a drink," Tibby said, sidling toward the door. "But I'm really worried. I can't imagine they'd all miss the match. If you don't mind, I'll take a rain check and go home."

"I'm right behind you," muttered Cole. "You go on. I'll load our clubs."

On the one hand Tibby regretted cutting short her time with Cole. On the other she felt very uneasy as she drove to Yaqui Springs. Wavering between regret and worry, Tibby had pulled to a complete stop in front of the store before the ugly truth rose up and smacked her. A huge gaping hole had been hacked into one wall of her office.

As if in slow motion, she climbed from the station wagon. Suddenly, as though the film had sped up, their post office—a building she had just won the right to keep intact—weaved drunkenly across her path. Eight men, the very men she'd been worried about, struggled to balance the structure.

Now Tibby noticed Ralph Hopple near the yawning hole. His gnarled hands beckoned the transporters. He yelled for them to place the building on two rows of concrete blocks protruding into her parking lot.

Beyond a haze of disbelief, on some other plane, Tibby sensed that Cole had driven in. His car door banged at the precise moment Exterminator snapped his cable and charged hell-for-leather across the lot. Except instead of greeting Cole, which had seemed his intent, the dog veered off toward Fred Feeny. Fred tried valiantly to juggle the back left corner of the wood framework and stave off the dog.

Tibby flinched. There was a growl, a rip and a series of colorful curses, seconds before the structure began to wobble crazily. Amid confusion and a mad scramble of bodies trying to get out of the way, the building toppled.

Tibby heard herself scream. The ground beneath her

feet shook as the post office cracked and splintered apart like kindling.

Exterminator streaked past Tibby, his booty in his mouth—an open pack of red licorice, unless Tibby missed her guess.

She realized from all the shouting and cursing that no one had been seriously hurt, thank goodness.

Except for her heart. These were people she'd loved and trusted. Every one of them.

Whirling, Tibby vented her frustration on the man she believed had masterminded this scheme. Cole O'Donnell.

"You," she said, pointing a quivering finger. "No wonder you were so magnanimous about my win. It didn't matter one little bit. You had your bases covered." Then, because her heart, like the building, had fractured and her voice failed, she spun and ran after her wayward dog, closing her ears to Cole's protests.

CHAPTER THIRTEEN

HER SPIRIT utterly destroyed, Tibby returned to the disaster site after capturing the Great Dane. Her red-tongued dog gleefully licked his lips because he'd devoured most of the hijacked red licorice sticks before his mistress nabbed him.

While Tibby was chasing her pet, the women drove up. They gestured at the ruins and yelled at the men, who shouted back.

As the decibel level rose, chills marched up Tibby's spine. She saw again the evidence of discord in Yaqui Springs. "Stop it. Stop it and go home," she ordered. "This post office has caused wholesale insanity. Gram would have hated it. We'll drive to Brawley every day for our mail. I don't care anymore. Just go. I have to find someone to clean up this mess or people will get hurt walking into the store. You," she said to Cole, "take your...your chicanery back to the coast where people understand backstabbing. This doesn't honor your grandfather. It dishonors him—and you."

"Tibby." He reached for her hand, but she jerked away. The dead look in her eyes convinced Cole it was useless to try to talk to her. He watched her stumble over Pete's chain saw and ran to yank it out of her way. Telltale chips from her office wall were still embedded in its links. Cole found himself angry that the men had gone ahead with their cockeyed plan. How could they have done this to Tibby? To him?

Winnie glared at the jumble of men, all of them wearing identical hangdog expressions. "Whose bright idea was this?"

Several sets of feet shuffled. Chins dived into shirtfronts, but no one spoke.

"Cole?" The feisty lady rounded on him.

He continued to stare after Tibby's retreating form. "I honestly thought I had them talked out of it. But it doesn't matter. Tibby's right. Basically I'm to blame. I should have redrawn the plans for placement of the clubhouse in the beginning. I looked for the easiest way out for me in terms of dollars and cents. She's paid the price."

Mabel laced her hands over her stomach. "How much do you think it'll cost to clean up and rebuild all this? Tibby has no spare cash. And we're all on fixed incomes."

Joe tugged on one ear. "If we all gave up golf for a year, it might cover the expense," he said, eyeing his pals.

"It wasn't our fault," blustered Fred, shaking the torn pocket of his shirt. "We were going great guns till that danged dog tried to eat me alive."

Pete cleared his throat. "We can't give up golf—our fees are paid in advance for the year. No sense laying blame at this late date. What we need is a solution."

"What we need is money," said Ariel. "Cole?"

He heaved his shoulders. "Ultimately it all comes back to me. Shall we clear a path to the door until I can hire a professional cleanup team? I don't know how long it'll take to find a group willing to drive out here."

"You buy the lumber and we'll do the work," said Joe.

"No, you won't," declared his wife. "The post-office boxes are all bent. I'll bet half the combination locks are jammed. We need an expert. Cole, are you able to take on this expense alone? We all thought Yale left you his money, but Tibby said he left the bulk of it to research.''

"Yes. It always bothered him that there was no cure for the blood disease that killed my father. I'm not complaining, mind you. Frankly, I was surprised by his generosity. Believe me, I had no designs on his wealth.''

"It's tacky to ask after your finances, but we're all friends, right? According to Justine, you've sunk every penny into this golf course. Is that true?''

True or not, Cole kept remembering the lack of life in Tibby's lovely eyes. To hell with his golf course. It had become personal. "I said I'll take care of paying damages and I will. Tibby's the injured party. An innocent caught in the middle. We've hurt her with our thoughtless actions—all of us. I want to make amends, and I want all the petty bickering to stop. She deserves better from her friends.''

Henrietta and Mabel exchanged interested glances, but it was Winnie who approached Cole with a gleam in her eye. "Could it be that you've fallen in love with our sweet Tibby?''

Cole started to laugh. Until the truth of her statement hit him between the eyes. He *was* in love with Tibby— had been falling in love with her for weeks. Love wasn't an emotion he'd had much experience with, outside of the bond he'd forged with his grandfather. "Ye-es,'' he said slowly, like a man emerging from a coma. A man who suddenly understood that love drove his desire to be with Tibby every waking minute. To have meals with her even if he had to cook. To buy her presents that made her eyes sparkle. To share stories he hadn't shared with anyone. To simply make her smile. Love. He felt like he'd been sucker punched.

Confounded, Cole left the group staring after him, scratching their heads. At least the men were. The women babbled excitedly and dabbed at happy tears.

As usual Winnie came to her senses first. "You men do what Cole said. Clear a pathway to the door. Ladies," she said, calling them aside, "knowing what we do, it's up to us to fan the spark we just saw ignited. Tibby is angry at Cole, and hurt. If we don't convince her he's blameless, our hopes of getting them together will be lost."

"Yes," agreed Henrietta. "We'll never hear the patter of little feet in Yaqui Springs unless someone sets Tibby straight."

"Winnie," they all chorused, "you got rid of Cicely. Handle this."

"All right. But Cole may need a push, too. It would be nice if he really sent her flowers this time. In fact, a new florist just opened at the resort in Bogey Wells. I'll bet if Cole phoned right now they'd deliver a bouquet today. Give me a few minutes to think the rest through." She paced to and fro, massaging her forehead. "Listen, I've got it. Mabel and Ariel, you pop in on Cole and give it to him straight. Don't let him wiggle off the hook. Rosamond, Justine, Henrietta and I will pay our Tibby a visit. We'll convince her Cole isn't at fault. We'll keep at her until we wear her down."

Mabel accepted the flower shop's business card that Winnie produced from her purse. The others studied the mess. "Don't worry if we're not home for dinner," Winnie told the men starting to clear the rubble. "We're going to rectify this mess you made."

Eight pairs of eyes glanced up hopefully.

COLE HAD SHOWERED and was poring over his ledgers when Ariel and Mabel converged on him. "Don't tell me there's more trouble afoot,'' he exclaimed upon opening the door to their insistent knocking.

Mabel pressed the business card into his hand. ''Monetary restitution will only cut so much ice with Tibby, upset as she is. Her heart aches, Cole. Our men could send a dozen roses and probably should. But it wouldn't help because she believes in her heart that you were the ringleader.''

''She feels betrayed from all sides,'' Ariel added.

Cole scooped up the cat, who was trying to escape. When he straightened, he dashed a wistful glance toward Tibby's house. ''Flowers, huh? How will she know I sent them for real this time?''

Mabel flushed at his subtle barb, but Ariel snapped her fingers. ''Tibby doesn't know you're fixing everything. Tell her on the enclosure. You owe her that much.''

Cole accepted the card and their advice. The minute they left, he sat down and phoned the flower shop. He didn't order roses, but a basket of white daisies with a few marigolds and cornflowers thrown in for color. He made the clerk taking his order repeat exactly what he wanted written on the card. That accomplished, he leafed through the phone book and started calling local contractors for approximate repair costs.

In less than an hour, Cole had all the estimates spread before him. They weren't a pretty sight. It wasn't only the cost of rebuilding the post office or of repairing Tibby's office wall that gouged holes in his budget. Selling the Jag would cover that. But to build his clubhouse elsewhere, he'd be looking at an added hundred grand for delays and excavation. Using Yale's house—Tibby's suggestion—was too impractical; renovating would cost almost as much as a new building and leave him without a place to live. Plus, he'd need another hundred for a dedicated left-turn lane, a commercial driveway and a parking lot. Prohibitive costs when he'd gone into this on a shoestring.

Borrowing wasn't an option. From experience, Cole knew banks considered golf courses bad risks. Especially public courses that lacked the potential revenue of selling memberships.

As he'd feared all along, there was simply no way to pull it off.

If only the women hadn't exposed his true feelings for Tibby. That made his decision to abandon his dream ten times harder. Or maybe not. She loved Yaqui Springs exactly as it was, sans golf course. Suddenly her happiness meant more to him than anything. "Bum," he said to the cat curled into a ball on his lap, purring like a motorboat, "we have nothing to offer the lady. Not now. Maybe not ever. Thing is, I can't bear to tell her goodbye." His voice stumbled. He stood up, moved to the window and gazed at her house for a long time.

TIBBY, WHO'D SPENT the past hour miserably tending her herb garden, had finally begun to relax. She'd even managed to see a modicum of humor in the post-office calamity. Fred had looked so funny when Exterminator grabbed hold of his pocket and literally ripped it from his shirt to get at the treat. Of course, what the men had taken upon themselves to do was dangerous. Tibby was thankful no one had been hurt.

Now that she really thought about it, she didn't see Cole's being party to anything that risky. If, as he claimed, he *hadn't* been privy to what the men were planning, then she should be ashamed, accusing him as she had.

Absently she picked old buds off the fresh clover and

set them aside to dry. Bees supped from her peppermint plants. Tibby bypassed them, instead loosening the earth around the roots of her lemon balm.

Engrossed in her thoughts and her work, she was surprised to see the Moped Mavericks converging on her. She stood, nervously brushing soil from her knees. What now? she wondered. Winnie, Rosamond, Henrietta and Justine approached in single file, picking their way through the waist-high corn with an obvious sense of purpose.

Winnie reached Tibby first. "Thought we'd find you out here. In some respects, you're exactly like Lara."

"In some," Tibby agreed, peeling off her gloves. "Grandmother wouldn't have been caught dead in these shorts, however."

"They look great on you, dear," Rosamond said. "Times have changed. Lara was progressive in many ways. In others she was downright old-fashioned."

Tibby studied each woman in turn. "Are you here to discuss my grandmother?"

"We're here for tea. If we're not interrupting." Henrietta agilely sidestepped Tibby's question.

"I'll save you ladies time and effort. I know I overreacted. I intend to apologize to Cole."

"Good. That was on the agenda." Smiling, Winnie linked arms with the younger woman, deftly weaving them toward the house. "The men, bless their balding heads, are attempting to clear a path to the store. Joe is going to nail some sheets of plastic over your office. They feel terrible, Tibby. They only meant to help."

"I know that. At least on a deeper level. And I underestimated how badly they wanted Cole's golf course."

Exterminator barked dutifully when the women entered

Tibby's kitchen. Seeing his mistress, he promptly went back to his rawhide doggie bone.

"I'm hoping if he chews on that till his teeth fall out," Tibby said wryly, "he'll quit craving candy. His sweet tooth is the bane of my existence."

All the women laughed and settled themselves around the table as Tibby filled the kettle with water. A series of sharp raps at her front door forestalled further conversation. She picked up a tray of cups and spoons, expecting someone else to answer the door. When no one got up, she plunked the tray in the center of the table and dashed off to do it herself.

Tibby returned, frowning and carrying a basket of flowers. "You ladies really should save your money," she said, brandishing a card bearing Cole's name.

"Scout's honor, Tibby, we didn't send these. That's partly why we're here," Winnie admitted. "To set you straight. We confess to sending the roses. But Cole really did order these."

"He did?" Tibby tapped the card against her lips. "He says here that he's paying to have the post office rebuilt and everything put to rights." She set the basket on a windowsill. "I'd decided he wasn't involved. Guess I was wrong."

"He wasn't involved," Henrietta said forcefully. "He's paying to fix things because he cares about you."

Winnie jumped up and snatched the whistling kettle off the stove. As she poured boiling water over the tea leaves, she said, "Henrietta's being wishy-washy. Cole admitted he loves you, Tibby. *L-o-v-e!*" She bent to spell the word in Tibby's ear.

Tibby sank into a chair, her lips and hands trembling. "Don't tease. I know you all rolled out the welcome mat for Cicely. It's her he wants."

Rosamond distributed the teacups. "I suppose it's time for us to confess all. I won't go into details, but suffice it to say, Ms. Hollywood got a poor view of Yaqui Springs. We did it for you, dear. You and Cole belong together."

Tibby flopped against the cane backing and gazed at the ceiling. "No. You're wrong. It's hopeless. Any feelings between us are one-sided."

"Not any longer, dear." Winnie patted Tibby's hand. "Men are so dense when it comes to love—except for the bedroom part, that is. In the romance department, they need to have things…pointed out to them."

"How?" Tibby sat up straight.

"Nothing overt. More like a subtle assault on the senses. That's where friends come in. We'll start by curling your hair. Then we'll paint your nails. Flirty clothes and flirty eyes leave men putty in a woman's hands."

"Forget flirting. It's…it's manipulative and out-of-date and… Anyway, I don't know *how* to flirt. I always freeze up."

Rosamond scooted closer to Tibby. "You know your pink dress with the buttons down the front? Leave the top two open. Three at the bottom. Give a twitch to your hips. And wear an ankle bracelet to flash naughtily when you cross your legs."

Winnie scoffed. "Rosamond. No one wears ankle bracelets anymore—but I second the pink dress. It's perfect for a midnight supper. And Tibby? Flirting is just a means to an end. You're in love and you need to make that clear to each other. That's what flirting's for—and it's fun, too. Now, you need to invite Cole over here. We'll arrange candlelight, wine and classical music playing in the background. A setting like that provides ample opportunity. Tibby, you should speak softly, leaning toward him. Touch his collar or his shirt buttons as you talk.''

"Why, Winifred Toliver!'' exclaimed Henrietta, aghast. "You're setting up a seduction. Don't you want our sweet Tibby to be able to wear Lara's white gown at her wedding?''

"Pssht, Henrietta. Those rules are obsolete. Tibby needs to live.''

"Oh, sure.'' Henrietta grimaced. "You remember what happened to Agnes Gooch in *Mame?* Mame told *her* to live and Agnes ended up *pregnant.*''

"Ladies—'' Tibby laughed "—I'm not a starry-eyed teen. Thanks to you, I'm sensible. What's important to me in a relationship is that both parties care. If I thought for a minute he really *did* care...''

"I've already told you—'' Winnie began.

Rosamond interrupted. "Then you'll let us do this?''

Tibby glanced at the clock. "It's nearly six. A midnight supper might help clear the air. Cole loves to eat. What if I write him a note, thanking him for the flowers and his offer to fix the post office? In closing I'll ask him to dinner. Henrietta, will you deliver it for me?''

"Yes, but I still vote for letting nature take its course. I hope you remember that men are like streetcars. Be patient, dear, and the right one will come along.''

Justine thrust a scented note card and a pen into Tibby's hand. "Honestly, Henrietta, not even a bus comes to Yaqui Springs. You have to stop watching all those old movies. Modern women take command of their love lives. They don't sit and wait around anymore. They ask for what they want.''

Tibby let their good-natured bickering pass. What Winnie had said concerning Cole's feelings for her played repeatedly in her mind. With the note on its way in Henrietta's hands, why not enjoy an evening of pampering? The works. Justine's idea of taking charge appealed to a new side of Tibby.

Winnie insisted the meal include meat. To keep the peace, Tibby consented to fix halibut steaks basted in butter and basil, then cooked in parchment. With it, twice-baked potatoes and steamed garden veggies. Wanting to draw the dinner out, her friends decided she should start with an orange-and-endive salad, and end with coffee and sherry-glazed strawberries for dessert. Both the house and Tibby sparkled by the time the last Moped Maverick headed for the door at eleven-thirty.

"You look wonderful," said Winnie, pausing to fluff Tibby's bangs.

"Mm, you smell nice, too." Justine sniffed the air all the way to the door. "Remember, light the candles fifteen minutes before the witching hour. And uncork the wine to let it breathe. Smile," she added, playfully jabbing Tibby's ribs. "This is going to *fun.*"

"Yes, Mother." Tibby wrinkled her nose. "Kidding aside, I don't even know how to thank you." Her voice sounded rocky. Tears sprang to her eyes.

"Here, here, none of that," Winnie commanded. "Your mascara will streak."

Rosamond stumbled out of the bedroom, dragging a reluctant Great Dane. "I want your night to be flawless," she explained breathlessly. "So I'm baby-sitting the pooch tonight."

"Are you sure, Rosie? He always wants out at least once during the night."

"I'm sure. I don't suppose they make doggie diapers, do they?"

The trill of the women's laughter was cloaked as they all slipped into the velvety night.

Tibby leaned against the door, immersing herself in their words of encouragement and good wishes. Tempting odors wafted from the kitchen. Her friends had done so much to make this night succeed. Tibby and Cole O'Donnell had a nice ring. For the first time she truly believed a relationship between them was possible.

If she didn't panic. And she wouldn't!

Humming to herself, Tibby lit the candles and opened the wine. She glanced at the clock for approximately the hundredth time and remembered the turntable of CDs Winnie had carefully selected. At exactly five minutes to twelve she switched on the stereo unit. Schubert's ballet music filled the room.

At five after twelve she turned the oven down so the halibut wouldn't dry out. The music bumped from Schubert to Grieg. She straightened already straight napkins. Her hands wouldn't stay still.

A quarter after the hour Tibby shut the stove off completely and covered the dishes. Mozart eased the jumpiness of her nerves. She shouldn't be so anxious; according to Justine, men were habitually late.

By twelve-thirty the candles had begun to droop and so had Tibby. Either that, or Chopin's piano concerto had dulled the edge of her excitement.

Another fifteen minutes ticked away before Tibby amassed nerve enough to pull the curtain aside and check Cole's house. Not a single light glimmered through the trees. The entire corner lot was inky black. He'd gone to bed. Her heartbeat slowed to a painful stutter in an empty chest.

Just how long she stared into the darkness, Tibby couldn't say. Sometime after the old grandfather clock chimed one, she dropped the curtain. Refusing to think, she blew out the candles, put the food in the fridge and turned off the stereo, no longer noticing which composer was playing.

She sat at the beautifully arranged table in her finery for much longer. And she knew for sure something she'd suspected since Cole's return to Yaqui Springs—yes, hearts could be broken twice.

And the second time hurt worse.

CHAPTER FOURTEEN

GRITTY EYED, TIBBY FACED the morning reluctantly. In the wee hours, as she creamed off the makeup so carefully applied by her friends, she'd come to the decision that Yaqui Springs wasn't big enough for her and Cole. It was a decision that caused her a great deal of pain. But if she'd learned anything reading women's magazines all these years, it was that when it came to romantic breakups, a strong woman should know when to cut her losses and get on with her life.

The women in the articles blithely quit jobs and moved from one coast to the other. Of course, they all seemed to have marketable skills and lived in apartments that were easily left. Not rambling old houses they loved.

Sitting with chin in hand, Tibby breathed in the soothing steam from her peppermint tea. She missed Exterminator's comforting presence. Darn, those articles never mentioned moving pets. Goldfish, maybe, but not a Great Dane.

In one of her crazier moments, while staring at the moon, Tibby had actually worked out the sale of the store in her head. Her grandmother had been approached more than once by Bogey Wells board members who wanted to put in a general store for the convenience of their customers. Market studies showed the area wouldn't support two convenience stores. The board hoped to tear down the older one and build a modern Stop and Shop type.

Stop and Rob, Lara Mack had called them, greatly annoyed by the men's offer.

Tibby took a small sip of the now cooling tea. What about the house? Gram's husband had built it and the store with his own hands when they were still newlyweds. Leo had come home from the war with a lung ailment that forced him to seek a dry climate. Tibby never tired of hearing stories about the young couple's struggles or how much in love they'd been. Too much to notice the hard times.

Apparently love wasn't part of *her* story.

Depending on the price Bogey Wells developers were willing to pay, perhaps she'd go to college as Gram had wished. Nursing. California offered some good programs in cities where a woman alone needed a big dog for protection. A nursing degree opened infinite job possibilities. Opportunities to meet new people. *Doctors.* Why didn't that excite her? Why did she feel as if the bottom were dropping out of her world?

Tibby heard the putt-putts of several mopeds, and she broke into a cold sweat at the thought of facing her friends. Shortly after the noise throttled down, someone tapped on her kitchen door. A host of someones, and they'd brought Exterminator home with them. Tibby might have tried ignoring them, but her dog set up a racket loud enough to wake the dead. Besides, Winnie carried a key for emergency purposes.

Footsteps dragging, Tibby crossed the room and opened the door to a ring of smiles. Exterminator leaped up to lick her face. Unable to help it, she burst into tears.

Winnie stepped inside and threw her arms around Tibby. "We expected you to be walking on clouds, child. My land, what's wrong?"

"I'm not a child," Tibby said stoutly. "I'm a woman! That's the trouble."

Henrietta hurried into the room. "You're the one who deliberately set her up for seduction, Winifred Toliver. You-know-who probably did you-know-what and then skated. You heard the meter man when we asked why he was reading Cole's meter before the end of the month. He said it was a close-out reading."

Justine frowned. "Man's dumb as a post. Why would Cole order a close-out reading? Tomorrow, he and I are shopping for sand for the greens."

Rosamond snatched a box of tissues from the top of the fridge, pulled out three or four and handed them to Tibby. "Is Henrietta right, honey? Did that no-good Cole O'Donnell take advantage of you last night?"

Tibby shook her head vigorously from side to side. "That would be rather difficult. He…he didn't even sh-show up."

Winnie's brows shot up into her short bangs. "How can that be? Henrietta, you delivered the invitation, didn't you?"

"Yes. Although Cole seemed a bit distracted. He didn't *open* the envelope while I was there. He laid it on the kitchen counter. I went to his back door," she explained.

"Did you tell him it was an invitation?" Ariel prompted.

"Why would I? It wasn't my place. He asked if Tibby had received his flowers. I said yes. Then he asked if she liked them. I pointed to the envelope and suggested she might have written it better than I could relay her thanks."

Winnie sighed loudly. "There you have the problem. He probably assumed it was a thank-you note. Men, unlike women, aren't bothered by unopened mail."

"So now it's my fault?" Henrietta bristled.

"I'm not laying blame, only trying to make Tibby feel better. It boils down to a simple communication mix-up. A shame, after all our work, but certainly not the end of the world." She snapped her fingers. "Come, come, ladies. Tibby needs to get ready for work, and if we don't leave now, it'll be too hot to ride." She lagged behind, after directing the others out. "A cold compress on your eyes will do wonders, Tibby. And wear the pink dress. I predict Cole will be waltzing into your store with egg on his face once he does read your message."

Tibby nodded, but she didn't feel at all reassured. Why wasn't Cole out throwing dirt over the last few pipes of his sprinkler system? And why would a meter reader come out from Brawley to do a closing read if he didn't have orders?

A cool elder-flower compress eased the swelling and grittiness of her eyes, enabling her to open the store on time. By noon, Tibby grew weary of explaining the plastic-covered hole in her wall and the splintered building outside to travelers she'd never see again. If Cole changed his mind about paying for repairs, why not just call and say so? On the other hand she could as easily walk over there and let him know she didn't want his money.

She'd do that as soon as she got rid of the talkative couple from New York. Their youngest son, stationed with the navy in San Diego, had asked them to visit. While they detailed their life story, another customer walked in. This one was handsome, sun-tanned and blond. The poor man was trussed up in a blue three-piece suit, a starched white shirt and a tie. He looked hot and uncomfortable.

"Excuse me," Tibby murmured to the couple. "Sir," she addressed the man in the suit. "There's bottled water and soft drinks in that case behind you. If you need anything else, I'll be with you in a moment.''

"We don't want to keep you from your business," said the man from New York. "We appreciate all the information you gave us on Anza-Borrego park. Our son misses the mountains. If he doesn't have all our days planned, we may be back to hike."

His wife wasn't in any rush to leave. "Our son's twenty-eight. He's not married," she said. "Nice girls are so hard to find these days. You've been very helpful, Ms....Mack? Are you engaged or anything?''

"Louise," the man admonished sharply. "Don't mind her," he said to a blushing Tibby. "My wife's on a crusade to marry off the last of our four sons."

"No such thing, Samuel. But he's a good boy and a long way from home. This young woman is pretty and polite. If we come back to the park, what's wrong with introducing them?"

Tibby smiled gently. "Perhaps your son's already found a nice woman in San Diego. That may be why he's anxious for you to visit."

"Oh, Samuel." The wife's face crumpled. "He wouldn't get serious over a girl we've never met, would he?''

Her husband rolled his eyes toward heaven and hustled his distraught wife past the newcomer—who tipped his frosty bottle of Perrier in a gesture of sympathy.

At Tibby's gigantic sigh, the stranger shifted his steely blue gaze her way. "Do you get that often?" he asked. "Marriage proposals from frantic mothers?"

In spite of her weariness, Tibby chuckled. "That's a first. I've had to search the aisles for a hungry boa constrictor some teenager let out of his cage. And once, a family of eight left a child behind. If I had the time, I'd write a book. It's plain to see why their son joined the navy, isn't it? Your drink's $1.29. May I help you with anything else?''

"I came to help *you*." He reached for a briefcase Tibby hadn't noticed and plunked it on the counter, followed by the money for his drink.

A salesman, she thought with a sinking feeling. Usually she spotted them the minute they walked in. Tired as she was, she hoped for both their sakes that he was selling something interesting. "I've been on my feet since early this morning. Do you mind if I make a cup of tea and join you at that table?" She pointed. "Will that allow you room to display your samples?"

He glanced up. "I don't have samples. My name is Lane Davis."

She reached for the hot water and poured it over a cheesecloth bag filled with wood betony, linden flower and chamomile. A tea she recommended to relieve stress. "Lane Davis" had a familiar sound, though she was quite certain they'd never met.

"If you're a valley craftsman, you're a tad over-dressed."

"I'm an attorney."

Tibby blanched, sat down quickly and clung to her cup with both hands. "I see. This is about Grant Carlyle's BMW? I can't deny that Exterminator chewed holes in his leather seats. So I guess my limited insurance policy didn't cover it. Are leather seats costly?"

"I don't know. Who's Exterminator?"

"My Great Dane. But if you're not here about Grant's car, why else?"

"I represent Cole O'Donnell." He dug out a packet of very legal-looking forms.

Tibby's mouth rounded in shock. "Cole? Ah, so he's

had second thoughts about covering the damages." Her wave took in the mess outside the store.

"On the contrary. Cole was sitting on my doorstep when I arrived at the office this morning. I assure you, he's most anxious to take responsibility. Too anxious, I thought, after I got the entire story out of him. So I came to assess the situation for myself. But now that I've seen you, I think I understand. Here are the estimates he secured. The check is made out to you. You're to call me in case of cost overruns."

With each successive word, Tibby's brows knit more tightly. "Exactly where is your office, Mr. Davis? Indio?" She knew that no one in Brawley dressed like Lane Davis in the heat of summer.

"Beverly Hills. Is that a problem?"

Not even a soothing sip of tea relaxed the knot in her stomach. "I find it odd that Cole didn't handle this transaction over the phone. And you're one hundred percent correct. He shouldn't accept responsibility. It wasn't his fault."

Lane Davis leaned forward, wiping condensation from his half-empty bottle. "I can see you aren't aware that Cole has abandoned his property here. I'm not in the habit of breaking a client's confidence. However, the news will soon be common knowledge. Cole asked me to pull together a package to place in the hands of a local realtor."

"No." The word emerged as a dry whisper. Tibby shook her head repeatedly. "But why? He's already invested a lot of time and money into building his golf course."

"You'll have to ask him," Lane said, taking a long drink from his bottle. He set it down and looked her square in the eye. "It's none of my business, Ms. Mack, but Cole wore a similar expression. I'd describe it as…shattered. If this is a personal matter that you two can work out, I'd advise you to get on the phone. I'll delay compiling the paperwork for a few days. Here's the number at his condo,'' he said, jotting it down.

"I'll admit we've had a few disagreements and a misunderstanding or two, but…'' Dazedly Tibby outlined some of their recent history. It sounded like an Abbott and Costello movie by the time she'd finished.

"You beat Cole in a fair golf match? Ho, ho—sneaky devil didn't mention that.'' Lane gazed at her with new respect.

"You don't think his losing triggered—''

"No, I don't,'' Lane cut in. "I shouldn't be telling you this, but his reasons are rooted in money. I can't say any more. Call him, please.''

"I will.'' She stared at the check. "I know he was playing his finances close to the wire. Here, take this back. As I said, it wasn't Cole's fault.''

"Keep the money. It's just the tip of the iceberg, Ms. Mack. If Cole sells his Jag, he'll still be 150 grand short. I agree, it's a shame. Especially since he's invested all his savings. I don't know who'll buy a half-finished golf course, do you?''

Tibby bit her lower lip. "Unfortunately, yes. I heard that a pig-and-goat farm in the valley wants to expand out here. You said you'll give me time to talk to Cole?''

"Gladly.'' He stood and shook loose the crease in his pant legs. "Here's my card.'' He pulled one out of the case and placed it beside Tibby's cup. "Now, indulge me, please. Is there something going on between you and Cole?''

Tibby swallowed twice, feeling her face flame. "I… ah…'' She gave up and shrugged. "I guess not.''

"I see. That, of course, is none of my business, either.

Only I've been dating a woman Cole used to see. With him back in town... Well, never mind.'' He buckled his briefcase. ''That's *my* problem.'' He nodded toward the collapsed building. ''Looks like you've got enough trouble. While I'm here, I'm going to nose around Cole's acreage. Will I be in danger from that dog—the one you called Exterminator?''

''No. He's inside today. I just thought of something, Mr. Davis. A stray cat adopted Cole. He didn't happen to mention... No, why would he tell his lawyer that?''

Lane smiled. ''Actually he did. It surprised me about Cole, but he smuggled the animal into his condominium. No pets allowed there.''

Tibby reveled in that bit of news. Perhaps it said Cole hadn't wanted to sever all his ties to Yaqui Springs. ''Have a safe trip home,'' she murmured, following Lane outside. ''How did you get here?'' She gazed around, looking for an automobile.

''I flew and rented a car that I left at Cole's house. Whose old woody is that? It's in great shape.'' He circled the station wagon.

''It belonged to my grandfather. It's mine now.''

He whistled through his teeth. ''If you ever need some quick cash, give me a jingle. My brother wants one. He'd pay the going price.''

''What is that, exactly?'' She'd never believed Cole's assessment.

''Good as that one looks, at a rough guess...forty thousand.'' When her jaw sagged and she gripped the wall for support, he smiled. ''You have my card,'' he reminded her as he slipped off his jacket and strode off in the direction of Cole's place.

Tibby braced a hand on the station wagon. Feeling suddenly faint, she went back inside, where she paced, trying

desperately to get a handle on the information Lane Davis
had given her regarding Cole's financial bind. With the
number of courses he'd designed, how had his cost estimates been so far off the mark? Justine said Cole kept
precise records, like Yale had. Tibby didn't see how a
shortfall of that magnitude could be linked in any way to
the post office. Yet she continued to feel responsible.

If Cole cared for her as Winnie said and Lane insinu-
ated, why would he take off without giving her a chance
to talk things out?

Thankful that the store remained empty for the moment,
Tibby took the papers Davis had left and Cole's phone
number, and went into her office to call him.

She connected with his answering machine.

Sometime after three, she tried again. This time she left
a message. At five o'clock he still hadn't returned her call.
Tibby decided she'd fretted by herself long enough. It was
time to rally the residents.

She closed the store at six and walked the two blocks
to the town's recreational center. The chairs were set up
and the seats nearly filled. No one questioned her right to
call a meeting of the residents' association on short notice.
It was how things operated in Yaqui Springs.

Tibby went directly to the podium, but before she said
a word, Joe Toliver got to his feet. "Winnie told us about
the meter reader. Pete and I drove to Brawley and checked
at the utilities office. It looks like Cole skipped town.
We're damned sorry, Tibby. We'd already discussed fund-
raisers. You know we wouldn't have let him pay for our
mistake." He sat as the others rumbled in agreement.

Tibby clasped the podium with both hands as the front
row swam through the tears that sprang to her eyes.
"Cole's lawyer delivered me a check today to pay for
repairs."

"He did? Then why'd the boy run off?" Pete asked, looking confused.

"That's what I hoped you might be able to tell me. His attorney said he needed a couple of hundred thousand to complete his golf course."

"Maybe he thought he'd have to buy back the hill," Justine said.

Tibby shook her head. "He has a deed he thinks is good. Neither of us ever found Yale's letter—the one that says he's donating the land."

Winnie hopped up and waved. "That letter is here in the residents' association files. Lara was afraid she'd lose it. Would it help to send Cole a copy?"

"Yes. I'll mail a copy to his lawyer," Tibby said. "But Cole seemed resigned to leaving the post office where it sat. Could it have been something else?"

The men all looked to Joe, who'd set up the deal with Cole. But it was Fred Feeny who jumped to his feet. "The golf pro at Bogey Wells told me Cole hoped to share the store's left-turn lane. You know what a stickler the county is, Tibby. They'd charge him an arm and leg to put in a second access."

Pete slapped his knee. "Same for adding a parking lot and traffic lights. I know he wanted to lease part of Tibby's parking lot until the course started making money."

Tibby stared at them, bewildered. "He did? He never mentioned it to me."

"Because you always jumped down his throat, dear, any time the subject of his clubhouse came up." Mabel's statement drew a nod from everyone.

"I'll admit I've been a mite closed-minded," Tibby muttered. "I'd have said yes if he'd just asked."

"Sounds like you're changing horses in midstream, gal," accused Ralph Hopple.

"With good reason," Tibby returned. "Cole's lawyer is drawing up a package to send to a local realtor. He all but said Cole's broke. The way I see it, I can look out my window on a golf course or a pig farm. Which horse would you bet on?"

"No contest," shouted someone from the back row. "Only, isn't it a little late to try and make amends? What can we do if he's made up his mind to sell?"

"Change it," Ariel Pulaski cried. "Help him raise the funds he needs."

"Not quite that simple," Joe snorted. "Somehow I don't think a craft fair or the bake sale we proposed is relevant now. The boy'll need some hefty cash."

Tibby pounded on the podium. "We're on the right track, though. On the way over here, I had an idea. What if we approached the board at Bogey Wells about holding a golf tournament? Cole knows some big names. Enough to warrant charging players and spectators alike. I propose we call it the Cole O'Donnell Open or something."

The men glanced at one another. "Might fly. Except we need seed money. Tournaments cost big bucks."

"They also earn big bucks," Tibby reminded them. "How much do we need? Someone offered me forty thousand for my station wagon."

"You're kidding!" Fred gasped.

"It seems there's money in classic cars. Plus, I have the check Cole sent to repair the post office."

"Yes, we're handling those repairs," chimed in George Gordon, Rosamond's normally quiet husband.

Joe dug in his pockets for a piece of paper. Winnie handed him a pen and he spent a few minutes doing calculations. "We'll still need corporate backing. If we can find a sponsor to underwrite the prize money in exchange for advertising, it might work. Will Cole buy into it? I wouldn't want to use his name if he didn't.''

"I've left a message for him to call," Tibby said. "Are we in agreement to proceed? I kid you not, it'll be work. A lot of work. Everyone will have to pull together as a team. We can't have people going off, following their own agendas." Her gaze settled on the men at length before skipping to the women. "Think it over. Talk among yourselves. Then we'll vote. A yes vote is a commitment for the duration."

Tibby stayed out of the discussion. Little by little, talk died. Finally Winnie got to her feet. "We're ready to vote. To keep any hint of coercion out of it, we'll use ballots." She went into the small office and returned with ballots and a box and a copy of Yale's letter for Tibby. The voting went fast. Henrietta and Mabel collected the ballots and started counting them. Tibby fidgeted, thinking of Cole. She'd probably missed his call. And frankly she didn't know if this would change his mind. He might be too fed up with Yaqui Springs and with her. All she knew was that she had to try.

"All votes are in favor," Mabel announced. "One hundred percent. More than half wrote that Tibby should coordinate things. Tag, you're it," her former teacher teased.

"I accept. Yale explained to me once how tournaments are set up and run. I'll work on individual assignments tonight. I assume we'll exclude Mildred, as she isn't here to vote. She's not ill, is she?"

Justine spoke up. "I offered to bring her. She doesn't like to go off and leave her dog. She's so afraid something's going to happen to Peek-a-boo."

"I hope nothing does," Tibby said quickly. "She can't handle losing another pet. I'd feel terribly responsible."

Winnie stood. "Nonsense. Your thoughtful gift gave

Millie a reason to want to live. And that dog is too spoiled to die. She's already in heaven.''

"I'm glad something I've done lately turned out right," Tibby mused. "Speaking of heaven, Gram and Yale must be laughing at all our screwups."

"Or suffering heartburn," said Pete in his candid way.

His statement seemed a fitting closure to the meeting. Tibby jogged home, planning in great detail how she'd approach Cole. She just knew he'd called.

But he hadn't.

Disappointed, Tibby tried him again. His phone rang and rang. People kept late hours in Hollywood, she told herself, trying not to wonder where he was or with whom.

She worked for a while on committees, then on an article for the newsletter. It was midnight when she glanced at the clock again. Too late to call him now. Anyway, she was beat. She'd had so little sleep last night. Better to tackle her conversation with him tomorrow.

Tired though she was, sleep didn't come easily. Cole haunted her waking thoughts and her dreams, as well. His face floated around in her head. His quirky half smile. Hair that needed cutting—hair she itched to rumple with her fingers. These visions lingered even after Exterminator awakened her at first light begging to go for a run.

She'd intended to call Cole early. But what with one thing and another, it was midmorning before she got around to it. Again, no answer. Her stomach knotted. Maybe he'd slept somewhere else last night.

It helped that the store was busy all day. Residents dropped by singly or in groups to pick up their assignments. Everyone wanted to understand how these various pieces fit into the whole of the tournament, which entailed many lengthy discussions. By nightfall, Tibby's throat was raw.

She'd left Cole another message. And intended to leave him several more. Let him get sick of hearing her voice. Not that she tired of hearing his—even if it was only his brief "I'm out. Leave a message."

Next day, able to stand it no longer, she called Lane Davis. Afraid the first words out of her mouth would be to ask after Cole, she plunged right into the second reason for her call. "Is there any way you can delay putting Cole's land on the market for a while longer?"

"How long? I might get away with saying I've been tied up in court."

"We need until September. Don't tell him, but the residents here are planning a golf tournament to raise money to help him out of his bind. Do you play, by the way?"

"No. Tennis is my game. But I'll have my secretary send you some names."

"Any and all are welcome. It'll be pricey, however."

He laughed. "I'll see the list includes only my rich friends. Say, that reminds me—my brother went crazy when I mentioned your car."

"Really? That was going to be my next question. We need a grubstake to get this tournament off the ground. I'm ready to sell the woody."

He whistled. "You're throwing personal money into the pot? Is that wise?"

"It's imperative. How soon can your brother come take a look at it?"

"Um…is tomorrow OK?"

"That would be great. By the way, I mailed you a copy of an old letter from Cole's grandfather—regarding the land he donated. I don't really expect it to change anything, though."

"All right. I'll see he gets it."

"Thanks, Mr. Davis—for everything."

"Call me Lane. And I won't charge if you ask me to knock some sense into Cole's head. I wonder if he knows what a gem he left behind."

Tibby felt the blush start at her toes. She was awfully glad videophones hadn't been perfected. After repeatedly telling herself to play it cool, her next remark just sort of popped out. "How is Cole?"

Lane's tone grew guarded. "I thought you knew. He's leaving any minute to design a golf course in Singapore. I recommend reaching him soon, or it'll be too late."

"I've left messages on his recorder. He hasn't returned my call."

"Look, Tibby—may I call you that?"

"Please."

"I just want to say, hang in there and don't write him off. In case you think I'm saying that because of my feelings for Cicely, believe me, I'm not. You know," he said after a pause, "Cole's mother really did a number on him."

"I know. He let a few things slip."

"Did he tell you the first girl he dated in college obsessed over him? She stalked him, then threatened suicide if he didn't marry her." He paused. "She didn't, of course—he talked her into seeing a shrink. But the whole thing was pretty nasty. Scared him off anything serious where women were concerned."

"How horrible for him."

"Pity isn't what I was getting at. He needs a woman he can trust. A woman willing to go all the way."

Tibby breathed in sharply, picturing herself in Cole's bed.

"Hey, don't get me wrong. I don't just mean climb in the sack together," he said. "I meant that if you're going to get Cole to the altar, you might have to do the asking, er, proposing yourself.''

Tibby imagined Lane's tanned skin growing as red as her face must be by now. "I don't know that your advice pertains to me," she managed at last. "Will you be with your brother tomorrow?" It felt safer to change the subject.

"No, unfortunately I'll be in court all day. For several weeks, remember?" He laughed. "But I'm the shy one in the Davis family, so watch out for my brother. Alec is working his way through the female alphabet. He has a computer-generated black book. I hate to use the term 'playboy' to describe my own flesh and blood, but—''

Tibby broke in, "Message received. I'll dig out my granny glasses, a gray wig and keep the car between us. Is his check good? That's my question.''

"He owns two of the biggest car dealerships in Southern California. He's good.''

"Mm. Does he golf?''

"Like a pro. Or says he does.''

"When you call him, mention that I'm looking for sponsors for our tournament.''

"Will do. Soak him a bundle. If you're not tied up tomorrow, you might talk him into a game. It'd do my heart good to hear that you trounced him.''

"Not a smart move if I hope to part him from some of his cash.''

"I suppose not. I have to admit I got carried away for a minute. He's two years older than me, you understand.''

"Yeah. I also know this call is costing me prime dimes. Thanks again for your help, Lane.''

"No problem. Goodbye.''

Tibby had customers lined up at the register. It was late in the day before she tried Cole again. She was almost ready to hang up when a woman with a low breathless voice answered the phone. Tibby gripped the receiver so tightly her fingers went numb. "Sorry, wrong number," she mumbled. Clicking off, she closed her eyes. She'd only met Cicely Brock once, but her voice was the sort you remembered.

Poor Lane. You'd have to be blind not to see how much he cared for Cicely. But so much for the lawyer's advice that she should ask Cole to marry her. A man had to be willing first. Obviously Cole hadn't left anything of consequence behind in Yaqui Springs—like his heart, for instance.

She eased the phone into its cradle, locked up the store and went home. Now what? She hadn't seen the residents this excited in a long time. What would happen to them if she canceled the tournament? They'd found purpose again. Cole might not care about a few old people's health and happiness, but she did. Let him be an absentee landlord if he liked. Maybe he didn't owe her anything, but after promising the residents a golf course in Yaqui Springs, he owed them, by heck.

Dry-eyed, she snapped the leash on Exterminator and ran with him until her heart was too exhausted to ache.

CHAPTER FIFTEEN

COLE STOOD on the balcony of his hotel room and gazed at the stars twinkling above the busy city he'd called home for the past month and a half. His work here in Singapore was almost at an end, and he had to decide whether to take an offer recently faxed to him from Japan. It was a good opportunity and it wasn't like him to vacillate. But today he'd heard some disturbing news that added to his indecision. The backers of this latest course had flown in a golf pro to do some advance PR work. The man had expressed surprise at seeing Cole still on-site. Said he thought Cole would be stateside, preparing for a big golf tourney bearing his name. All the top players had been contacted, and many were going. At first Cole thought the pro was joking—until he mentioned where this supposed tournament was taking place. Bogey Wells.

Cole hated appearing stupid, but in truth he'd been flabbergasted. The time difference between here and California irritated him. He'd stomped around his room until one in the morning so he could call the resort and ask what in hell was going on. Now he wished he hadn't bothered. A sweet-voiced receptionist had told him there was indeed going to be a Cole O'Donnell Open, and if he wanted particulars, to contact Tibby Mack.

Cole stared at the half-empty bottle of guava juice in his hand—*her* choice in a bottled drink, not his—still trying to get a grip on the grief he'd felt hearing that bit of news. He'd come halfway around the world to get the woman out of his system. And she still wasn't out. So many things reminded him of her. Simple things. A pot of tea. A basket of herbs. Unicorns. Just last week he'd passed a jade display. Hard to say what prompted him to browse, but he had. The shop had a million intricate carvings. Pagodas. Dragons. He recalled Tibby saying she'd coveted a jade unicorn. Then he'd spotted one the exact shade of her eyes. He'd left the store with it. And more. A ring. One set with a perfect jade stone. Cole knew then that he had it bad.

Now this. Of all the people he knew, she was the one he'd least expect to do something so sneaky and underhanded. Using *his* name for her own purposes. What was it this time? Had she decided Yaqui Springs needed a fire station to go with its post office? It cut him to the quick. What would she do if he showed up unexpectedly and called her bluff?

The longer Cole smoldered, the more he thought that dropping in on the tournament was a very good plan.

Cicely wasn't going to be able to live in his condo and take care of Bum much longer. He'd have to make other arrangements by the end of September, anyway—after she and Lane got married. This way, he'd be home for the wedding, too. Since he'd let her stay in his place rent free in exchange for cat-sitting, maybe she'd do him one more favor. Cicely already sported a rock the size of Plymouth on her left hand. Besotted though the future bridegroom was, Cole figured Lane would understand the need for a man to keep his pride intact. The residents of Yaqui Springs were already aware of his history with Cicely. Why not borrow her as fiancée for a day? After all, someone had borrowed his name—without asking—and he didn't appreciate it.

Since he was still up, he might as well call and secure Lane's OK. Kill two birds, as it were. They hadn't talked in some time about prospects for the sale of his land. Frankly, it was going more slowly than Cole would have figured. Wanting to be fair to Tibby, he hadn't discussed the letter from the pig-and-goat farm with Lane. But after this crap Tibby was pulling, he might.

He'd thought Tibby was different—sweet, like everyone in Yaqui Springs had said. Honest. He didn't understand why she'd go behind his back. In fact, he didn't understand *what* she was doing behind his back. But he intended to find out.

Lane's private number rang five times before his secretary picked up. "I'm sorry, Mr. Davis is speaking at a law conference in San Francisco. He won't be back until after Labor Day. May I have him call you? You're still in Singapore, aren't you, Mr. O'Donnell?"

"Yes, but I'll be home soon. I'll catch him later. Did Cicely go with him?"

"No, she's doing a final shoot on a TV show, and she's got the last fitting for her wedding dress. Would you like me to give her a message?"

"I'll call her myself." She'd kept his phone number rather than make a temporary change. Cole thumbed the plunger a few times and redialed.

Surprisingly Cicely caught the phone on the first ring. "I thought you were my caterer." She laughed. "He's trying to substitute squid for smoked salmon at our reception. You know, Cole, you don't have to call every week to check on your cat. Although if he destroys another pair of my silk hose while they're on my legs," she drawled, "he's going on my hit list. Just below the caterer."

"Well, you won't have him much longer." Cole explained why he'd called.

"I'm not keen on visiting Yaqui Springs again, what with all the rattlers, scorpions and pack rats," she said. "But I'll do it, just because Lane says you're marrying that store clerk and I say he's dead wrong."

"Cicely, you're always going on about rattlers and scorpions."

She filled him in on everything Winnie and her friends had said the night they delivered dinner. It took Cole a moment to piece things together. When he did, he realized Winnie Toliver's troops had been up to far more mischief than merely sending flowers in his name. Suddenly it struck him what else Cicely had said. "Where did Lane get the idea I'd marry Tibby? Never mind, when I see him, I'll set him straight. Hey, thanks for being a pal, Cicely. I'll call you later with my flight times."

Hanging up, he gave some hard thought to those senior-citizen con artists. He should have washed his hands of the whole bunch. Well, he would soon.

TIBBY HAD FULLY EXPECTED coordinating a golf tournament to be time-consuming. If she'd known how many hours it'd actually take, she never would have suggested it. Especially since she was also struggling to keep the store open, oversee the men's rebuilding of the post office and handle the finishing touches on the greens.

The last was Justine's idea. She pointed out that Cole had already paid for the sand, fertilizers and seed. And the sprinkler heads chewed by coyotes had all been replaced—twice. Tibby decided nothing was ever as simple as it sounded. Spreading sand on eighteen greens was backbreaking work. Then all the coyotes, raccoons and opossums for miles around considered it their personal litter box. Nightly she pored over the *U.S. Golf Associa-tion's Greens Guide* when she should have been sleeping.

What kept her going was a picture of Cole that she'd clipped from one of Ralph's golf magazines, framed and placed on her desk. That, and the seniors who had begun to glow with good health. They'd trimmed down and in many cases their blood pressure had dropped. Except for Justine. Dealing with slow-moving county clerks to secure signoffs at every stage of the work left her a basket case. Between fumigation, sterilization and sowing seed, Tibby added county-clerk duty to her roster of golf-course chores. One trip putting up with their repeated delays, and she got wise. She carted reams of papers needing notari-zation into their office at five minutes to five on Friday afternoon. It was amazing how fast her stuff was pro-cessed after that.

The worst thing that happened—other than Fred Feeny's hitting a skunk with his golf cart on the ninth green and halting work for a week—was that the com-puterized sprinkler-control panel went berserk, nearly drowning their seed. Then the company didn't ship the new unit on time. If half the town hadn't been willing to water by hand, the seed would have fried in the mid-August heat wave.

Well, that was behind them now. Tibby paused to gaze at herself in the mirror. No wonder she looked like a zom-bie and had lost fifteen pounds. What really depressed her was that all this work might be for nothing. There was no guarantee Cole would choose to open the public course. No guarantee at all. Tibby clung to the hope that if they handed him the money from the tournament to build his access and parking lot and if the residents were willing to manage the whole operation, he'd decide to go ahead with it.

She wished someone besides her could present him with the idea. But who? Surely, in the interests of business, Cole would recognize the value of having the loyal residents run his course. It was exactly the type of part-time work they all needed. But even if he refused and insisted on selling, with the improvements they'd made there was a better chance he'd sell to someone wanting a golf course, wasn't there?

Sighing, Tibby ran her finger over the glass covering his picture. If only there were fairy godmothers. Then he'd come back, and the two of them would marry and live happily ever after. If there were fairy godmothers.

Pipe dreams. Fairy tales, all right. Cicely awaited Cole's return—in *his* condominium. A fact not likely to change. Quite frankly, if Tibby had the brains God gave a bat, she'd thank providence that Cole was a safe seventy-five hundred miles away right now. Because she had other worries. Like making it through the welcoming reception at Bogey Wells tonight, followed by three grueling days of tournament golf.

Stifling a yawn, Tibby stroked Exterminator's head before hurrying out to wait on the last straggling customer. Then she'd lock up and go home to change for the big event. The beginning of the first ever—and last, she hoped—Cole O'Donnell Open.

MIDWAY THROUGH the evening gala, Winnie sidled up to Tibby, raising her voice to be heard over the crowd. "Isn't this a toot?"

"I've been thanking my lucky stars we've only got two hours to go."

Winnie chucked Tibby under the chin. "I'd offer tooth-picks to hold your eyes open, kiddo. Except then everybody'd see they look like road maps. I wish you'd relax and try to enjoy the party.''

"I finally ditched the tag that said, 'Welcome, I'm the tournament coordinator.' I had no idea Cole knew so many golfers. They're all asking when he'll be here.''

"Ouch. What have you been telling them?''

"The truth,'' she murmured, crossing her fingers behind her back. "That he's in Singapore, and due to some unforeseen problems, may be forced to extend his regrets. I'm hoping that by tomorrow they'll all be so engrossed in the game, no one will notice he's missing. I hardly think anyone will back out now. They've already paid registration and fees. A tidy sum, I might add.''

"Thanks to your hard work, Tibby. If Cole doesn't show up, I'm tempted to call him. His up and leaving the way he did still seems foolish to me. I suppose he got cold feet after admitting he loved you. In my day, when a man reached thirty, he was anxious to settle down. Today they're just interested in trying every chocolate in the box before they pick one.''

Tibby wanted to defend Cole—to say he wasn't like that. She held her tongue because she hadn't told anyone he'd gone back to Cicely. Like she'd conveniently failed to mention that Cole hadn't given them permission to use his name for the tournament. Everyone thought she'd arranged it through Lane Davis. They'd know everything soon enough, though, when not even the money brought him back from the coast. Tibby sighed. So much depended on her ability to sell him the idea of retaining the course and letting the seniors manage it for him.

Joe and Pete came by just then, carrying stacks of empty hors d'oeuvre plates, headed for the kitchen.

"I'm in hog heaven,'' Pete said. "In the space of half

an hour I've met Cory Pavin, Guy Boros, Mark Brooks, Jeff Hart and Fuzzy Zoeller.''

"Yeah.'' Joe grinned from ear to ear. "Curtis Strange asked *my* advice on how to play the twelfth hole. He and some of the others got here early and walked the course.''

Tibby lowered her voice. "Out of curiosity, what are they saying? They've played on some of the best.''

"So far, so good,'' Pete replied. "Nary a negative word. In case you haven't noticed, all the board members look pretty darn satisfied. Good thing you drilled into everyone not to mention how you beat Cole in that match. Oh, and some of the guests asked why he selected Bogey Wells, instead of Palm Springs. We explained that he owns property nearby.''

"I'll be glad when this is over.'' Tibby lost her battle with a yawn. "I feel some disaster is sitting out there, laughing, waiting to dump on us when we're not looking.''

"This from our calm efficient Tibby?'' Peter chuckled. "Accept that everything is running like a well-oiled machine. Cole may not be here, but think of the positive publicity he'll get for letting us use his name. And entrants still get what they paid for—a good game and decent prize money to the top six.''

Tibby felt her color drain. That minor detail again—Cole hadn't authorized using his name. Blessedly none of the entrants had asked where the profits were going, either. It was quite possible they wouldn't like their money going to fund a public golf course.

"Hey, this tray is getting blamed heavy,'' Joe complained. "Mabel and Henrietta will have our hides if we bring them too many dishes at one time. Winnie, dear,'' he said, "has anyone checked the coffeepots recently?''

"Slave driver," she murmured, rising to her toes to give him a quick kiss.

Tibby smiled to herself long after her friends had gone their separate ways. Winnie and Joe enjoyed the type of relationship she envisioned for herself. They were openly and unabashedly in love, yet they weren't so wrapped up in each other that they lost their individual identities. Tibby's smile dissolved slowly. Why did she persist in torturing herself with ridiculous dreams? Dreams that had no possibility of coming true. She found it impossible to imagine loving any man but Cole.

At the appointed time Tibby and her helpers cleaned up around the few people, guests and hangers-on, who hadn't wandered into the bar. "My feet are killing me," Tibby whispered. "I don't know how people wear heels day in and day out."

"I saw a young man—one of the sponsors, I believe—eyeing your legs a time or two," Rosamond said. "I also saw you give him the brush-off."

"That's Alec Davis. He has a black book the size of the L.A. telephone directory. His own brother warned me off. Alec bought my station wagon. And since we're on that subject, who's giving me a ride home?"

"I will," said Ariel. "I'm just so glad to hear you aren't spending the night here fussing over the banners, the drink carts, the scorecards, whatever."

"I probably would if Exterminator hadn't learned how to shake all the food out of his automatic feeder. He's such a bad dog."

"Amen," said Justine. "I read an article the other day, Tibby. It said some big dogs owned by single women are jealous of their boyfriends. Your dog mauled Cole. Then he ate Dr. Carlyle's expensive car and ran him off. At this rate, how will you ever find a husband?"

Tibby glanced around her circle of friends, waiting for someone to laugh. No one did. They all bobbed their heads in agreement. Tibby crossed her arms and tapped her toe. "To tell you the truth, Justine, I hadn't planned on looking for a husband. I figured I had all of you doing that for me. By the way, the dog isn't negotiable. He stays."

No one said a word. Most, however, looked sheepish. Winnie broke the silence. "Um, it's getting late. We have to be back here early tomorrow. Shall we leave?"

"When this is all over, Tibby," Ariel said on the drive home, "I'll spend some time helping you train your Great Dane. It's true some big dogs get possessive."

Tibby opened one tired eye. "It's all right, Ariel." She yawned sleepily. "It's just going to be Exterminator and me rattling around in that big old house forever. I'm never getting married."

Ariel drove past the store and stopped under the light illuminating Tibby's back porch. "Never say never, sweet Tibby. Everyone I've heard making *that* statement ended up married before the year was out."

Tibby crawled tiredly from the car. "There's a first time for everything, Ariel. Mark my words, I'll be the exception."

The older woman smiled. "Your grandmother used to say, 'Too many of us expect miracles to be like greeting cards—one for every occasion.' Truth is, miracles come when we least expect them."

"Yeah, well, it'll take one to get me up in the morning. What unholy hour will you be here to collect me?"

"Betty, the receptionist, told one of the board members that the TV station out of Indio wants to set up at six. He said the press will be right on their heels."

"Ugh. Those folks I can do without. They're pushy."

"Ah, but they give our sponsors a lot of publicity."

Tibby yawned again. "OK. I'll be ready at a quarter to. Notice I didn't say bright-eyed and bushy-tailed." The two waved and Ariel waited until Tibby unlocked her door and went inside.

Exterminator was glad to see her. In spite of her weariness and the late hour, Tibby pulled on sweats and took him for a run. The moon was nearly full. It was a beautiful night. Feeling energized, instead of sleepier, Tibby dragged him to a walk. He was heeling better, she thought as they sauntered along the golf course where, yesterday, the men had set some of the bunkers and spread sand for several traps. It wouldn't be long before it'd be time to mow. Therein lay another major problem. A commercial mower cost a mint, and Cole hadn't gotten that far in his ordering process. She sighed and turned back for home.

As soon as she got in, she noticed the light on her answering machine blinking. The caller was Lane Davis. He said he was at a conference in San Francisco and needed to talk with her. Odd. Unless Cole was pressuring him to find a buyer for the property. *Please, Lord. Not now. We just need a few more days.* It was after midnight—too late to call. Lane must have forgotten this was the weekend of the tournament. Anyway, if it was bad news, Tibby didn't want to hear it tonight. She'd find time to call him from the club tomorrow.

What she really needed was a warm bath. She dumped in a lavender oil infusion to help her relax. Her body relaxed, but her mind ticked away like a reliable clock. She didn't often suffer insomnia; for people who did, she recommended nightcap and passion-flower tea, which was what she made for herself now. Two teaspoons of mix steeped five minutes in a tisane cup. She strained the liquid and carried the cup to her bed. Less than thirty

minutes later she drifted gently off to a land filled with
pleasant dreams of Cole.

THE MOON WAS STILL a gray haze in the sky when Tibby's
alarm went off. Tea, toast and a bracing shower revived
her. She dressed with care in a new outfit Winnie had
helped her buy. Actually she had three new outfits, one
for each day of the tournament. Today she chose her favorite. It was a cool leafy green batik—a crinkle shirt-
and-shorts duo. Winnie had said the shirt should be worn
loose over an oyster white shell. New white sandals with
squishy inner soles promised an easier day for her feet
than yesterday's heels. She braided her heavy hair in two
plaits, then wound them together in a figure eight. Mabel
and Henrietta had bought her a hand-crocheted raffia baseball cap. They said if she was going to ramrod things, she
needed to look like an umpire. Mabel did tend to get her
games mixed up.

Tipped to one side, the cap shaded her eyes, yet looked
kind of smart, Tibby thought. Even if it'd looked ghastly,
she'd have worn it rather than hurt those dear ladies.
Tibby didn't kid herself that her friends would live forever. But what would she do without them? Losing her
grandmother and then Yale had been hard. Like shedding
pieces of her heart. And now Cole. Soon she'd have no
heart left.

Fortunately Ariel honked, saving her from getting too
maudlin. Ariel, never at her best before noon, compli-
mented Tibby on how she looked, then said nothing, only
drank coffee for the remainder of the drive.

The receptionist at Bogey Wells had been right; the
press were already setting up cameras, and it was barely
five minutes after six. Tibby hit the ground running. She

managed to evade the reporters until the first round of players gathered on the patio ready to tee off.

"Ms. Mack." A heavyset fellow stuck a microphone in her face. "You're coordinating this shindig, right?"

She stepped back and nodded as a television camera crew closed in from her right.

"Come on, Ms. Mack, we can't hear you nod." The chunky man laughed at his lame joke.

"Yes," she said, freezing him with a frown. "I'm the coordinator. But the residents of Yaqui Springs are the ones doing all the work. They're wearing gold name tags should anyone need assistance."

"That's nice. Is there one in particular who can direct me to the elusive Cole O'Donnell? At the desk they said you'd know."

Caught off guard, Tibby choked. "Uh, well, uh, Cole is...he's had some problems on a design project in Southeast Asia."

"Interesting. You've raised considerable money in his name and he's not here? Does this man exist?" he asked around an oily smile.

Tibby tried her best to stare down the fat little weasel. In the process she ignored a sudden disturbance at the door leading to the patio. But all at once the crowd shifted and separated like the parting of the Red Sea. Tibby's gaze was drawn to a man whose broad shoulders filled the doorway, leaving scant room for the slender blond woman at his side.

"Cole." His name rasped from her lips as the room spun. Overhead the chandelier rocked. But it wasn't the flash of the chandelier making her dizzy. It was the glare from the diamond on Cicely Brock's third finger, left hand.

"Cole?" muttered the reporter, turning to see what he

was missing. "Is the good-looking dude with the snazzy babe Cole O'Donnell?" But by the time he'd spun again and carried his question back to Tibby Mack, she'd disappeared.

He elbowed his way to the newcomers. "You'd be the late Mr. O'Donnell, I presume." Again the cocky reporter seemed to be the only one who found his repartee funny.

Cole, not yet recovered from his first brief glimpse of Tibby, shuttered his eyes lest they reveal his scattered feelings. He focused on the loud man with the microphone. "The 'late Mr. O'Donnell' would be my grandfather," Cole snapped. "A wonderful man who played a lot of golf at this club."

"Then why didn't you name the tournament after him?" the reporter shot back. "It's your name that drew all these great players. Either that or the charity to which you'll donate the profits—a nebulous entity, to say the least. Perhaps you'll be more specific than your coordinator's been."

Cole, who'd managed to focus his anger at Tibby now that he didn't have to stare into her stricken green eyes, opened his mouth to denounce her as an opportunist.

His speech was interrupted by a roar of motorbikes arriving outside the patio. The crowd began to twitter as the riders' helmets came off and a troupe of gray-haired ladies, dressed in matching navy shorts and white blouses, weaved through the press and the waiting players.

Winnie spotted Cole the minute her eyes adjusted to the subdued light. Her smile erupted. "Cole! We were afraid you weren't going to make it. Tibby will be so relieved. Now you can present the cash awards." Her smile dimmed noticeably as her attention lit on the woman in the short dazzling white dress who clung possessively to Cole's arm. "Cicely, dear, I'm sure our local press hasn't yet realized we have a budding television star in our midst." Deftly Winnie Toliver peeled the woman off Cole's arm and urged her a short distance away, where she beckoned reporters. "This is Cicely Brock, gentlemen. She's playing a villainess in my favorite daytime soap. A walk-on part, but with her talent, it won't be long before someone realizes she should have a starring role."

Cicely appeared flustered by Winnie's glowing compliments and the crush of reporters descending on her.

"What's your relationship to Cole O'Donnell?" an eager young reporter asked. "Is that an engagement ring you're wearing?"

"I, ah, yes," she said softly, flinging a helpless gaze over her shoulder at Cole.

"So when's the wedding?" asked a woman holding a video camera.

The reporter who'd given Tibby a bad time barged in with his mike. "Is it safe to say you and O'Donnell are combining the tournament with an early honeymoon?"

A fair-haired man sporting an even tan strode from the sidelines to tower over the obnoxious reporter. "Print that if you want your employer to be sued, buddy. I think my brother would object vehemently, since he put that ring on Cicely's finger. Lane Davis, a prominent Beverly Hills attorney. They're to be married at the end of the month."

"Alec?" Cicely clutched her throat. "What are you doing here?"

"I might ask the same of you, little sister-in-law-to-be," he growled near her ear, simultaneously darting Cole a glare.

Cole, however, missed the daggers, for he was being whisked away by a mob of gray-haired elves.

Winnie closed the door to a coatroom used only for winter gatherings.

Cole cleared his throat. "I have to tell you," he said dryly, "there's not a soul who'll pay ransom for my safe return."

Henrietta shook her finger under his nose. "I should think not, you naughty boy. Running off, making our Tibby cry."

"Cry?" His whole demeanor changed. He seemed confused.

Winnie motioned for the women to give Cole breathing room. "We were all disappointed when you left so suddenly, Cole. But we don't have much time to get to the whys and wherefores. Tibby will be needing our help. She's almost killed herself making this a success."

"What exactly is *this?*" Cole bracketed his hips with his hands. "I don't like that nasty reporter's charge—that I'm profiting from the tournament."

"Oh, but you are," Winnie said. As the other ladies nodded at intervals and sometimes interjected a strong word or two, she filled Cole in on all that'd happened. Ending with, "Are you staying at the house? Have you seen the golf course? It's ready to play except for a clubhouse. Everyone helped, but our sweet Tibby did the most, including keeping us all on track."

"I still don't understand why. I asked Lane to put the property on the market."

"Tibby talked him out of it. She'll say it's because she didn't want some pig-and-goat farm moving in. Truth is, it's a labor of love. She thinks we don't see her mooning over the picture of you she cut out of Ralph's golf magazine. She misses you, Cole. You miss her, it's plain to see. Quit pussyfooting around and come back here where you belong." Mabel leveled one of her finest teacher glowers on him.

He spread his hands. "Starting a golf course is a risky

business. Tibby's store is doing well. Do you think I'd live off her largesse? Not on your life.''

"You still don't get it," Justine said, advancing on him. "Building the Yaqui Springs Public Golf Course was your dream. Tibby knew that. She is also well aware that those of us on fixed incomes won't be able to afford the rising cost of private courses much longer. She's worn herself out seeing to everyone else's needs. Our sweet Tibby is like that. Love is a powerful motivator. She's giving you every cent of profit from this tournament, and if you're the man we think you are, Cole, you'll accept.''

"Oh, by the way," Winnie said as she opened the door. "Tibby put up the check you sent and sold her station wagon for seed money to get this off the ground. I helped tally receipts yesterday. When all is said and done, we earned just enough to cover your cost overruns."

They disappeared silently, leaving Cole alone with his thoughts. Black thoughts, aimed at himself. He didn't deserve to have his sorry ass saved, but he was thankful Winnie had intervened before he'd opened his mouth to that reporter. His lack of faith would have done Tibby a grave injustice. He'd come so close to ruining the tournament. Everything she'd worked for. His very presence here was hurting her. Her mossy eyes were so easily read. There'd been a glimmer of pleasure when she'd first seen him, but it hadn't lasted.

Why? Of course—*Cicely.* He hadn't been fair to her, either. But now she had Alec to run interference. Tibby, he owed an apology. More than an apology.

Cole set out to find her. The going was slow. Golfers he knew but hadn't seen in some time stopped him to swap stories. He ran into Joe, Pete and Fred. They weren't quite as direct as their wives had been, yet Cole walked away feeling as if he'd been chastised by three doting fathers.

The woman herself continued to elude him.

Some three hours later he still seemed to show up wherever she'd just been. He went into the bar, hoping it'd throw her off track if she had lookouts posted. He threaded his way through clusters of men discussing the scores of the contest's front-runners. Cole smiled, realizing the winner to date hadn't matched Tibby's score the day she'd beaten him. A heavy hand descended on Cole's shoulder, wiping away his smile.

"So, good buddy, you'd better cop a feasible plea for taking a hike with my fiancée, or I'll be forced to rearrange your pretty mug."

"Lane? Cicely said you were in San Francisco for another week. What are you doing here?"

"Cicely told me you were on your way home. She didn't mention the two of you running off together. I called Tibby last night because she wanted to know when you got back to the States. I reached her answering machine. She called back a few hours ago. Imagine my surprise when she consoled me and said you were here with your fiancée, er, *my* fiancée. I caught the next flight to Palm Springs and rented a car. Would it be too much to ask what the hell is going on? Where's Cicely?"

"With Alec," Cole said glumly. "I've been looking for Tibby all day to straighten out this mess. You haven't seen her, have you?"

Lane gazed at his friend a moment, then smiled wickedly. "You have that man-in-love look if ever I saw it. So she finally wormed her way into your heart, did she, you pigheaded Irishman? I'll drink to that. Even stand you one. What'll you have?"

Cole slumped into a chair at the bar. "You know about all this, too?" His wave took in the room.

"'Fraid so. And I've got to tell you it has nothing to do with that damned post office. She sent me a copy of a letter from your grandfather deeding her the land. No, the whole truth is she's nuts about you, man. And you know what? I'm beginning to think you may finally deserve her. Want my advice? You'd better brush up on your golf. A man's reputation with his kids is likely to suffer if they see Mom wax his tail too often at some silly game."

Cole lifted a brow. "Very funny. Now suppose you convince me that Tibby deserves a jerk like me."

"Only she can convince you of that, Cole. I take back my drink offer for the moment. We'll celebrate later. I did see her. Outside where the caddies check in."

"Wish me luck?" Cole stood and held out his hand. Two people clapped when Lane clasped Cole's hand. Glancing over, Cole saw that the measured applause came from Alec and Cicely. Judging by her smile, she had apparently accepted the idea that he was marrying Tibby—and moving to Yaqui Springs.

Cole slipped out a side door. He saw Tibby. Alone. Her back was toward him as she gazed out over the golf course. His heart lurched. Always slender, she'd lost weight. A lot of weight. His fault. She'd taken on all this extra burden for him.

Walking softly, he slipped up behind her, caught the arm with which she shaded her eyes and spun her around. Fear flashed across her face a moment, then her green eyes leaped in recognition. "Tibby," he breathed. The spark he'd seen winked out. He swallowed his lengthy apology and acted, instead, gathering her close for a kiss. Bending her over his arm, he poured every "I'm sorry" he could muster into that kiss. In the process, she lost the silly straw baseball cap sitting atop her braid. He didn't bother to pick it up. Neither did she.

Her hands slid up his arms and locked around his neck, and their bodies melted together. Eventually they both gasped for air. The first to regain her senses, Tibby sank back on her heels, a hand fluttering to her mouth. "Oh, Cole, you can't kiss me like that. It's not fair when you're engaged to Cicely."

It took some time for her words to register. Cole's thoughts couldn't seem to get any farther than the next kiss. Except that she looked so distraught he knew there'd be no more kissing until he set matters straight. Gently he led her to a bench shaded by a huge mesquite tree. Not sure where to begin untangling threads, he started at the point in Singapore when he'd first learned of the tournament and worked his way backward, to why he'd left Yaqui Springs.

Halfway through his explanation, she'd gathered one of his large hands between her smaller ones. At the end of the story, she held her breath—waiting for him to admit that he loved her. She felt it in the rapid beat of the pulse at his wrist.

Still the silence lengthened.

If not Cicely, what barrier stood between them? Ah. *Trust.* Lane Davis said Cole needed a woman he could trust.

"I'm sorry I used your name on this tourney without permission, Cole. I left messages on your recorder, asking you to call. I did it for you, and for the seniors, and for Yaqui Springs." Her lips trembled. Tears glistened in her eyes.

Cole wiped them away "I signed a contract to go to Singapore and immediately sublet the place to Cicely. She didn't mention a call."

"She wouldn't if she wanted to get back together with you."

"It wasn't like that. She'd already planned to marry Lane. Cicely wants a big wedding. They're expensive. So she agreed to cat-sit in exchange for free rent."

"Oh. I didn't know. The last time I phoned, she answered. I'm afraid I got the wrong idea and hung up. It hurt, Cole. I never tried again."

"Lane should have told me."

"He wants you to have your golf course—so he kept our secret. About the tournament, I mean. He just wants you to be happy, Cole." That was when Tibby remembered something Lane had said—that Cole might be too wary of women to ever make a commitment. Well, darn. She felt her palms grow damp. The strain of waiting for him to express his feelings was getting to her.

"Cole," she said abruptly, "Winnie thinks you love me."

Cole's hand gripped her elbow. "So it seems. Half a world away I thought about you day and night." With his free hand, he traced the earnest features of her face.

She sighed. "I love you, too, Cole. So much." After that she assumed their conversation would get personal, that it'd progress. It didn't. It died, and the only sound she heard was the sigh of an afternoon breeze rustling through the branches. Although Cole's fingers toyed with tendrils of hair that'd tumbled loose from her braid. His slightest touch sent prickles of awareness up her spine. Tension rose in her as she waited—until finally, she reared back and smacked his shoulder, hard. "Darn you, Cole O'Donnell. Why didn't you just come to my midnight supper the night of the post-office disaster?"

He rubbed his arm, looking blank. "I wasn't invited."

"Henrietta hand-delivered the invitation. A note in a pink envelope."

"Oh, that. I thought it was a thank-you for the flowers. She said you liked them."

"I did. And I like your cooking—and the gift of the unicorn. I like the way you treat the residents—and our animals. I like the way you make me laugh...and the way you kiss me." Pausing to haul in a deep breath, she slowly let it out. "Cole, will you marry me?"

Seconds ticked by while a nerve jumped erratically in the hollow below Cole's ear. After several more seconds his eyes blazed like polished silver, and he framed her trembling chin with both his hands. Leaning forward, he kissed her. At first softly. Then a devouring kiss that left them both shaking by the time it ended.

Her voice was barely a whisper. "Is that a yes? For once I need you to say it."

He felt like laughing. Felt like shouting. But the moment was too serious. Instead, he drew her face against his chest and let her feel the thunder of his heart. "Yes," he breathed. Then he said it again, solemnly, emphatically, so she'd be sure to hear. *"Yes."*

This time Tibby initiated the kiss—one designed to knock his socks off.

Little by little, golfers dragging in off the course spoke in hushed tones and tiptoed past the couple. But Cole and Tibby were too engrossed to notice.

Inside the clubhouse the residents of Yaqui Springs pressed their noses to the window and exchanged knowing grins.

A beaming Lane Davis set up a pool to name a date for Cole and Tibby's wedding.

"Soon," Winnie said. "We're not leaving something that important to chance. We'll get busy right now and plan it." She snapped her fingers, and the Moped Mavericks formed a tight knot.

EPILOGUE

THE WEATHER WAS SUNNY but cool. A lovely November day—perfect for a wedding. The very same month and day that Tibby's grandmother, Lara, had wed the love of her life. A good omen. Not that Tibby needed any extra luck, weighed down as she was with borrowed items, blue items, old and new ones, thanks to the excited ladies of Yaqui Springs. And she wore the jade engagement ring Cole had purchased in Singapore. Proof that marrying her had been on his mind, even though she'd done the asking.

Winnie fussed with Tibby's hair, rolling the thick tresses around Tibby's head. A 1940s style that was perfect with the high-necked, white satin gown her grandmother had worn.

At the dining-room table, Mabel and Henrietta tied long satin ribbons on the bridal bouquet—a gift from the flower shop in Bogey Wells. Since his return, Cole had been their best customer. Not only did he ply Tibby with flowers, today he'd bought corsages for every woman in town, as well as boutonnieres for the men.

Ariel reached around Winnie to pin her own mother's cameo at Tibby's throat. Rosamond and Justine adjusted the draped skirt. Millie Hopkins had left Peek-a-boo long enough to join the festive occasion. She kept dabbing her eyes with a hanky.

Tibby felt thoroughly pampered as the hour of her wedding to Cole drew near. Following a simple service at the chapel, she and Cole would host a reception at the spiffy new clubhouse—previously Yale's place. The dear ladies in this room had planned every last detail. Nothing pleased Tibby so much as the fact that Cole and the men had finished the work in time—except maybe the knowledge that Cole had taken her suggestion for renovating Yale's house. They'd make their home in hers.

Cole had done it all to please her.

Tibby smiled, knowing her husband-to-be was receiving the same treatment from the men, whose idea of a bachelor party yesterday had been to play eighteen holes of golf on Cole's new course. She had to start thinking of it as hers, too. The O'Donnell-Mack Public Golf Course. Cole insisted on naming it for Yale and Lara.

"Tibby," Winnie murmured, stepping back and turning her toward the mirror. "I've never seen you look more radiant. Lara would be so pleased. I do believe you're the spitting image of her on her wedding day. Like she looked in the photo downstairs."

"Oh, Tibby," sniffled Justine, "we've all been dreaming of this for so long."

Mabel nodded. "We'll have to do something special for Joe. He's the one responsible for enticing Cole to town, you know."

"Not so," said Winnie. "Who planted the idea in his head after we decided to find Tibby a husband?"

"True," Henrietta agreed. "Give credit where credit's due. Winnie's a genius."

Tibby gasped. "You mean your matchmaking started that long ago?"

"Why, certainly, dear," cooed Rosamond. "If we'd left it up to you, Tibby, we'd never hear the scampering of little feet. Babies," she said dreamily. "I'm volunteering now to be the first to baby-sit."

Tibby burst out laughing. "Do you mind if I get married first?"

They all smirked. "It's time," announced Winnie, ever the one to take charge.

The chapel was beautifully decorated with tall baskets of white roses and blue Dutch irises. But Tibby saw nothing except the man who waited at the altar, a look of pure adoration on his face as she walked slowly down the aisle toward him.

Because she had so many "fathers" to choose from—and choice was impossible—Tibby had elected to take the walk alone. She hadn't expected her knees to shake like this. It was a good thing Cole ran up the aisle to meet her. A romantic gesture not lost on the weeping women in the audience.

Lane Davis stood up for Cole, returning the favor Cole had granted him the previous month. As Tibby had no girlfriends her own age, she'd asked Cicely to be her matron of honor. Cicely had agreed and now she, too, smiled at the glowing bride.

The kiss, following the pastor's presentation of the newlyweds to the congregation, went on so long that people began to shuffle their feet and clear their throats until the two finally took the hint and broke apart.

On the short drive to the reception, Cole couldn't keep his hands off his wife. "Do we have to attend this part?" he muttered as he nibbled at her neck.

Tibby smiled shyly. "It would suit me to skip it. But the ladies worked so hard."

"You're right. This isn't just our wedding. It's a community affair."

Colorful balloons floated to the club's high-beamed ceiling. Baskets of lavender and honeysuckle freshened the rooms. The doors stood open to a welcome breeze and a host of revelers. People from Bogey Wells and Brawley joined the residents of Yaqui Springs, talking and laughing.

Joe Toliver popped the first champagne cork and gave the toast. "May life bring you nothing more stressful than sinking a hole in one," he said, holding his glass high. It seemed as if everyone in the room had a golf joke to add.

"Time to cut the cake," someone shouted after the laughter wound down.

Cole and Tibby took their places behind the cake, eyes skimming each other with love. Cole's hand covered Tibby's on the knife and they were posing for the photographer when through the front door raced a fat yowling cat. *Bum.* Hot on his tail was a clumsy barking Great Dane, whose big feet slipped on the polished hardwood floor. A length of chain attached to his collar clanked noisily behind him.

The cat leaped for the table—and all four feet landed in one of three sheet cakes that'd been precut to feed the crowd.

"Look out!" Cole yelled, thrusting his bride aside. He snatched up the tiered cake, and none too soon. "Dammit, Bum, how'd you get out?"

Exterminator seemed bent on following the cat. Or he did until he smelled the cake. Stopping dead in his tracks, he planted both paws on the table and buried his snout in frosting already tracked by Bum. Cole tried but failed to shoo him away.

Fred and Pete saved the remaining two sheet cakes. And it was a good thing, too, because Cole and Tibby had their hands full keeping the tiers upright. George Gordon grabbed the cat, and Ralph Hopple wrested the Dane away from the table. But not before his new blue suit was liberally smeared with cream-cheese frosting.

Getting a rein on her laughter took some effort. When at last Tibby managed a straight face, she sought out Rosamond Gordon. "Since you couldn't wait for the scamper of little feet, Cole and I accept your offer to baby-sit our two little darlings. Bum and Exterminator are yours for the duration of our honeymoon. But I promise his obedience training will have top priority the minute we get back."

Taking his cue from that, Cole scooped up his sweet bride and the two of them escaped. They got as far as the front porch, and then, because each looked back wistfully before their eyes met, Cole cleared his throat and planted a drugging kiss on Tibby's lips. "We don't have to go away for two weeks," he said. "Everything I've ever wanted is right here in Yaqui Springs."

Ten thousand declarations of love would not have meant more to Tibby. She hugged him tight, wriggled down, and the two of them went back to party with the matchmakers who'd brought them a lifetime of love.

EVER HAD ONE OF THOSE DAYS?

TO DO:

✔ late for a super-important meeting, you discover the cat has eaten your panty hose

✔ while you work through lunch, the rest of the gang goes out and finds a one-hour, once-in-a-lifetime 90% off sale at the most exclusive store in town (Oh, and they also get to meet Brad Pitt who's filming a movie across the street.)

✔ you discover that your intimate phone call with your boyfriend was on company-wide intercom

✔ finally at the end of a long and exasperating day, you escape from it all with an entertaining, humorous and always romantic Love & Laughter book!

ENJOY
LOVE & LAUGHTER™
EVERY DAY!

For a preview, turn the page....

Here's a sneak peek at
Colleen Collins's RIGHT CHEST, WRONG NAME
Available August 1997...

"DARLING, YOU SOUND like a broken cappuccino machine," murmured Charlotte, her voice oozing disapproval.

Russell juggled the receiver while attempting to sit up in bed, but couldn't. If he *sounded* like a wreck over the phone, he could only imagine what he looked like.

"What mischief did you and your friends get into at your bachelor's party last night?" she continued.

She always had a way of saying "your friends" as though they were a pack of degenerate water buffalo. Professors deserved to be several notches higher up on the food chain, he thought. Which he would have said if his tongue wasn't swollen to twice its size.

"You didn't do anything...bad...did you, Russell?"

"Bad." His laugh came out like a bark.

"Bad as in *naughty*."

He heard her piqued tone but knew she'd never admit to such a base emotion as jealousy. Charlotte Maday, the woman he was to wed in a week, came from a family who bled blue. Exhibiting raw emotion was akin to burping in public.

After agreeing to be at her parents' pool party by noon,

he untangled himself from the bed sheets and stumbled to the bathroom.

"Pool party," he reminded himself. He'd put on his best front and accommodate Char's request. Make the family rounds, exchange a few pleasantries, play the role she liked best: the erudite, cultured English literature professor. After fulfilling his duties, he'd slink into some lawn chair, preferably one in the shade, and nurse his hangover.

He tossed back a few aspirin and splashed cold water on his face. Grappling for a towel, he squinted into the mirror.

Then he jerked upright and stared at his reflection, blinking back drops of water. "Good Lord. They stuck me in a wind tunnel."

His hair, usually neatly parted and combed, sprang from his head as though he'd been struck by lightning. "Can too many Wild Turkeys do that?" he asked himself as he stared with horror at his reflection.

Something caught his eye in the mirror. Russell's gaze dropped.

"What in the—"

Over his pectoral muscle was a small patch of white. A bandage. Gingerly, he pulled it off.

Underneath, on his skin, was not a wound but a small, neat drawing.

"A red heart?" His voice cracked on the word *heart*. Something—a word?—was scrawled across it.

"Good Lord," he croaked. "I got a tattoo. A heart tattoo with the name Liz on it."

Not Charlotte. Liz!

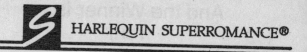

HARLEQUIN SUPERROMANCE®

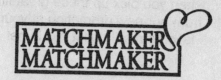

MATCHMAKER MATCHMAKER

When love needs a little nudge...

SWEET TIBBY MACK
by Roz Denny Fox

Tibby Mack is, at twenty-seven, the youngest resident in Yaqui Springs, a retirement community near California's Salton Sea. The folks there have become her family, her friends...her matchmakers. But what chance do they have of finding Tibby a husband when the youngest man in town is sixty-six?

Then Cole O'Donnell arrives. *Age:* 30. *Looks:* good (make that great). *And* he's inherited his grandfather's property in Yaqui Springs. He's the answer to their prayers. Not Tibby's, though.

But the matchmakers know that these two should be in love and that once in a while, love needs a nudge....

Watch for *Sweet Tibby Mack* (#746) by Roz Denny Fox

Available in July 1997 wherever Harlequin books are sold.

And the Winner Is...
You!

...when you pick up these great titles
from our new promotion at your
favorite retail outlet this June!

Diana Palmer
The Case of the Mesmerizing Boss

Betty Neels
The Convenient Wife

Annette Broadrick
Irresistible

Emma Darcy
A Wedding to Remember

Rachel Lee
Lost Warriors

Marie Ferrarella
Father Goose

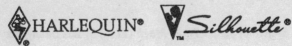

Look us up on-line at: http://www.romance.net   ATWI397-R

Let's Celebrate!

LOVE & LAUGHTER™

invites you to
the party of the season!

Grab your popcorn and be prepared to laugh as we celebrate with **LOVE & LAUGHTER**.

Harlequin's newest series is going Hollywood!

Let us make you laugh with three months of terrific books, authors and romance, plus a chance to win a FREE 15-copy video collection of the best romantic comedies ever made.

For more details look in the back pages of any Love & Laughter title, from July to September, at your favorite retail outlet.

Don't forget the popcorn!

Available wherever
Harlequin books are sold.

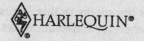 HARLEQUIN®

Look us up on-line at: http://www.romance.net

LLCELEB

HARLEQUIN SUPERROMANCE®

MARRIAGE OF INCONVENIENCE

SHOTGUN BABY (#750)

by Tara Taylor Quinn

FBI agent Con Randolf is desperate to claim his abandoned infant son—a child he didn't know he had. Yet as far as the state is concerned, Con doesn't have much to offer a child—he has a risk-filled job and he's single.

Con doesn't know a single woman who would marry him—or whom he wants to marry. But he does have a best friend—Robyn Blair—who could benefit from a *temporary marriage of convenience.*

Watch as the sparks fly this August 1997. Available wherever Harlequin books are sold.

HARLEQUIN WOMEN KNOW ROMANCE WHEN THEY SEE IT.

And they'll see it on **ROMANCE CLASSICS**, the new 24-hour TV channel devoted to romantic movies and original programs like the special **Harlequin** Showcase of Authors & Stories.

The **Harlequin** Showcase of Authors & Stories introduces you to many of your favorite romance authors in a program developed exclusively for Harlequin readers.

Watch for the **Harlequin** Showcase of Authors & Stories series beginning in the summer of 1997.

If you're not receiving *ROMANCE CLASSICS*, call your local cable operator or satellite provider and ask for it today!

Escape to the network of your dreams.

HARLEQUIN AND SILHOUETTE
ARE PLEASED TO PRESENT

Love, marriage—and the pursuit of family!

Check your retail shelves for these upcoming titles:

July 1997
Last Chance Cafe by Curtiss Ann Matlock
The most determined bachelor in Oklahoma is in trouble! A
lovely widow with three daughters has moved next door—and
the girls want a dad! But he wants to know if their mom needs
a husband....

August 1997
Thorne's Wife by Joan Hohl
Pennsylvania. It was only to be a marriage of convenience—
until they fell in love! Now, three years later, tragedy
threatens to separate them forever and Valerie wants only to
be in the strength of her husband's arms. For she has some
very special news for the expectant father...

September 1997
Desperate Measures by Paula Detmer Riggs
New Mexico judge Amanda Wainwright's daughter has been
kidnapped, and the price of her freedom is a verdict in
favor of a notorious crime boss. So enters ex-FBI agent
Devlin Buchanan—ruthless, unstoppable—and soon there is
no risk he will not take for her.

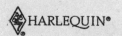